The Waynflete Trilogy

VOLUME 2

Deidamia's Surprise

N.E. Miller

Published by Clink Street Publishing 2021

Copyright © 2021

First edition.

The author asserts the moral right under the Copyright, Designs and Patents Act 1988 to be identified as the author of this work.

ISBN:
978-1-913340-23-0- paperback
978-1-913340-24-7 - ebook

Acknowledgements

Nothing about computer viruses or spyware could have been built into this story without the help of Ed Skoudis, author of "Malware: Fighting Malicious Code" and "Counter Hack Reloaded" (Prentice Hall). I also owe a debt to the countless people who made my many Internet searches so interesting and informative.

The author

Norman Miller is a doctor and medical scientist. In the 1970s, he and his brother discovered the link between 'good' cholesterol and protection against heart disease, their paper on which became the most cited ever published in The Lancet. This important discovery was to form the bedrock of a distinguished research career in the UK, USA, and Australia.

He was the scientific adviser and presenter for two award-winning documentaries on the prevention of heart disease, and was an expert consultant to the biotechnology company that developed the first gene therapy to be approved for human use in Europe.

He turned to writing fiction when a Visiting Fellow and Waynflete Lecturer at Oxford University's Magdalen College.

He is a Fellow of the Royal Society of Medicine and Royal Society of Arts.

Chapter One

When Giles Butterfield had walked through Magdalen College's gates for the first time in so many weeks, his great adventure and the drama of Stockholm behind him, his sentiments had been curiously similar to those on his very first day in the College. Despite his standing in the world of genetics, he had always been conscious of the limits of his talents and achievements. After being headhunted by Sir Quentin, a physicist whose name was familiar to every science journalist in the land, most would have waltzed through the Porters' Lodge off High Street brimming with confidence. But in spite of the romantic streak that fuelled his lifelong passion for poetry, he was also very much a realist. He knew that it took three things to get to the top of the academic tree. Intelligence was certainly an asset, but rarely sufficient on its own. Equally important were hard work and good luck. Those endowed with a hefty helping of the third floated from gossamer to settle on the highest twigs. The brightest flittered between the branches and leaves with effortless agility. But for many, of whom he was undoubtedly one, it was a scramble from the roots upwards, collecting a few scratches on the way, and more often than not a bruised finger or two from the attentions of competitors.

His recent ascent to unwanted celebrity status had been little different. As far as he was concerned, the supposed investigative genius proclaimed by journalists simply did not exist. It might approach the truth in Fiona's case perhaps. But for him, it had been mostly unrelenting toil that had got him there. That and good fortune. For how much would he have achieved if his brother Conrad had not been an expert in computer malware and been willing to get involved, or without Fiona's bold dash to Washington and her late nights on his laptop?

And so it had been only with trepidation that he had glanced towards the windows of the President's Lodgings, as he followed the well-trodden route across St. John's Quad to his office. His greatest worry had been how Sir Quentin, such a stickler for doing things the "proper way," might have reacted to the news of his methods. As Fiona had quipped during his call from the Sheraton, there was no escaping the fact that in the eyes of the law he was now a criminal on four counts. He was a burglar, who had broken into an office in the US National Cancer Institute; a thief, who had stolen a document while he was there; an accomplice to a computer hacker; and a fraudster, who had falsified evidence to gain approval for a second cyber-attack.

He was also painfully aware of the manner in which he had lied his way out of one tight spot after another with such facility and effect that he had begun to fear it was his natural bent. Nobody of importance to the success of the mission had been spared his trickery—not his secretary Jane, the Director of the National Institutes of Health Hank Weinberg, Stephen Salomon's research fellow, the porter at the National Cancer Institute, Conrad, or Gunnar Eriksson, Chairman of the Karolinska Institute's Nobel Prize committee no less. The list had seemed endless. But the deception foremost on his mind upon reaching St. Swithun's Tower had been that of duping Sir Quentin into believing he was at Georgetown University working on a grant application, even emailing fictitious progress reports as evidence. How had the old shrew reacted to that one?

To add to his torment, there had been other preoccupations. How had Fiona been getting on with Aram, after finding copies of her latest lab results in one of his computer files? She had questioned his honesty so often without getting the response it merited from her chief that she was entitled to be in a huff. And had Jane become aware of the true reason for her sudden absence, and been broadcasting it to other secretaries? Star of chat shows, interviews, and documentaries he might have been in Sweden, but back inside Bishop Waynflete's walls he had never felt so vulnerable.

But the extraordinary spectacle that had greeted him as he stepped from under the tower into St. Swithun's Quad had swept away all doubts about his reception. The College could not have witnessed such a scene in its half millennium. The square, normally empty and rather sad that time of the year, had been overflowing with smiling faces beneath a banner proclaiming "Welcome Home, Magdalen's Great Hero!" Where had they come from? And in front of them all, with Fiona at his shoulder jumping with excitement and discreetly blowing kisses, was Sir Quentin, beaming like a beacon and clapping furiously.

Sir Quentin's long speech the same afternoon in the Great Hall after the first "Giles Butterfield Dinner," an event henceforth to be held on the same date annually, had said it all.

"Here is a man, ladies and gentlemen, who has shown to the world that Magdalen College Oxford is much more than a place of great ideas. It is also a place of great *ideals*, and of people who have the guts to be true to them—whatever the cost, whatever the difficulties, whatever the risks…in short, whatever it takes. Ladies and gentlemen, I give you, Professor Giles Butterfield."

In his brief reply, Giles had insisted he was neither a superman, nor a hero. Once he had picked up the courage to set off on his journey, it had all been down to dogged perseverance and good luck.

"What if Dr Salomon had taken the all-important website report with him on his lecture tour," he had asked, "instead of carelessly pushing it behind his office curtain? What if my brother had gone to Cape Town to be a programmer for mobile phones instead of a computer security expert? What if Professor Eriksson in Stockholm had refused to meet me, assuming I was a crank with a chip on my shoulder? And what if Dr Cameron over there had not had the initiative and the courage to follow me? For it was she…not I…who, burning the midnight oil in a Washington hotel, unlocked the secrets that were hidden in the depths of Stephen Salomon's hard disk.

"Thomas Jefferson once said, 'I'm a great believer in luck, and I find the harder I work the more I have of it.' That's the spirit that kept me going—from the moment I closed my office door behind me after a long and tormented night to when Henrik Olsson dropped me off at what is now the most famous bus stop in Sweden, if not the world— that and the knowledge that as soon as I stopped…I'd have to return to this bloody place and you bunch of boring buggers!"

Now recovering from an emotional and hectic day in the quiet solitude of his office, he marvelled at how his light-hearted gibe had seemed to offend so many. Clearly, nothing much had changed in the old place. But there again, why should it have?

"Talk about dropping a clanger!" he called back to the Marchese, as he returned from the reading room with a mug of coffee. "People can be so bloody sensitive. I wish you'd been there. You could have heard a pin drop. One thing's certain, this time next year, I'll keep to two glasses of D 'n' S…well, three anyway."

The atmosphere in his office—dimly lit to avoid being disturbed by an unwelcome visitor, a touch damp after his long absence, the only sound the whistle of the winter wind through the window frames—took him back to the night he had endured before his fateful departure for Heathrow. His mind raced through the events that had followed: his shock on reading the note on the back of the *Achilles* gene report in Steve's office; the difficult meetings with Hank Weinberg in the National Institutes of Health; the shock, relief, and joy of seeing Fiona in the lobby of The Jefferson; his amazement on learning the results of her computer work; lunch with Hank and his wife in Chevy Chase, when they'd tried every trick in the book to get him to drop the case; the long journey to Cape Town, uncertain of how Conrad was going to react to his proposal;

the agonising wait for his decision at the Cape of Good Hope with Fiona; their emotional parting in Frankfurt airport; the cold encounter with Gunnar Eriksson beside the lake in Stockholm; their visit to the "Toppen av isberget" coffee bar to view what *Adonis* had supposedly sent from Steve's laptop; the excitement in Gunnar's study, as Conrad controlled Steve's laptop from a surgical trolley in Cape Town's Groote Schuur hospital to reveal the damning evidence; the hair-raising ride through Stockholm's narrow streets on Henrik's crossbar; the scenes outside the Concert Hall, as Steve had been led away by the police. It all seemed too fantastic to be true. If he had seen it in a movie, he would have mocked its implausibility.

He thought also of the major players in the saga, their present circumstances, and their futures. How was Steve coping? Had Hank survived professionally? As Director of the NIH, and therefore Steve's boss, he'd almost certainly lose his job, if he hadn't done so already. Was Conrad's wound infection clearing up after his appendectomy? Was little Jabu still enjoying his computer in Cape Town? Could it be true that Henrik and Eir had decided to name their baby Butterfield, as they had written…whatever the sex? Butterfield Olsson…poor child!

The stack of unanswered letters that Jane had arranged neatly in the centre of his desk seemed to glower at him. Perhaps he would put them through the shredder? After all, most of them would be junk, wouldn't they? And anything important would arrive again sooner or later.

After dropping them into a cardboard box that once held six bottles of Gosling's Black Seal rum, he raised his eyes to admire the vase of Christmas rose and wintersweet flowers that Jane had brought from her cottage. He had known from his occasional visits for afternoon tea that nobody could cultivate a better winter garden than she. Judging from the blooms on display, he imagined this year's must be prettier than ever.

He looked around for a better home for the sprigs of winter honeysuckle she had laid on the hearth. After rejecting a Nescafé tin, he reached for his briefcase to take out the empty bottle of Svaneke Session pilsner he had rescued from the trash bag during the flight from Stockholm. Its association with Ahmad's last moments in Sorrento had been far too poignant for him to leave it behind. Although his intention had been to add it to his collection of improvised paperweights in the rosewood bookcase, he had since realised it was unsuitable for that purpose. After trimming the wintersweet stems with his penknife, he arranged the flowers in the bottle as best he could, and placed it on the mantelpiece between the two brass candlesticks. The finishing touch, he decided, would be a brief dedication to Ahmad, preceded by a few carefully chosen lines of verse.

He drew the curtains across, switched on the Anglepoise lamp, and took a few index cards from a desk drawer. Thinking he owed it to Ahmad to do a good job, he stretched to the windowsill for his father's Augustus Teetgen tea caddy that contained the qalams, likka, and inkwell he'd bought for calligraphy as a young man in Cairo. After pouring just enough black ink onto the silk fibres, he closed his eyes in search of inspiration.

"I know, a few lines of Rossetti's 'The Honeysuckle' would be perfect," he enthused. "What could be more appropriate?"

After practising several letters on a scrap of paper, he wrote with meticulous care.

> 'I plucked a honeysuckle where
> The hedge on high is quick with thorn,
> And climbing for the prize was torn,
> And fouled my feet in quag-water...'

"No, that won't do, will it?" he gasped. "Ahmad drowned, remember. I'd better skip a few lines."

He took another and recharged the reed with more ink.

> 'I plucked a honeysuckle...
> Thence to a richer growth I came,
> Where, nursed in mellow intercourse...'

"Intercourse? Jesus! Forgot about that too. Couldn't bear the sight of Jane's beetroot cheeks every time she passes by."

He dropped the card to the floor, and grasped a third.

"Okay, forget about Rossetti. Let me think. Ah, yes… Freneau's 'Wild Honeysuckle' should be safe."

> 'Fair flower, that dost so comely grow
> Hid in this silent dull retreat…'

"No, that won't do either! Some of today's lot will surely drop in tomorrow, and accuse me of getting in a dig. I can hear Nigel Johnson now. 'If you still think it's so bloody dull around here, Giles, why don't you go back to Merseyside?'"

He ripped the card into small pieces, and picked up a fourth.

"Sorry, Ahmad, but I live under difficult circumstances. This'll have to do."

IN MEMORIAM
AHMAD SHARIF

Propping the card against the bottle, he paused to enjoy the perfume of the pink and yellow flowers. But inevitably, it was not long before his eyes dropped to the bottle itself. He pictured Ahmad refusing a glass of wine in the bar; resisting the olives that were on offer because of Ramadan; and arriving for his lecture a few minutes late after being delayed by his Dhur prayers. Was it possible that someone who had adhered to the Shari'a so conscientiously in public would have been drinking beer on his own late at night? They may have chatted for only a few minutes, but Giles had lived in the Middle East long enough to recognise a closet boozer when he saw one. And drinking directly from a bottle…*Ahmad*? Yet there was no escaping the fact that the laboratory in Naples had found alcohol in his blood. They couldn't have got that one wrong surely…could they?

Snapping out of his daydream to look at his watch, he saw it was 3:25 a.m. Should he stay where he was, and sleep on the couch again? Or make his way home? Deciding it would be too cold on the sofa, he donned his duffle coat, and moved next door to collect his scarf and gloves from Jane's desk.

Peering through the window, he watched the sleet swirling around the holly tree in the centre of the lawn, illuminated by the lights from the students' rooms.

"Looks ghastly!" he groaned, turning towards the Marchese. "But here goes. What did Captain Oates say—I'm just going out, and may be some time? But I won't be as long as him, I hope."

Chapter Two

During the flight from Stockholm, Giles had decided his first job in Oxford would be to take Aram to task for copying Fiona's data. Only when that was out of the way would he be able to focus on the task of rustling up support for Rashid Yamani's Nobel Prize nomination in recognition of MECCAR's discovery of *Achilles*. As time was short, he would have to get on with it.

After calling Fiona over breakfast to advise her to keep out of the way until around midday, he arrived in the New Building to find Aram busy on his mobile phone at the far end of the corridor. Summoning him with a gesture, Giles entered the lab to find the small table that served as Aram's desk covered in papers with his open laptop in the centre. Glancing at the screen, he saw the title page of a document.

صـــفحة 1

للغايـــــة ســـرية

البيانـــــات لمعالجـــة تعليمـــــات

"What the…?" he gasped.

Before he could look at the next page, Aram came running through the door looking flustered.

"Good morning, Professor," he stuttered, before coughing loudly.

"Morning, Aram. Oh!"

"What, sir?"

"Your laptop seems to be shutting down."

"Yes, probably. It's programmed to do so whenever it hears a cough."

"Never heard of that one before! Why on earth…?"

"All of the laptops MECCAR gives its fellows are like that. It's an emergency security feature. But it can be a bit of a problem if the sensitivity is set too high."

"They seem to have thought of everything! Damn good idea though. We all need to avoid prying eyes these days. I could do with that system when my housemaid stops for a chat while I'm checking my bank statements. They seem to attract her like a magnet."

"Oh, don't misunderstand, Professor. I didn't do it deliberately. I must have caught Dr Cameron's virus. There was nothing confidential on the screen. From *you*…how could there be? It was just a booklet MECCAR sent to us all, giving advice on laboratory equipment—operating instructions, accessories, troubleshooting. That sort of thing."

"I see. Sounds very useful. Can anyone use it, like me or Dr Cameron?"

"Yes, of course, but unfortunately it's in Arabic. I'm not aware there's an English version. Sorry!"

"What a pity. Never mind. Now, to get down to another security matter, Aram, Fiona told me you'd inadvertently sent her a file containing data you'd copied from her laptop without her knowledge. Is that true?"

Aram's eyes dropped as he propped himself against the table.

"Yes, I'm afraid it is, sir. I wanted to have copies so that when I'd done the same experiments myself, I could see if my results agreed with hers. She was at a lecture at the time, you see. But I should have waited until she'd returned, shouldn't I?"

"Absolutely! But she also said that, although you'd copied the results of several experiments, you haven't got around to doing a single one of them yet. Why's that?"

"I haven't had the time, sir. I've had a lot of reading to do. So much is being published."

"I see. Well, I appreciate your diligence in keeping on top of the journals, Aram, but doing what you did was not just an invasion of Dr Cameron's privacy, it was actually a form of theft. What's inside someone else's computer is no business of yours. If you're caught again, I'll have to report it to Professor Yamani."

"Professor Yamani, not Sir Quentin?"

"Yes, they're the rules. It's in the contract. MECCAR pays your stipend. So, he's the first port of call. Understand?"

"Yes, sir. Thank you."

"There's nothing to thank me for."

"No, I just…"

"Aram, did I see you smirking?"

"Smirking? What does…?"

"A smirk is the smile of a smart aleck, Aram."

"A smart what, sir?"

"Never mind! I'm letting you off this time, but it's a very serious matter. If it ever happens again, you'll…"

"I wasn't smiling, sir. I promise."

Giles stared at him inquisitively.

"Okay, back to your work!"

As he made his way down the gravel path that leads from the New Building towards the Cloister, pensively kicking pebbles to one side or the other, so many unforeseen questions were running through Giles's mind. Why had MECCAR gone to the trouble of installing such an extraordinary security feature in its fellows' laptops? And why had Conrad not mentioned this to him when they were in Cape Town? If it was so confidential that he dared not mention it even to his brother, what could it mean? And what was the supposed booklet really all about? Not what Aram said it was, that's for sure.

Upon arriving at the New Library, he could hear Fiona on the other side of the door saying goodbye to a couple of students. As two boys carrying books passed by to descend the steps, she remained in the doorway with arms crossed and an expectant smile, as if waiting for gratifying confirmation that Aram had been given a good hiding. But when their eyes met, she knew it had not gone as she'd hoped.

Giles beckoned Fiona to accompany him to one of the benches overlooking the lawn. Glancing towards the bay window of his office on the other side of the square, she could see Jane arranging a pot of flowers on his desk and gave her a little wave.

"Looks rather damp," Giles said, stopping at the first bench. "Better sit on this."

He pulled a plastic supermarket bag from his pocket and put in place as best he could in the wind.

"Thanks. You seem very quiet. How did it go?"

"I gave him a strong message. But to be honest, I wasn't too hard…because I think we should continue with business as usual while keeping an eye on him."

"Why?"

"Three things are worrying me. As soon as we met, he immediately switched off his laptop using a fancy security programme that responds to someone coughing. He said it was unintentional. He wasn't trying to hide anything. It was just that he'd caught your virus. Obviously, that wasn't the case, and he certainly didn't look ill to me. Second, a document in Arabic had been open, which he said was booklet on lab equipment that MECCAR had sent to all its fellows. But it wasn't. The title said 'Instructions for Data Processing,' and above that, 'Highly Confidential.' Of course, he doesn't know I can read Arabic."

Fiona stared at the path beneath her feet, still wet after an early morning shower, and rubbed her shoe into the moss and lichens. Stooping to pick up an empty snail shell, she tossed it onto the lawn, disturbing a crow into flight.

"That's pretty suspicious, isn't it? And what's the other thing? You said there were three."

"I may have misunderstood his body language, but when I threatened to go to Rashid Yamani if we caught him stealing your data again, he didn't seem worried in the least."

Fiona rested her chin on her hands, saying nothing until a gardener had passed carrying a basket of weeds.

"He's definitely up to something, Giles. What Conrad said about their laptops' security systems was pretty extreme, but this is extraordinary. And why did he lie about the document?"

Fiona covered her face with her notebook, as a gust of wind swept through the branches of a nearby birch tree, scattering leaves in her direction. She picked them off her white lab coat one by one.

"As you said, Giles, we should definitely keep an eye on him. Here comes the gardener again. Let's go for a coffee, and continue wherever we end up."

***

Settled in a corner at the far end of the Grand Café in High Street, next to a large gold-framed wall mirror, their coffee and pastries being prepared, Fiona was keen to return to her thoughts on the matter.

"I think there are two possibilities, Giles. The first is he's cooking, perhaps even completely inventing, some of his lab results. Whenever he gets the opportunity, he takes a look at mine. If his don't agree with mine, he fudges them or makes them up. Have you noticed whenever you ask the two of us to do the same experiment independently, he usually gives you his results a week or two after mine?"

"Yes, I have. But there could be other reasons, couldn't there? As he's less experienced, perhaps he just takes longer. Or he needs to repeat a few measurements."

"Possible. Nevertheless, the next time you get two sets of data from us, why don't you see if there's a mathematical relationship between them— if he was adding a constant number to my data, for example, or multiplying them by a common factor, or both."

"But he might be smarter than that. What if he added or subtracted random numbers, for example, that were large enough to make them look like two different data sets, but small enough for the outcome of his experiment to be the same as yours? It wouldn't be so easy to detect."

"That's true, but it's worth a try, isn't it?"

As the waitress had just arrived, they waited while she arranged the table and poured the coffee. When she'd finished, Giles's face showed only painful disappointment.

"Don't let it get you down, Giles. It's worrying, I agree, but as you know, I always had my suspicions about…."

"It's not that," he sighed, waving a limp hand over the table. "From one end of Oxford to the other, it's always the same fancy cakes, isn't it—French, Austrian, Italian, German, anything but traditional British fare. One day, I'll get my Mavis to bake a batch of her Northern specials— Goosnargh cakes laced with caraway seeds, Manchester tart, parkin squares oozing molasses and ginger, Bury simnel bursting with sultanas, and a few others—and put a plate of free samples on that glass counter over there. She'd have them queueing up overnight."

"Mavis's baking is marvellous, I agree, Giles. But I must say I'm rather partial to this sort of thing too. Sorry to disappoint!"

Fiona's eyes lit up, as she dithered between a slice of crostata al limone and one of Black Forest gateau, finally settling on both.

"Mmm! Now, where was I? Oh, yes. Another possibility is he's sabotaging our data to slow us down. If every Alhazen Fellow around the world got up to that sort of trick, the aggregate effect would be to give MECCAR a big advantage over the rest of us."

Giles frowned at her over his glasses.

"Bit farfetched, isn't it? Apart from the fact it would be contrary to everything MECCAR is supposed to stand for."

"I don't think it is farfetched. Sabotage happens in labs. Human nature being what it is, it would be surprising if it didn't. Only a few weeks ago a case was reported in Nature. Someone in the University of Michigan was convicted, in a court of law no less, of adding alcohol to a postgrad student's cell culture media. As far as I know, Aram's not interfering with my experiments, but what if he copied one of my spreadsheets, altered the results, and then replaced the original file in my laptop with that one? In all the jumble of numbers I get from the analysers, I probably wouldn't notice. It would be easy to send us up the garden path. From now on, whenever I return to a spreadsheet, I'm going to check the date and time stamp to see if it's been altered."

Giles smiled wryly.

"And hope Aram doesn't know any of the tricks you learnt in The Jefferson!"

"Good point. I know, every time I've finished with a spreadsheet, I'll copy it into a memory stick. Then when I go back to it, I'll compare the numbers in the two versions."

"Every one?"

"Yes. There's software for that sort of thing."

"Okay, do that. Not a bad idea. Now, having got that out of the way, while you're busy this afternoon, I'll drum up support for Rashid's Nobel Prize nomination. Gunnar gave me a call last night, and urged me to get on with it. First stop will be Sir Q."

"Good luck!"

Chapter Three

As a physicist, Sir Quentin could not nominate anyone for a Nobel Prize in Physiology or Medicine, but as he was such a big name in science, destined it was rumoured for the House of Lords, Giles knew his backing would carry immense weight. And as the President of one of Oxford's most prestigious colleges, a job that involved a hectic round of social engagements, he also had a plethora of influential connections. If Giles could tell the local nominators, all appointed personally by the Nobel Committee, that Sir Quentin was behind him, he would be halfway there.

And so it was to his delight that same afternoon, as they shook hands on the doorstep of the Lodgings, after no more suffering than that inflicted by a glass of Sir Quentin's cheap sherry, that his visit had secured more than mere support. Always a man to get on with things, Sir Quentin had promptly telephoned Professor Lars Walldius, a member of the Nobel Assembly, followed by two of the biggest names in physiology, Henry Waterstone in Boston and Nigel Ford in London, whom he had met at a congress on medical physics a few years back.

"Well, that's one vote and two nominators in the bag already," he declared proudly. "Not a bad start, eh, Giles? Normally, I'm averse to lobbying. Quite dishonourable in my view. But this is different. I wouldn't call it lobbying at all. More like leadership. I haven't coerced anyone. No arm-twisting or arse-licking. I just presented the facts, and offered them an opportunity to make history. With the discoverer of that Bedouin gene dead, it's only right his boss should be next in line. And between you and me, I'm all in favour of the top dog sharing the biggest bone anyhow."

After such a triumph, Giles strode confidently to the Grammar Hall, just a few yards away, to knock on the door of Sir Cardew Wilberforce, an Emeritus Fellow who'd been awarded a Nobel himself twenty-seven years ago. The fact that the reliability of his research had since been questioned by an American university was not important. Once you had one, you had it for life, and all that goes with it. A nomination from him would carry as much weight as any other.

Working on an article with a deadline just two days away, with a student about to arrive for a tutorial, and his secretary unable to understand his latest dictation, Sir Cardew was in no mood to spend much time on a nomination for someone whose work he knew nothing about.

"Love to help, Giles, but you know me, can't stand the sight of application forms. So why don't you complete it, the whole lot. Sally over there will give you one. I'll probably be on my way to Argentina by the time you've done it. So, she'll forge my signature—she's an expert, don't worry. I trust that'll be okay? Now, if you don't mind, I must get on with a few other things. Bye for now."

Having good reason to believe his next target would be equally pliable, Giles was confident the whole business was going to be a cakewalk. Dieter-Nicolas Alessi was the son of a wealthy Swiss industrialist who, hoping his son would become a famous geneticist, had ensured he had the perfect initials for the job. However, unlike Michael Colin Cowdrey, the English batsman famously guided from birth to membership of Marylebone Cricket Club, Dieter had not been so amenable to parental ambition, preferring sexually transmitted diseases to DNA. "In more ways than one!" his students were inclined to gibe, given his notoriety as a philanderer. But in spite of his dark side, Dieter had achieved international standing as an expert on AIDS. Although he had no experience of cancer research, the fact that he shared MECCAR's other field of interest was important. For Dieter would certainly hope that Rashid would eventually learn of his role, and that was an investment he would not want to miss. Almost important was the fact that his long-suffering wife was Lebanese. The combination of self-interest and spousal pressure should make him easy meat.

Sure enough, by the time the waiter was collecting their plates in the Randolph Hotel, Dieter had been hooked. Dessert, coffee, and liqueurs were spent chatting about rugby and Dieter's other favourite sport, until he realised he was going to be late for his train to Kingham. As they said their goodbyes outside the station, Giles was congratulating himself. Three nominations was perfect. More than that would look excessive.

***

Come the weekend, Fiona flew to Inverness to spend Christmas with her father. As Bill Eccles had gone down with sinusitis, Giles's customary visit to his finca in Majorca's Tramuntana mountains had been cancelled. Fearing that Christmas on his own in Oxford would be dead after the excitement of the past few weeks, he decided to spend it in Little Compton, where at least he would have the company of the villagers.

As the Austin Healey's road licence had expired while he'd been in Cape Town, he left the car in the Fellows' car park and took the train to Moreton-in-Marsh. The long walk from the station to the village down the A44 reminded him of how appealing the English countryside could be even in the middle of winter. The smell of grass and rotting vegetation drifting from the hedgerows, the feel of wet grit and soft clay beneath his heavy shoes, and the cawing of rooks in the treetops kindled memories of his schoolboy hikes with Conrad in West Sussex, before he had joined his parents in the Middle East.

Approaching the empty cottage, the bay windows on either side of the low door appeared to stare at him solemnly. The drops of water on the panes from the last downpour, glinting in the weak winter sunlight, drew his eyes to the emptiness that lay beyond. Stopping a few yards from the entrance, he dropped his leather suitcase onto the drive, not heeding the muddy puddle that splashed his trouser legs. The clack of its brass studs against the cobbles scattered a group of chirping sparrows from the Virginia creeper over the porch. As they rose into the sky, their fading song intensified the feeling of isolation that had overcome him when the latch of the gate had dropped into place.

If only Fiona could have been there. As much as he liked the cottage, it was more for its rural setting and quaintness than for its qualities as a home. Since Hillary's passing, he had never really enjoyed being there alone. Apart from reminiscing about their weekends together, he had a habit of ruminating about the old building's history and its former occupants. For no apparent reason, especially during the long winter evenings, his mind's eye would picture an imagined event from the distant past. It might be of a terrified cobbler and his distraught wife bolting the front door in a desperate attempt to keep the Great Plague at bay, as it marched north from London, ravaging village after village. Or of a young farming couple a century later, warming themselves by the fireplace, as they pondered the impact on the local wool trade of Richard Arkright's new invention in the North. Or another hundred years on, a group of lads from Hitchman's Brewery in nearby Chipping Norton, gathered in the kitchen, mugs of stout in hand, commenting on the sale of the Manor House to Ann Fowler after so many years of wrangling with the Church.

It was the same with the antique pieces that Hillary had collected. What letters had been written on his desk by candlelight, its surface strewn with quill pens, parchment, and sand? What emotions, pleading, arguments, and explanations had been expressed in them? Who had sat in the same spot, looking through the same glass panes at the same stone church? What incidents, many years apart, explained the stains, scratches, and chips on the mahogany dining table—a petulant child tossing a plate of porridge aside, the shaking of a horse-drawn cart as it carried a young couple's furniture from one town to another, a tragic incident of domestic violence?

And what faces, young and old, had looked out from the Victorian mirror in the hallway, expressing the whole range of human emotions—unbridled joy, sadness, anxiety, curiosity, devastating grief—each with its own story? It was haunting.

He put these habits down to being a geneticist. Perpetually thinking about family trees, inheritance, and evolution, he was forever conscious of the past, and of how in every one of us our ancestry is recorded in the tiny strands of DNA that are passed down from one generation to the next. As he gazed at the leaded, crooked kitchen window where Hillary had spent so many hours, he smiled as he thought of the occasion he'd brought all of this to her attention.

"Hillary," he had called, while stooping to poke the embers in the living room.

"Yes, dear."

"Do you have any notion of how many people who survived the Great Plague we've each inherited bits and pieces of genes from?"

"Bits and pieces of what?"

"Genes."

"How should I know? You do ask some funny questions, Giles. I'm more concerned with how many potatoes to peel this minute."

"Believe it or not, it could be as many as fifteen thousand. And if you go back to the year Marlowe and Shakespeare were born, it might be four times that number. Isn't that something? To think that when Will was penning Macbeth, all those people, perhaps sixty thousand of them, about two per cent of the population of England at the time, were going about their lives, destined to pass on copies of some of their DNA to you. And they're there, in every one of your cells. All it took was time, chance meetings of men and women, and a bit of the other—in fact, rather a lot of the other—and eventually there was you. Wouldn't it be fantastic to go back in time, and meet them all, say hello, shake their hands?"

"Five potatoes or six, Giles?"

While all this had been running through his head, it had started to rain again. But he had hardly noticed the fact. His coat had remained unbuttoned, his umbrella unfurled, his Barmah hat rolled up inside his pocket. Had it been a mistake after all? Should he go back to the station, get the next train to Paddington, and take a flight to Majorca? He'd probably catch a cold between now and the end of January anyhow. So if he caught Bill's virus over Christmas, would it matter? And the weather would surely be more clement.

He was still hesitating, when the wife of the cabinet maker next door drew back her net curtains with a toddler in her arms. The little girl's big smile and her mother's enthusiastic wave reminded him of how much life there was in the village, and how warm and friendly the people could be. He waved back, and pulled a funny face at the child. His mind was made up. He would change his clothes, and then set off for the Red Lion to learn what the landlord had organised for Christmas Day.

***

Overflowing with excited children, and with passable food brought to a banqueting table by the landlord's daughters dressed as Elizabethan serving wenches, the pub proved to be a good choice for Christmas lunch. The only downside was the impact of his new celebrity status, something he had not expected deep in the heart of the Cotswolds. He had always disliked the celebrity culture that pervades British life, and to have it thrust upon him towards the end of a long career in the serious business of science was painful.

"The really annoying part," he confided to the landlord over a glass of his usual after the others had dispersed, "is you have no bloody say in the matter. The media simply do it to you for their own benefit. I never looked for it, and I don't want it. But I can't get rid of it. There's nowhere to run. Becoming a hermit wouldn't do any good. The mere fact of my disappearance would be a huge story in itself. And when the bastards eventually found me, I'd be an even bigger celeb. If I went out of my way to tarnish my reputation, get into some sort of scandal, it wouldn't achieve anything either. They wouldn't drop me. Quite the opposite. The magazines would be competing for a photo shoot. It's a dungeon with webcams, from which there's no escape."

His mood had been soured by his experience during the meal. Hoping most of the others would lose interest with so many children within earshot, he had responded to the clamour for an account of his adventure by quietly confessing to a "multitude of dishonesties" during his quest for the truth. But to his dismay, rather than dampen their enthusiasm, it had served to fuel it. His later revelations that he had absented himself from work, trespassed into somebody's office, stolen a document, hacked into a computer, falsified evidence, and lied to colleagues, friends and relatives on three continents had elicited only expressions of admiration. "That's the spirit!", "Jolly good show!", "Good for you, old boy!", and "I wish this weak-kneed, jelly-bellied husband of mine had such guts" had been accompanied by roars of approval, stamping of heavy shoes, and bursts of applause.

By the time they had reached the plum pudding, there had been unanimous agreement that a second session would be essential to do the story justice. After a snap vote had been taken for the best time and place, the landlord had reached for the phone to book afternoon tea the following day in The Manor House up the road. Desperate for an escape route, Giles had promptly raised both arms to quell the excitement, and stood up so all could witness his sombre mood.

"Dear friends, fellow villagers, ladies, and gentlemen, I would dearly love to tell you more about my experiences tomorrow. Indeed, there is nothing I would enjoy more. But alas, I cannot. Why? For the reason that it's about to go into my autobiography, Memoires of a Pox-Hunting Man—yes, that is really the title—and I'm afraid my publisher would lynch me if I said any more, even in this little corner of the world. You see, the Internet has changed our lives forever. Even places like Little Compton, only a few years ago known to very few, are now part of the big wide world. News can travel fast—literally as fast as electrons down wires, light through fibre-optic cables, and electromagnetic waves through space—to all corners of the globe. And publishers don't want people to know too much about what's in a new book before it's in the shops and Amazon's website. If I were to give you the complete unabridged story, my publisher would have my guts for garters. So, I'm very sorry, but I'm afraid you'll all have to wait until it's in print. Sad, but that's the way it is. Tomorrow, instead of enjoying myself with you all, I'll be at my desk, nose to the grindstone, writing the next few chapters. So, who's for a game of draughts?"

***

Boxing Day was much more tranquil. Keeping to his word, Giles returned to his autobiography. Working at the mahogany dining table by candlelight until after midnight, he got as far as the moment in Frankfurt when he and Fiona had said their emotional goodbyes. Next morning, he was up before sunrise, packed his suitcase, and took a taxi to the station.

Editing the previous day's writing over a cup of coffee as the train made its way through the Gloucestershire countryside, he felt a great sense of relief that Christmas was over at last. It had never been his favourite time of the year. Even as a child he had not enjoyed it, pretending he was having fun just to please the grownups. What he disliked most was the predictability of everything: the same boring cousins on the doorstep, the same carols with their silly lyrics and simple music, gifts he had little interest in, endless turkey. He had never revealed it to anyone but Conrad, but the prospect of avoiding the annual ritual for a few years had been a significant factor in his decision as a young man to accompany his parents to the Middle East.

Raising his eyes to admire the reflections of weeping willows in the Evenlode's slow-moving surface, his thoughts turned to those who had made the latest adventure of his eventful life such a success. He wondered how the Salomon family were getting on, as they struggled to come to terms with the ruin of Steve's career and his reputation. He might not be the best geneticist in the world, but he wasn't a bad one either. Who knows what he would have achieved in the years ahead? Nothing had been heard of him since Stockholm—no press releases, no interviews, no statements by attorneys. Was it possible the claim he had made to the Swedish police had been true—that when he discovered Ahmad Sharif's writing on the back of the website report, he felt a moral obligation to make the results public in the only way possible without getting MECCAR into hot water with the tribal elders?

As soon as he stepped onto Oxford station's platform, he called Fiona's mobile number to see if she was back from Scotland.

"Giles," she shrieked with surprise. "How lovely!"

"How was Christmas, dear?"

"So, so, thanks. With my father not being very well, a few long lost uncles and aunts turned up out of the blue. And you know what? I discovered something."

"What's that?"

"Einstein was right. Time goes much more slowly when you're with relatives."

"Ha!"

"And yours?"

"Best forgotten—Christmas that is, though the same applies to most of my relatives. Where are you?"

"Have a guess."

"On top of Ben Nevis?"

"No. I haven't been on top of a Ben for weeks—a Hamish and a Mungo, but not a single Ben. Actually, I'm soaking in a hot bath in the flat. Cousin Ivor gave me a Vodafone bluetooth goose for Christmas. It floats with my phone between its wings. Then when someone calls, it quacks and paddles around in circles. Isn't that cute?"

"Very. Reminds me of Hank Weinberg's computer. Must remember to get a flock. But I thought Ivor was a successful lawyer. Is that all he gave you?"

"No. There was also a Harrods gift card worth five hundred pounds, and the key to his new studio apartment in Knightsbridge, which he said I could use for the New Year sales. Hold on, I'll switch on the speaker...there. Now I'm getting out."

"Fiona, listen, I called Conrad from the cottage and..."

"Sorry, me first. This is too important. Prepare yourself for a shock."

"Why?"

"Rashid Yamani has posted a message on MECCAR's website saying that the genetic code that Ahmad Sharif wrote on the back of the *Achilles* website report was not... repeat not...the Bedouins' DNA switch after all."

"WHAT! You're having me on?"

"No, I'm not."

"Hang on, I need to sit down on this bench...but that would mean..."

"That what Steve reported in Science and called *Deidamia* really *was* an artificial switch for *Achilles*. It wasn't his invention. Nothing changes that. But it wasn't the Bedouins' switch either. He jumped to the wrong conclusion, just like the rest of us have ever since."

"But...but...but where the hell did it come from then?"

"The website doesn't say. I guess Ahmad must have been working on alternative DNA switches for *Achilles*... presumably with success."

"But if that was the case, why didn't MECCAR lay claim to *Deidamia* when they saw Steve's paper?"

"Perhaps Ahmad had developed it on the quiet. If he'd used the Bedouins' code as a starting point, and played around with the base sequence in the hope of finding one that worked just as well, he might have got lucky. It's not impossible, is it?"

"No, it isn't. This is extraordinary. Okay, I must go now. There are two huge Irish wolfhounds here sniffing me all over. Must be the rural pong on my shoes. Bye."

"Hold on! You'd started to say something before."

"Oh, yes. I called Conrad over Christmas and told him about Aram's laptop. I had to prise it out of him, but it's true about that system that responds to coughs. And he said something else. Apparently, his company set up another system for MECCAR, this time for the transfer of encrypted information between the fellows' laptops and their server in Wadi Rum."

"That sounds a bit suspicious too. Why encrypted?"

"Good question. Okay, I'm off, before I'm buried in dog hairs. See you soon."

***

As soon as he was in his office, without stopping to remove his hat or coat, Giles went to his desk with the intention of sending MECCAR a request for more information. However, when he went to his emails, he saw that his inbox contained a message from Rashid Yamani with the subject line "Urgent rendezvous."

> "Dear Professor Butterfield,
>
> You will have learnt from MECCAR's website that what Dr Salomon called his *Deidamia* insertion was NOT the Bedouins' enhancer, and you will no doubt be wondering where it came from. Normally, I would not be permitted to comment on such a matter, but in view of the extraordinary effort you have made to protect my institute's intellectual property and reputation, I have been given permission to discuss the matter with you under conditions of strict confidentiality.
>
> I am staying in the Hôtel de Crillon in Paris for talks with the chairman of our trust. If I could meet you here during the evening of December 29, we could talk about it. I have already booked

a table for 8:00 p.m. in Les Ambassadeurs, and a suite for you in the hotel as my guest.

I apologise for the very short notice, but I have been waiting for some news from my staff in MECCAR before contacting you. More when we meet.

Kind regards, Rashid Yamani.

PS: I shall be in the bar from 7:20 pm. As we have never met, I have attached a photograph of myself. I am sure to recognise you from your famous picture in Stockholm. I hope the bus did not take too long to arrive!"

Chapter Four

Paris was wet and windy when Eurostar glided into the Gare du Nord. Giles took a taxi as far as the Louvre before completing his journey to the Place de la Concorde on foot. By the time he was inside the lobby of the Hôtel de Crillon, he was already five minutes late. Dropping his overcoat, hat, and overnight bag with the concierge, he hurried to the washroom to brush his hair and straighten his tie.

He approached the bar feeling strangely apprehensive. The sound of piano music, conversation, and laughter, softened by the upholstered chairs, thick carpets, and walnut panelling, had for him an unwelcome, almost alienating, quality. This was not his natural scene at all. Like most academics, he had stayed in many plush hotels for international congresses, but even the smartest had a very different atmosphere when overflowing with excited scientists sharing discounted rooms in place of the regular well-heeled clientele.

On entering the crowded room, uneasily dusting the sleeves of the same tweed jacket he'd worn during his fateful journey to Washington, his eyes settled on a distinguished middle-aged man, impeccably dressed in a light blue suit and gold silk tie, sitting on his own on the far side. Tall, good looking and well built, without being overweight, with greying hair, a neat black moustache and heavy tortoiseshell spectacles, it was unmistakably Rashid Yamani. Engrossed in a recent issue of the Journal of Human Genetics, he didn't notice his guest until he was on top of him.

"Professor Butterfield!" he gasped with a start, rising from his chair to shake his hand. How wonderful it is to meet you at last."

"Call me Giles, please."

"Thank you…and likewise. I feel that I know you already anyhow. Your great achievement has been given so much publicity in my part of the world that you're something of a celebrity there. Don't be surprised if you bump into a statue or two of yourself next time you're in Amman!"

After lifting a couple of glasses of fresh fruit juice from a passing trolley and placing them on the table, Rashid withdrew two copies of a confidentiality agreement from his attaché case, and offered them with an uncomfortable smile.

"Sorry about the formalities, Giles, but MECCAR takes secrecy very seriously, as you know."

After signing them and pushing one across the table, Giles sipped his juice nervously, as he waited for the news.

"Thank you for coming," Rashid continued, crossing his legs and making himself comfortable in his chair. "You must be very confused. So I'll waste no time and get straight to the point. It's to do with the nucleotide base sequence of that *Deidamia* insertion. You see, it's a bit of a puzzle. I said on our website that it wasn't the Bedouins' switch for *Achilles*, which is true. But there's more to it than that. It also had nothing to do with MECCAR. Neither Ahmad Sharif nor anyone else in my institute had been working on artificial switches for *Achilles*. I'm absolutely certain of that.

"You see, when we discovered the *Achilles* gene in those Bedouins, that's as far as we wanted to take it. Our policy when we make a breakthrough is different from yours in the West. We immediately move onto something else. As far as we were concerned, it was time for others to take over, people like you and that Alhazen Fellow of ours. How's he doing by the way?"

"Aram? Quite well, thanks."

Giles sipped his juice again, while hesitating to move onto his next question.

"Do you think Ahmad could have been doing it behind your back, Rashid? He was a dedicated scientist after all. Scientific curiosity can be an irresistible force. As you know too well, once you get started on something, it's difficult, sometimes impossible, to break off."

"I know what you mean, Giles. But no, definitely not. In MECCAR we keep meticulous inventories of all laboratory consumables—when they were ordered, by whom, when they were received, who used how much and for what purpose, what happened to the surplus, and so on. Everything is accounted for, from disposable pipette tips to the last few drops of an antiserum. My laboratory managers keep a database of the whole lot, which our auditing department checks regularly. On top of that, all our laboratories and offices have 24/7 CCTV, and all our computers work through a central server that records every keystroke of every keyboard. So you see, it would not have been possible for Ahmad to do such work without my knowledge."

"So, what's the explanation?"

Rashid leant forwards, beckoning Giles to move his chair closer to the table.

"There can be only one explanation," he whispered. "I'm afraid somebody must have given Ahmad the information in Sorrento. He jotted it down on one of the copies of the *Achilles* report he'd taken along to hand out to people, and by accident he gave that particular one to Dr Salomon."

Giles was about to suggest there may have been a deal between the two of them, but then decided against it.

"Why are you so sure Ahmad got the information in Sorrento, Rashid, and not before then?"

"He couldn't have taken it with him, not a chance."

Rashid raised his left hand to start counting his fingers.

"One, that trip to Italy was the first time I'd given him permission to attend an international meeting. Two, in accordance with our security procedures, which apply to everyone, all his mail, telephone calls, faxes, texts, and emails had been monitored. And three, his bags and clothing were searched at the airport by two of our aler'eah."

"Aler'eah? Shepherds?"

"That's right. That's what we call them. Your Arabic is pretty good! Whenever any one of us goes to a meeting, two security officers accompany us to the airport. One of the things they do is to check our bags and clothing in the departure lounge. I know it sounds extraordinary, but that's the way we operate. Such restrictions apply to everyone in MECCAR. We have a very efficient security department, run by an ex-senior KGB officer, and we also have very severe penalties for transgressions."

"Okay, well, let's assume you're right, and Ahmad got the details during the Sorrento symposium. Why would anybody want to give away such valuable information? An academic would have a career path paved with gold with a discovery like that under his or her belt. It doesn't add up, does it?"

"Good questions, Giles. As I would expect from you, very good questions. There is one scenario that I think can explain everything."

Rashid glanced over his shoulder before continuing.

"I'm afraid the sad truth is that Ahmad must have been acting as a fence."

"A fence? What do you mean?"

He leant forward again, gesturing to Giles to do likewise.

"A go-between."

"A go-between? In what way?"

"You haven't heard about the recent spate of DNA peddling?"

Giles raised his eyebrows in surprise, shaking his head.

"No?"

Embarrassed by his apparent ignorance, he tried to laugh it off.

"The only peddling I've encountered lately was when I was perched on the frozen crossbar of a certain Swedish bicycle."

"Ha! Yes, I can imagine the seat in that bus stop must have been heaven after Dr Olsson's favour. The point is this, Giles. These days there's big money in what's being called the gene trade. Corrupt biotech companies, mostly in China and Mexico, will pay huge sums for the details of hot DNA sequences. I attended a workshop on the subject in Singapore in November. Most of the information is supplied by crooked academics, who choose to sell the results of their work instead of publishing them. These rogues are often quite senior, even full professors, making preparations for a comfortable retirement. The rest are mostly research fellows worried about job security, and unemployed scientists who plant themselves in laboratories to spy in the guise of non-academic staff. In December we caught one among our cleaners, a Tunisian. She had not written anything down, just memorised the entire sequence of 857 nucleotide bases of part of a gene we'd been studying in our AIDS programme."

"Extraordinary!"

"Not in her case. She was a huffaz. If you can memorise the entire Qur'an, you can commit anything to memory. One night, she took a torch onto the roof of the main building, where we have a terrace, and started flashing the sequence in Morse code to an accomplice in the desert. Adenine, abbreviated to A, was dot-dash. Cytosine, C, was dash-dot-dash-dot. And so on. My helicopter pilot spotted her from a distance, when I was returning from Aqaba one night. Now she feeds the cacti in our residential complex."

"She's a gardener?"

Rashid dropped his eyes, as he needlessly adjusted his cufflinks in silence.

"Let's move on. She's not important any more. The young postdocs are the most successful peddlers. As they're not yet known on the international circuit, they can network more freely in the meetings. They can be very smart. Apparently, one of their tricks is to disguise the sequence of a length of DNA as something completely different, even colours in a picture, or as fake barcodes or QR codes on a piece of merchandise. Sometimes, they throw in some 'noise' — irrelevant colours, numbers or letters that are filtered out by whoever receives the information."

Giles fidgeted in his chair, as he became more and more embarrassed by his ignorance.

"I'm beginning to feel pretty stupid, I'm afraid, Rashid. I knew nothing about this business. How long has it been going on?"

"Not very long, but it's growing fast. So far, most of it's been to do with plant genes—genetically modified crops, and so on—which is why it isn't common knowledge among medical people like you."

"I see. But where does all this leave Ahmad?"

"I was coming to that. The postdocs prefer not to go to the companies directly. They like to stay in the background and pay someone else to do that job, somebody who already has a scientific reputation and will be taken seriously at the other end. The greater the credibility of the fence, the more money they can get out of the companies. It's all to do with confidence. Every case is different. In this one, I'd say somebody attended the Sorrento symposium with the sole intention of recruiting Ahmad. He wasted no time making contact, softened Ahmad up by questioning the morality of withholding the details of the Bedouins' switch from the world when it has the potential to save millions of lives, told him about the artificial one he'd invented, and made his proposal. Once Ahmad had been hooked, they met again to agree on the finances. Then he disappeared, telling the organisers he had to rush off for some reason—a message from home, sudden illness, anything. I'm sure that's what happened. There have been a few similar cases."

Giles looked aghast.

"Ahmad doing a deal with one of those crooks? Is that possible?"

"I understand your surprise, Giles. It's sad, very sad. But I'm afraid it's more than possible. There's no doubt in my mind that that's what must have happened. You see, Ahmad had never been happy with my promise to the Bedouins about never publishing anything special about their DNA. To be honest, I hadn't been too comfortable myself, but I had no choice. It was either that or no project. But Ahmad thought I should have tried harder. He felt deeply about that.

"Unfortunately, he was not very good at keeping his opinions to himself, and went as far as expressing them during an interview on German television. There was nothing wrong with that, of course. He was quite entitled to say how he felt on the matter. All I demand from my staff is that they adhere to the rules. They don't have to like them. But perhaps word got to the wrong person, who concluded that Ahmad would be a soft target.

"The other factor, of course, would have been the money. Chinese companies in particular will pay a fortune for this sort of information."

"Do you have any idea where the crook might have come from?"

"Most of them, of course, are from the countries with the best records in molecular biology: the USA, Switzerland, UK, Germany, Japan."

Giles closed his eyes, as he tried to take it in.

"I'm stunned, Rashid. I don't know what to think. You knew Ahmad much better than I did. In fact, I hardly knew him at all. But he didn't strike me as someone who would betray MECCAR for money. He seemed like a dedicated scientist."

"You're absolutely right, Giles. He was. His work was everything. The problem was not him. It was his wife, who I assume you have not had the misfortune to meet. While Ahmad was in Sorrento, she was with their children in a lakeside suite of the Villa Principe Leopoldo in Lugano. You can't do that for much less than two thousand Swiss francs a night."

Rashid gulped some of his juice, before crunching a mouthful of ice with such vigour that he hurt his gum in the process.

"Ouch! Damn bitch! Sorry, Giles, but that's what she is. Just the mention of her name makes my blood boil. Poor Ahmad was perpetually under pressure from her. She made his life hell. Shortly before going to Sorrento, he told me she was obsessed with putting their children into Le Rosey. Heard of it?"

"No."

"They call it Switzerland's 'school of kings,' the most expensive school in the world. MECCAR pays its staff very well, but not that well."

"But Ahmad told me she's a historian. She's published a book on the Bisistun Inscriptions."

"Yes, she is. And she has, a very good one as it happens. But her ambition is to write books on archaeology in the style of your country's Victorian scholars—in a large mansion overlooking beautiful scenery, interrupted only by cocktail parties and the occasional expedition to far off lands."

"And you think she could have pressured Ahmad into what you're suggesting?"

"No doubt about it. It was a bizarre marriage. He was incurably in love with her, and yet at the same time the cow was driving him to despair…with apologies to the real ones out there. He would have done anything to satisfy her wishes."

Giles scratched his head in disbelief.

"This is utterly bewildering, Rashid. If your theory is right…"

"I wouldn't call it a theory, Giles. It has to be right."

"But how could the creator of *Deidamia* have achieved it so quickly, in a matter of weeks? Steve tried to fool us into believing his fictitious computer programme was the key to success. But you're suggesting somebody actually did it in that time without one. How?"

Rashid shrugged his shoulders.

"Another very good question, Giles. And this time one to which I don't have the answer. There's a very smart geneticist out there somewhere. Very crooked, but also very smart."

"And very lucky, I'd say."

"Agreed. So far, at least!"

Giles hesitated before making his next point.

"Rashid, I hope this won't upset you. Please don't think I'm being critical, or casting aspersions, anything like that. It's just that I don't understand why, given what you knew about this DNA trafficking business, and the fact you had reason to believe Ahmad might be vulnerable…"

Rashid held up both hands to stop him asking the question.

"I know exactly what you're going to say. Why did I let him out? Yes?"

Giles nodded.

"I thought you'd ask that. It must look a little foolish, or at least reckless, on my part to have let him go to Sorrento. Yes, it's true that Ahmad was vulnerable. I thought about it long and hard before giving him permission. I had to weigh the chance of this sort of thing happening, which was very small, against the possibility of upsetting him, which I didn't want to do. I knew it was mostly thanks to his hard work that MECCAR had achieved so much and all that goes with it. So, I thought I owed it to him. And there was another factor in the equation. Like the rest of us at MECCAR, but particularly in his case I would say, Ahmad was very devout. His faith was extremely important to him. From what I have read about your youth in the Middle East, you must know that in Islam honesty and integrity are extremely important virtues. Indeed, they are more than that. They are essential. The Holy Qur'an makes it clear. Our great scholar al-Muhâsibî, founder of the Baghdad School of Islamic Philosophy, put it succinctly when he said, 'For honesty to be complete, it must exist in three things…in the heart as one's faith…in the intentions behind one's deeds, and…in the words that one speaks.'

"And there was something else. I knew Ahmad was committed not only to finding a cure for cancer, but also to our wider mission of returning Islamic scholarship to the pinnacle it once occupied, when we led the world in intellectual pursuits of every kind. By setting an example to universities in the Middle East, MECCAR has the potential to ignite another explosion of academic excellence throughout Islam. Ahmad was very much married to that idea. And so I convinced myself that his dual commitment to his faith and the ideals and ambitions of MECCAR would steer him from temptation, should it ever arise. But I think I was wrong. Unfortunately, these things happen in life. It is very sad.

"Excuse me, with all this talking, my mouth is dry."

"Mine too, but for another reason!"

As they finished their drinks, Giles reflected on how Rashid's belief in Ahmad's commitment to his faith dovetailed with the impression he had gained in Sorrento. But was it all a façade to cover up his true character? If Rashid was right about what had happened in Sorrento, could his death have been connected with it in some way? Had he become enmeshed in organised crime? After all, it had happened in southern Italy, hadn't it? Was the bottle of Svaneke Session pilsner, still collecting dust on his office mantelpiece, the key to the puzzle?

"My, that was good!" Rashid resumed, his glass drained dry. "Eight parts orange, one of lemon, one of lime, and one of grape juice. The girl behind the bar told me last night. By the way, did you know that every one of those fruits was originally brought to Europe by Arabs?"

"Yes, I did actually. Perhaps that's why you gave Ferdinand and Isabella the pip!"

"Ha ha! I must remember that one…very good! Except it can't be true, of course, because they also expelled the Jews. What a tragedy! Before those two came along, everyone was happy in the south of Spain. Jews, Muslims, and Christians living in harmony built a wonderful place, while the rest of Europe festered in ignorance and mediaeval squalor. Imagine what could have been, if that doctrine of tolerance and cooperation had spread throughout the world, instead of what we have.

"Okay, now that we've finished, let's go and enjoy the culinary delights of Les Ambassadeurs. All this talking has made me hungry. Or do you have more questions?"

"Just two."

"Fire away."

"Why have you confided in me, Rashid? Why didn't you give the full story on your website? Or call a press conference to give the same message? Why only me?"

"Two reasons, Giles, two very good reasons. Obviously, it would not be good for MECCAR's reputation for it to be known far and wide that our most famous scientist had been lured into the DNA underworld. Can you imagine how the world would have reacted to such news? I can hear them now. 'They cannot be trusted,' they would cry. 'Their faculty has links with criminal groups, exploiting medical research for personal wealth.' At the same time, Muslims everywhere would have said we have betrayed our faith, disgraced Islam. No, it would have been a disaster. We are a very wealthy institute, but we are also a very young one. We have had one great success with *Achilles*, but we want to survive long enough to have many more.

"Apart from that, I want the crook to be caught and punished. People like that are despicable. They make themselves rich by trading in something that belongs to humanity and has been paid for by charitable foundations, benefactors, and taxpayers. And they don't care to whom they sell the information, what it's used for, or what happens to it. We have to stamp it out, or it will spread like a forest fire. If I told a bunch of journalists what I've told you, there would be no chance of catching the rogue. Within hours, all the evidence would be destroyed without a trace.

"We're all at risk, Giles, including your famous college. But it's clear that MECCAR has already become the focus of attention. And more than anyone else, we cannot afford to lose one shred of our intellectual property. It is our life blood. If we lose that, we lose everything. Imagine if *Achilles* had been leaked. Right now, we have some very exciting discoveries on the HIV virus in the pipeline. I'm very worried about them, very worried indeed."

Rashid was trembling with emotion, as he felt in his pocket for the room key to show to the waitress.

"And there's another side to it, Giles, a very sinister side. If the trade is not stamped out, it won't be long before viruses engineered to deliver lethal genes into our brains, hearts, or liver are on the black market. DNA terrorism could be around the corner. The trade has to be killed before it's too late. If we catch whoever led Ahmad astray, it might help to take the lid off this underworld. And who knows what we might find inside. We have to catch the crook."

Giles looked over his glasses in earnest.

"I think you're right, Rashid. And by 'we,' I take it you mean me, yes?"

Rashid rose to his feet with a broad grin, and slapped Giles heavily on the back.

"Ha! Of course, Giles! Who else? You're the only person for this job. There's nobody with your gift for fishing in the murky waters of medical research. You've already hooked one big fish. These guys will be tiddlers for you, dangerous tiddlers, but tiddlers nevertheless. You know how academics think, how they tick, how they operate. You understand the science. You know your way around. You're a highly respected member of the club. You can go anywhere, visit any lab, infiltrate research teams, mix with congress delegates, probe, enquire, rub shoulders. The world of genetics is your world, Giles. And you've proved your worth. Interpol, the FBI, the rest—forget them! For this job, give me Giles Butterfield."

"Well, I must say, Rashid, I'm very flattered. I'll certainly think about it."

"Excellent! And your second question?"

Giles picked up his glass.

"Would you mind if I followed this with a large D 'n' S, and took it with me?" "What on earth's that?"

"Dark 'n' Stormy. Gosling's Black Seal rum, ginger beer, and a slice of lime. At times like this, it stops me from going off the rails."

"By all means. As long as I can stay with my usual, Veuve Clicquot."

For the rest of the evening, both Rashid Yamani and Les Ambassadeurs lived up to their reputations. The meal, though prepared with exquisite skill, was not to Giles's liking, but his new friend's company was more than compensation. Conrad had been right during their time in Cape Town. MECCAR had chosen an exceptional man as its first director. Under his watch, its success would surely continue. But in spite of his host's great intellect, erudition and charm, Giles would remember the occasion mostly for the turmoil that was inside his head.

The revelation about gene peddling had been shattering. How could he have been so poorly informed about something of such importance in his own back yard? Perhaps he had overlooked an editorial on the subject in one of the journals. And of course, for the past few weeks he'd been virtually out of action. With all that rushing around and so many problems to sort out, it had been impossible to keep up with the literature. Perhaps that's why he had missed it.

There were other concerns too. Was it possible, he wondered, that Aram's odd behaviour in the lab, and that of the other Alhazen Fellows Fiona had told him about, was tied up with all this? Could they have been fishing for information to put on the market?

Equally worrying was the prospect of being drawn into another detective hunt. He had not yet recovered physically or mentally from the first. Was he up to it? Was Fiona up to it? Would she agree to it? He would certainly need her help. She had been a tower of strength in Washington and Cape Town. Without her talent, initiative, and resourcefulness, Steve Salomon would surely have got away with it.

There was also their personal safety to think about. Hank Weinberg's veiled references in Bethesda to reprisals by Steve, his family, or those dependent on him professionally could have been mere bluster in the hope of frightening him off. But if Rashid was right about an illicit DNA trade worth millions, there could be a real risk this time. Thugs and crime syndicates must have got into the act by now.

And what about Sir Quentin? He had regarded the two of them as heroes up to now. But what if everything went disastrously wrong? How would he react then?

While Rashid was chatting about his childhood in Lebanon, his experiences as a student in America, and how he would like to spend some study leave in Magdalen, Giles's mind wandered back to the Sorrento symposium to picture the scenes in the hotel and congress centre—in the lobby, the bar, on the terrace, in and around the lecture theatres, everywhere he could think of. If Rashid had got it right, he must have set eyes on Ahmad's contact on at least one occasion during the event. Who on earth could it have been?

Giles was reflecting on the similarity of his present dilemma to the one he had endured in his office overnight before setting off for Washington, when Rashid tapped him on the wrist with his napkin.

"You haven't said much, Giles. Haven't been boring you with my life's story, I hope?"

"Of course not, Rashid. I've enjoyed the evening immensely. But I have to admit you've put a weight on my shoulders."

"What you need is a good night's sleep. Everything will look different in the morning. I won't be able to hold you back. You were made for this sort of thing, Giles. Go for it!"

A couple of hours later, Giles was admiring the lights of the Place de la Concorde through the suite's window as he continued to struggle with his predicament.

"Wait till Fiona hears about this," he remarked to his reflection. "So much for a conspiracy starring Steve, Hank, and Ted Crabb, with a supporting cast of the CIA, Swiss banks, and high-class tarts! Just when it seemed you'd dragged yourself out of the quagmire, Giles, you're sliding into another one. In fact, it's worse than that. You're already up to your neck in it, gasping for breath, looking for a lifeline as it sucks you down."

As it was too late to call Fiona, he decided to send her a text message.

"What shall I say? Can't give her the whole story. That'll have to wait. I know, what could be more appropriate than a line from Seamus Heaney's Bogland?"

He dropped onto the bed and sent his message.

> 'Black butter, melting and opening underfoot'
> See you soon!
> Giles.

"See if she can work that one out. The book I picked up in Frankfurt has earned its keep after all."

Chapter Five

"Paddington as fast as you can go!" Giles screeched to the driver as the black cab moved away from the forecourt of St. Pancras Station. "Can you believe the Eurostar arrived an hour late this morning, and the Northern, Victoria and Piccadilly tube lines are all paralysed with signal failures? It's absolute hell in there.

"On second thoughts, it'll take an age to get through this damn traffic. To hell with it! Take me all the way to Oxford. I'll use my credit card and claim it back. After all, it won't cost my host in Paris much more that his vintage champagne."

Within minutes of scampering through the College gates, Giles burst into Fiona's office to find her rummaging through her filing cabinet. After a quick kiss on the forehead, he hung his wet coat on the back of the door, and dropped onto a lab stool.

"I've just had a new experience, Fiona. Came all the way by taxi, can you believe? I'm sure Rashid will foot the bill. You should have seen the suite he put me in."

"Don't make me jealous! Coffee?"

"Yes, please. Well, I learnt something quite extraordinary last night, Fiona. You got my cryptic message?"

"Yes. Where did the quote come from?"

"Seamus, the College's very own Nobel in literature. You should read him. He grows on you."

"Really?"

"Absolutely. Listen to this."

Giles cleared his throat in preparation for a light-hearted tribute in the best Irish brogue he could manage.

"Like an ancient lichen clinging to the northern aspect of an ageing oak's gnarled and twisted trunk, slowly and imperceptibly it evolves to acquire a pure and simple beauty that belies the symbiotic complexity that lies within.

"See what I mean?"

Fiona placed a mug of coffee in his hand.

"If that's what it does to your voice, I think I'll give it a miss! Now, tell me all about last night. So it we're up to our necks in it again, are we?"

"You could say that. Let me start at the beginning. He's very impressive, and quite charming to boot, although I suspect there's a dark side to his character. I've never met anybody like him really. We got on pretty well, so much so he's thinking of spending a sabbatical here in a few years' time."

"That's good news. But what did he say?"

"We met in the bar. You should have seen it. Everyone looked loaded, even the barmaid. I learnt later that Saudis have just bought the hotel. So you can imagine…"

"Come one, Giles! I'm not interested in the barmaid or the hotel. What did he say?"

"Sorry! Well, first he confirmed what he'd said on the website, namely that Steve's *Deidamia* most definitely is not the Bedouins' DNA switch. And what's more, he was adamant that neither Ahmad nor anyone else in MECCAR had been working on anything to do with artificial switches for *Achilles*. Although Steve clearly got the information from Ahmad, about that there is no doubt, Ahmad definitely did not take it with him to Italy."

"What's the explanation then?"

"He reckons it must have been passed on to Ahmad during the symposium by the inventor."

"For a collaboration of some sort?"

"MECCAR doesn't collaborate. Remember?"

"Oh, yes. So?"

"He thinks it was probably a crooked university researcher, who was looking to sell the information to a biotech company, and needed a credible go-between. He told me about an illegal trade in DNA sequences. It was news to me. Have you heard about it?"

"Yes, I have. There was an article in New Scientist. Apparently, it's a big problem in plant genetics. To make matters worse, organised crime syndicates have been running protection rackets. Based on intelligence gathered by their hackers, they contact the perpetrators and threaten to expose them, and worse, if they don't play ball. The President of the Royal Society blames it on the low salaries and chronic insecurity of academic jobs. But don't worry, I'm not tempted!"

"That's good news! Clearly, I need to catch up. Well, Rashid believes one of those crooks must have attended the symposium in Sorrento, told Ahmad about his invention, and guaranteed him a chunk of the proceeds in return for finding a buyer. Apparently, the Chinese will pay eye-watering sums."

"Does Rashid have any evidence?"

"No."

"So, it's only speculation?"

"Strictly speaking, but he can't think of any other explanation. And he reckons Ahmad was under pressure from his wife to get rich quick."

"So, he thinks Ahmad was seduced into finding a buyer for the base sequence, jotted it down on the back of one of the *Achilles* reports he'd taken along to hand out, and then carelessly gave that one to Steve?"

Giles nodded.

"I hope he's wrong. It would be very sad. Given the organised crime that's infiltrated the racket, it also makes me wonder about Ahmad's death. Why do you think Rashid chose to tell you, and presumably nobody else?"

"He wants to keep a lid on it to protect MECCAR's reputation, while yours truly finds the villain."

"And what did you say?"

"That I needed time to think about it, and to talk to you."

"Certainly sounds like another worthy cause. But this one could be dangerous, very dangerous."

"That's what I thought too. But as you know, when I've started a job, I can't rest until it's finished. And clearly this one isn't. So, either I try to forget about it for the rest of my life, or we carry on until we're there.

"What do you think? Should we go for it?"

Fiona dropped onto a stool and held her head in her hands, her long red hair hiding her face and falling onto her knees.

"The decision's yours, dear. Think it over. If you say yes, we give it a go. If you say no, we don't. Simple as that."

Emptying his mug into the sink, he collected his coat and case, and placed a comforting hand on her head.

"When you've reached your decision, give me a call, either in the office or at home. Take your time."

He was halfway through the door, when she stirred.

"Giles."

"Yes."

"I've got a question."

"What's that?"

"When do we start?"

Chapter Six

Having agreed with Fiona that everything must be above board this time, or at least as much as possible, their first job after lunch was to tell Sir Quentin about the development and get his approval. After tidying her hair, applying some mascara and lipstick, putting on a clean lab coat, and dropping a plastic pipette, steel spatula, and felt-tipped marker pen into its top pocket to look businesslike, Fiona accompanied him to reinforce the message that this would be another team effort.

When Sir Quentin's secretary led them into his office, they found him in a restless mood. Continually drumming his fingers on the desktop, fidgeting, and moving his legs, his chair squeaked and groaned throughout the meeting. Giles guessed it was because the New Year's Honours List was about to be announced, always a stressful time for a man who craved for such accolades. Either that or his long-running divorce had run into more financial squabbling. Whatever the reason, he was in no frame of mind to hear the full story of Giles's trip to Paris.

"No need for the gory details," he spouted, as Giles began to describe Ahmad Sharif's wife. "I sympathise with the poor man. Some women can be so greedy. He should have told her to pack her bags long ago. Probably everything she owns was due to his hard work and dedication. It doesn't matter how much you do for some people, they're never happy. You put up with it for years, and then…never mind!"

He stopped talking to tidy up his pen pot, seemingly oblivious to his visitors, in a world of his own, until he knocked it over and spilled the pens and pencils on to the floor.

"Damn! Must get a bigger one. This one is useless. The thing is you've told me enough already, Giles. What Professor Yamani said is obviously very worrying. Why don't the two of you just get on with it. It's okay by me. But there are a few conditions. One, you must let me know whenever you're flying off somewhere. Two, as irksome as they can be at times, the students must never be neglected. And three, you must send me regular progress reports.

"Now, having settled that, why don't the two of you stop for a glass of sherry. I opened a new bottle last night."

Giles and Fiona glanced at each other as he collected a half-empty bottle from the bookcase behind him.

"Very kind of you Quentin. We'd love to, wouldn't we, Fiona. But we've an experiment running in the lab we must get back to."

"Fair enough. Let me show you out."

As they crossed the lawn, hand in hand, Sir Quentin waved and called to them from the doorway.

"And a bit of advice. Don't give Jane a hint of your hotel arrangements. Take it from me, it's not a good idea around here!"

As they made their way across St. John's Quad, the approaching archway under St. Swithun's Tower, only ten days previously the returning hero's triumphal arch, was now as a gateway to the unknown. The grassy square beyond, boxed in on three sides and the focal point of so many unseen eyes, with the open pasture of the Deer Park barely visible through the distant mist to the north, seemed to embody their new predicament.

Upon entering Giles's' office, his eyes were drawn to the Svaneke Session bottle on the mantelpiece, now containing only dejected twigs in a sea of fallen petals. It was a sad sight, but one that fired his determination to solve the mystery. And below it was good news. For attached to the mantelpiece was a note from Jane to apologise for not having had the time to reorganise and tidy the room while he'd been in Paris, as promised.

Confident it would still be under his desk, Giles dropped to his knees to retrieve the cardboard box in which he had dumped the programme and name badges from the Sorrento symposium, which as the Society's next Secretary it had been his job to archive. Taking it next door, they sat on the sofa and ran their eyes down the list of attendees in the programme. They had been cancer geneticists long enough to know they could exclude all but a handful of the names as potential sources of *Deidamia*'s details. There were just five whom neither had ever met: a Gaston Davignon of the Université Toulouse III, Prof Fernando Lopez of the Universitat de Barcelona, a Dr Gerhard Goldschmidt-Theissen of the Ludwig-Maximilians-Universität-München, and two research fellows from the Università degli Studi di Firenze. As Fiona jotted down their email addresses and telephone numbers, she suggested that Giles should telephone each of them to say he was thinking of organising a workshop on the *Achilles* gene, and was trying to gauge how much interest there would be in the idea. During the call, he could try and learn something about their laboratories and recent work.

By nine-thirty the following morning, everything had gone more or less according to plan. Four of the five names had already been eliminated. Giles was about to call the fifth, when Jane entered, earlier than expected. As she was hanging her hat and coat, Giles nipped into the next room while Fiona kept her chatting. A minute later, he reappeared, wiping his hands on the back of his trousers.

"Jane, before you get started, could you pop out for some coffee grounds? I've just seen we've run out, and I'm desperate for a cup."

"Are you sure, Professor?" she said frowning. "There were plenty before I went to London. Let me go and check."

Giles buried his head in the programme, while Fiona sorted through the name badges.

"That's very odd," she called back. "The sink's covered in coffee grounds."

"Really? I didn't notice." Giles mumbled. "Perhaps Sir Q's secretary dropped in for emergency supplies, as she sometimes does, and knocked the tin over. That would explain it. She has the key, of course."

"Never mind. The walk to the market will do me good."

As soon as her footsteps were no longer audible, Giles called the last person on his list, Gerhard Goldschmidt-Theissen in Munich. To his frustration, the programme had given only the university's main number, not his direct line, on top of which the operator, new to the job, hadn't heard of him. After some persistence, he persuaded her to put him through to the director of the Gene Centre Professor Anastasia Kohl, an elderly lady with a light Bavarian accent, answered and listened while he explained the purpose of his call.

"I'm afraid poor Gerhard is no longer with us," she sighed. "He died soon after returning from the symposium in Sorrento you mentioned. It was very sudden. Apparently, he was quite well when he left here, but became ill soon after arriving in Italy. He returned at once to see his family doctor, but he died the same night. I was told it was a subarachnoid haemorrhage. So sad. I gather he was very clever and had a bright future."

"What a tragedy! Just out of interest, Professor Kohl, do you know what sort of work he'd been doing?"

"I don't know the details, I'm afraid. It all happened before I moved here from Hamburg. But I do know it was to do with the regulation of gene expression—promoters, enhancers, transcription factors, that sort of thing."

"I see. What happened to his group? Perhaps I could I talk to one of them about my idea for a workshop."

"He didn't have one at the time. His grants had run out and he was short of money. It was just him—no research assistant or lab techs. I don't know what he was doing. Nobody seemed to know very much. By the time I arrived, his lab had been cleared, and another of our groups was moving in. It all happened very quickly."

"I see. Professor Kohl, what you said about his work is very interesting. Do you think I could pay you a visit?"

"Why should you want to do that, Professor Butterfield?"

"It's possible Gerhard may have discovered something very important about the *Achilles* gene. And if so, it might be sitting in his lab books, never to see the light of day."

"Why on earth do you think that?"

"A friend told me he'd travelled by train from Naples to the Sorrento symposium with a young German from Munich, who was in the middle of writing up some exciting findings on the regulation of the *Achilles* gene. Apparently, he was planning to submit it to Nature or Science. So it must have been very important. That's all he was told. No details. But I think it must have been Gerhard. Nobody else from Munich attended the symposium. If you'd let me go through his lab books, assuming they're still around, I could see what he was doing. If I found anything important, I could present it during my workshop—giving him and your institute full credit, of course."

"It's an unusual request, I must say, Professor, but I see no reason to say no. All his things are packed away in boxes in the basement. It will be very quiet here next week. Could you manage Tuesday? I'll be having a long New Year's weekend between now and then."

"Yes, I could, thank you. What time should I arrive?"

"Ten-thirty?"

"Perfect. I look forward to meeting you."

As he replaced the handset, Giles was convinced he was onto something. This had to be the German, whom Steve had invited to join Ahmad and the girls to discuss their work in Sorrento. If he'd been so short of money and was working on his own, the temptation to cash in on a discovery known only to him could have been irresistible.

Throughout the call, Fiona had been at Jane's desk in the adjacent room, on the lookout in case she made an early return via the Lodge, instead of her usual route across the Longwall Quad.

"You know, Fiona," he called, "I think Rashid made a pretty good choice with us. Do you remember I mentioned Steve had invited a German to discuss the girls' research projects in Sorrento?"

"Yes."

"But he had to go home early because of a headache, and Steve took his place?"

"Yes."

"Well, he's the man we're looking for, I'm sure. He must have been. He died from a brain haemorrhage after getting back to Munich. On top of which, his profile sounds perfect for a gene peddler—young, very smart, working on gene regulation, and desperate for money. What more could we want? Game, set, and match!"

Fiona eyed him sceptically from the doorway.

"Sounds too good to be true, Giles. Who told you this?"

"Professor Anastasia Kohl."

"What did she say about his work?"

"She didn't have any details."

"Pity! So what's next?"

"She's given me permission to go through his lab books in case there are some unpublished data on *Achilles* sitting there. After the weekend, I'm off to Munich to do exactly that. We could have gone together, of course, if you didn't have that report to finish for the Wellcome Trust."

"Never mind. I can do without all those sausages and sauerkraut. I'm trying to lose weight. At least you're not going tonight, and we can spend New Year's Eve together. What time should I expect you this evening?"

"Ten?"

"The haggis will be steaming in its pot."

Chapter Seven

After the best New Year's weekend he could remember in a long time, Giles arrived in Munich the following Tuesday with his pulse racing. Anastasia Kohl, a demure, slim lady with short white hair, was waiting for him outside the elevator, having been notified of his arrival by the porter.

"Good morning, Professor Butterfield, and a Happy New Year!" she said cheerfully, offering her hand. "My P.A. is off all week, so you can use my office. You will not be disturbed."

As she led him into a large room whose floor-to-ceiling windows overlooked the institute's leafy suburban setting, Giles was taken aback. In Britain, academics generally work in a sea of paper and books, more often than not in cramped space cluttered with dilapidated furniture. Window ledges are more likely to be occupied by coffee mugs than plant pots, and if there are any of the latter, their occupants would usually be dust-covered and dehydrated. Apart from the removal of rubbish, these rooms were no-go zones for cleaners. By contrast, many of his American friends had the benefit of a veritable home from home, comfortably furnished with their personal choice of anything from oriental lamps to hi-fi systems and rocking chairs. Although his temporary office in the NCI during his sabbatical with Steve had not been in the same category, the year had taught him how the right environment could enhance his productivity, a lesson he'd put to good use in Oxford.

But Anastasia Kohl's was unlike any office he had ever seen. In the centre of the polished wooden floor, six lime green leather chairs encircled a round glass table that reflected the morning sunlight onto a wall of stainless-steel shelves, each packed with books seemingly arranged according to their colour. A desk of walnut and tubular chrome, its surface empty but for a pot of artificial pansies, reminded him of one he had seen in a Bauhaus catalogue. Above the desk, a large Mondaine Swiss railway clock ticked loudly, far too loudly in his opinion, as if to impress upon all the importance of punctuality and good timekeeping. Apart from a matt black sideboard that accommodated a percolator, that's all there was. No easy chairs or coffee table, no rug, not even a desk lamp. The absence of a trash can was explained when she dropped a crushed Tchibo coffee box and empty Coca-Cola can into the deepest drawer of her desk.

As she busied herself preparing a pot of coffee, Giles toured the prints that adorned the plain white walls. A huge Kandinsky of twelve multicoloured bulls-eyes had pride of place opposite the windows that overlooked the garden. On the wall to its left was a chequered pattern punctuated by occasional black boxes with what looked like fungus growing from their tops, which Giles guessed was by Klee. On the other wall was a Mondrian of straight black lines and coloured rectangles. To him, they were all meaningless patterns masquerading as works of art by men whose reputations for genius were illusions born of a pseudo-intellectual clientele with money to burn. He reflected on how different they were from the Georgina Lara of an English farmyard scene that hung over his fireplace in the College, and James Docharty's atmospheric painting of the Trossachs that Fiona loved so much in his living room. He was about to launch into a discussion of the art world when he was interrupted.

"I know what you're thinking," she said with a twinkle in her eye, as she arranged the crockery on the table. "Every visitor loves them!"

Giles agreed that the best German porcelain is among the finest.

"Oh no, not the cups and saucers! I meant the paintings. I chose each one myself. I find them so comforting. The stress of budgets, rejected manuscripts, and university politics just melts away when I scan my eyes around these walls. And do you know? I'm so excited. My wealthy banker of a brother has just bought me an original— an *original* can you believe? — from Josef Albers' series Homage to the Square. Aren't you jealous?"

Having seen a few examples in a Christie's catalogue in his dentist's waiting room several years ago, Giles did not share her enthusiasm.

"Sorry to be a bore, Professor Kohl, and I hope this doesn't offend, but is there really any more to those paintings by Albers than three or four squares of different colours planted one on top of the other? You or I could do the same with one eye closed, couldn't we?"

"Oh dear, you're one of those, are you?"

"Yes, I am actually. Take that Mondrian, for example. If I painted a criss-cross of black lines on white paper, and then coloured in a few of the boxes with yellow, red and blue, it would be worth nothing. But simply because a rich American socialite with a vast art collection once admired his simple childish patterns, and made a noise about it, they now fetch millions. Did she ever explain why she thought he was a genius? Or what her qualifications were to make such a judgment? Has anyone ever questioned her motives?"

"Her motives? What do you mean?"

"Well, think about it. If someone owns work by an unknown painter that they bought for next to nothing, and then convinces the world that the artist is or was a genius, he or she is suddenly sitting on a gold mine. Right?"

"Er…yes…I suppose that would be true, in theory. I can see we must have a chat one day. We're clearly on very different wavelengths. But I do admire your frankness, Professor. I like that in a man. Your coffee will be ready soon. Meanwhile, I'll go and get what you came for. I asked my P.A. to put them in a cupboard in the corridor. Excuse me for a second."

She returned carrying five large notebooks covered in doodles of mathematical formulae and chemical equations, and placed them in the centre of the glass table.

"As far as we can tell, these record all the laboratory work he ever did. His experiments during the period from MECCAR's announcement of the discovery of the *Achilles* gene to the Sorrento symposium are in the red one. There are about one hundred pages of handwritten notes. Fortunately, his writing is very clear, and it's all in English. We couldn't find any computer files for this period. He used his own laptop, and his poor wife collected it along with his other personal effects."

"If I wanted to look in his laptop, would it be possible to contact her?"

"I think it might be difficult. She's Japanese, and has returned to Kyoto with their two children. So I'll leave you to it. I'm off to the library, and then to see a colleague. Help yourself to coffee, and there are biscuits in the tin."

When she returned, Giles had gone through every page that Gerhard Goldschmidt-Theissen had written during the weeks running up to the symposium, and was admiring the garden as he pondered the implications of what he had seen.

"Well, was it worth the trip, Professor?" she asked, clearly in a great hurry as she collected her hat and coat from behind the door.

"Yes, thank you. In fact, there was…"

"Sorry, not just now," she interjected. "Please forgive me. I'd love to know what you've found, but I should have collected my granddaughter ten minutes ago. She'll be waiting for me outside the building, wondering where I am. I'm terrified for her safety. Send me a message as soon as you're back in Oxford."

She withdrew a small photograph of a blonde toddler from her handbag.

"This was her a few years ago. Isn't she pretty? You wouldn't believe how ugly her father is. I think there must be a lot about genes we don't understand!"

"She's lovely. I'm sure you cherish every moment with her. Don't let me hold you up. I'll be in touch. And thank you once again. It's been most useful."

After a night in the Vierjahrezeiten as the university's guest, Giles arrived back at Magdalen at around three o'clock the following afternoon. To avoid passing Jane's window, he made his way to the New Building via the Cloister. Recognising his footsteps, Fiona ran into the corridor to greet him.

"Giles, welcome back!" she enthused, throwing her arms around him.

"Thanks. You look very excited. Do you have good news for some reason?"

"More than good. Are you ready for a big shock?"

"What about?"

"While you were away, I discovered something—something really important for both of us."

"What?"

"I'm expecting…"

"What?"

"I said I'm *expecting*…"

"Jesus! But…"

"Isn't it wonderful?"

"Er…well…"

Fiona propped herself against the wall, weak with laughter.

"Sorry, my little joke. I'm expecting…you to be happy that I've solved it."

"What on earth are you talking about?"

"*Deidamia*. You didn't find a trace of her in Munich, did you?"

"As a matter of fact, no, I didn't. I went through every page of his lab books, and found nothing to do with *Achilles* either. How did you know?"

"Because I've solved the puzzle of where she came from, or at least I think I have. The answer came to me yesterday, completely out of the blue. And it's nothing to do with DNA peddling, or anything like that."

"What is it then?"

"You'll have to wait until tonight," she teased.

"Why?"

"Too busy right now. There's too much to explain."

"But surely, you can give me a clue?"

"Sorry. If you come round tonight, I promise I'll give it to you. And if you're a good boy, it might be in more ways than one!"

"Well, there's no way I can turn that one down."

"I said *might*."

Chapter Eight

Ever since moving to Oxford, Fiona had rented the same cosy one-bedroom flat on the top floor of Number 2, Mansfield Road, a large detached house surrounded by mature well-tended gardens, just ten minutes by foot from the College gates.

Giles arrived as punctual as ever at nine o'clock, looking the worse for an unexpected downpour on the way. As he reached the top-floor landing, Fiona was waiting at the open door, hands on hips. Wearing a short silk Japanese dressing gown tied tightly around her waist, gold high-heeled slippers, long silver earrings, and rather more makeup and perfume than usual, she seemed ready for a very special evening.

"Look at you!" she sympathised, welcoming him with a kiss. "You're drenched. Leave your shoes and jacket here, while I get something for your head."

She returned giggling with a fresh towel in her arms.

"I almost said for your hair! There, polish it with that. Everything's prepared for you."

"So I see. But isn't there some work to do first?"

"Yes, there is actually. Sorry to disappoint. By the way, do you like my new earrings? I'm off to London tomorrow to find a matching necklace in the sales. I told you about Ivor's offer to use his new studio apartment in Knightsbridge, didn't I?"

"Yes, you did. And his Harrods gift card to go with it. Very generous, although I guess he can afford it."

"Even so, it's nice of him. Okay, help yourself to a drink, and we'll get started."

As Giles mixed a D 'n' S at the sideboard, he saw that she'd prepared the dining table for the occasion. Nothing unusual about that, except on this occasion it was not the familiar Tain pottery and tartan napkins, but a fountain pen, several sheets of lined paper, an open book, and a calculator. After dropping a couple of ice cubes into his glass and giving it a swirl, he was intrigued to see what the book was about. Lifting the cover, he read its title aloud.

"'Evolution: Possible or Impossible?' by James F. Coppedge."

"Do you know it?" Fiona asked as she reappeared from the kitchen drying her hands.

"Can't say I do."

"It's quite fascinating. But leave it for now. Its moment will come."

She offered him a chair at the table.

"Now, you'll have to forgive me if this sounds a bit like a public lecture. But there's a reason for that. As I've a sneaky feeling I'll be doing this for a few journalists very soon, I thought I might as well make it a sort of dress rehearsal."

Giles smirked as he adjusted his glasses.

"Which journalists: Playboy or Cosmopolitan?"

"I'll ignore that comment. Okay, here goes. But wait a minute. I'll get up. It feels strange sitting down."

Fiona moved to the side of the fireplace to stand in front of an antique copper floor lamp she had picked up in Morocco a few years back.

"Right, so…"

"Before you start, dear, could you switch that light off?"

"Sorry, is it disturbing you?"

"No, something else is!"

"What if I stand to the right a bit? Is that better?"

"Yes thanks, much better."

"Okay, here goes. Now remember, I'm imagining you're a journalist. The first thing I need to explain is that every piece of DNA is like a ladder, each side of which is composed of a string of sugar molecules. To each sugar molecule is attached a single molecule of what we call a nucleotide base, or just a base for short. Chemical bonds between the bases hold the two sides of the ladder together. So, each rung is made up of two bases. In nature there are lots of different bases, but only four of them are found in DNA. They're called cytosine, thymine, adenine and guanine, and the order in which they occur as you go up the ladder is what we call its base sequence, more commonly known as its genetic code. Parts of the DNA provide the recipes for the synthesis of proteins in other parts of the cell. These are the genes. Other parts regulate the activities of the genes. And still others have no known function."

She skipped to the table and turned over the top sheet of paper to reveal a simple diagram of DNA.

"What Stephen Salomon called *Deidamia* is one side of a short length of DNA, a single chain of sugar molecules with base molecules attached. When this is inserted it into the DNA of cells at precisely the right distance from the *Achilles* gene, the cell synthesizes the other half of the ladder. The extra piece of DNA so formed, what we call an insertion, then acts as a switch for *Achilles*. From then on, if the cell should ever turn into a cancer cell, the switch would detect certain chemicals it produces, and respond by activating *Achilles*, resulting in the death of the cell. You can think of it like a sprinkler system in a building. It does nothing for years. Then, when a fire breaks out in one room, it detects the heat, and immediately douses the flames to prevent the fire from spreading. The room is ruined, but the building is saved.

"Now, *Deidamia* is very small as strands of DNA go. It has just seven molecules of those bases in the order shown here."

She turned over the next sheet of paper to reveal the base sequence.

CYTOSINE–THYMINE–GUANINE–GUANINE–
THYMINE–ADENINE–CYTOSINE

"But of course, the usual way to write such sequences is to use the first letters only, and omit the hyphens between them. So the sequence then looks like this."

She turned over the third sheet.

CTGGTAC

"Which is what Dr Sharif wrote near the picture of the *Achilles* gene on the back of the now famous website report that somehow fell into Stephen Salomon's hands. So far, so good?"

"Yes, thank you, Dr Cameron," Giles answered, raising his hand to cover his eyes, "except you're standing in front of that lamp again!"

"Sorry, I'll switch it off…there. Now, let's move to Sorrento. Dr Salomon invited three people to meet Dr Sharif in private during the symposium. Their names were Carina Taricani, an Italian girl; Gerhard Goldstein-Theissen, a young German scientist from Munich; and a French girl called Amandine Coupe."

She wrote down the three names:

Carina Taricani   Gerhard Goldstein–
Theissen   Amandine Coupe

"Except, Dr Cameron," Giles interrupted flippantly, "it was Goldschmidt–Theissen, not Goldstein–Theissen."

"Thank you, kind sir. But as you'll soon see, it could have been Goldilocks– Theissen, and it would make no difference."

She pointed to the names.

"Notice anything else about them?"

"Yes," Giles quipped, "your writing never gets any better!"

"Giles, be serious!"

She drew a heavy circle around the first letter of each word.

"Notice anything now?"

"Yes. The first letters go C, T, G, G, T, A and C."

"And?"

"That's the same as *Deidamia*'s base sequence."

"So?"

"Quite a coincidence, isn't it?"

"Quite a *coincidence*? Is that all you have to say?"

"Yes. A remarkable one, but that's all it can be, surely? I don't see how the two could be connected, do you? Why on earth would Ahmad have written the initials of those three just above the picture of the *Achilles* gene?"

"Well, perhaps when Steve called him about the arrangements for their private meeting, Ahmad wrote the initials on the first thing that came to hand to remind him of who would be there."

"But why only their initials?"

"Maybe he was in a hurry, or perhaps Steve called him when he was shaving, about to go out, or about to say his prayers. Anything. There are all sorts of scenarios that could have led him to scribble down a note in shorthand."

"Well, it's an interesting idea, Fiona, I must say. But it's only speculation, isn't it? We don't have a shred of evidence to support it. And as long as it stays that way, I think we have to assume it was a coincidence. The scenario suggested by Rashid is far too serious to ignore. I don't think we can drop it simply on the basis of this, without anything else to go on. Clearly, my suspicions about Gerhard were wrong, but if Rashid was right, the crook who enticed Ahmad into his web of crime is still out there, and may have been linked to his death in some way."

"I agree some extra evidence would be a big advantage. But do you have any idea what the chances are of it having been just a coincidence?"

"Not off the top of my head, of course not. Do you?"

"Yes, I do actually. I've worked it out. Have a guess."

"Let me think—about one in five hundred?"

"Ha! Try again."

"Okay, let's say one in five thousand."

"Keep going."

"One in ten thousand?"

Fiona shook her head in dismay.

"It's pretty obvious you're not a statistician, Giles. And as it's not exactly my strong point either, I looked for some help in here."

She placed her hand on the open book.

"This chapter tells you how to calculate the likelihood of getting any given series of letters when they're taken at random from the alphabet. Let's work it out for this case. I think you're going to find it interesting. Are you sitting comfortably?"

"Yes."

"Right. How many letters are there in our alphabet?"

"Er…twenty-four."

"Wrong. Twenty-six. Therefore, under normal circumstances we would need to calculate the likelihood of getting any series of seven letters, when they're taken at random one after another from the twenty-six of the alphabet, in a situation where taking a letter once does not affect its chances of being taken again. However, this particular case is complicated by the fact that, unusual for a German, the man from Munich had a hyphenated name, on account of which we have to treat 'GT' as if it were a twenty-seventh letter. So, what we actually need to calculate is the likelihood of getting a six-letter word when taking letters at random from a twenty-seven-letter alphabet. And the answer to that is twenty-seven to the power of six."

Giles raised his eyebrows.

"Are you sure?"

"Yes. It's all in here, in this book. You can see for yourself later. So, we're talking about a probability of one in…"

She wrote it down, before working out the answer with the calculator.

$$27^6 = 27 \times 27 \times 27 \times 27 \times 27 \times 27 = 387,420,489$$

"Which means that, in round numbers, the likelihood of getting CTGGTAC in precisely that order purely by chance would have been about one in three hundred and eighty-seven million. Still with me?"

Giles stared at the numbers in silence.

"Now, obviously if Ahmad had been writing down their initials, he wouldn't have had to do so in that particular order.

Any order of the three pairs CT, GGT and AC would have done, remembering that although GGT looks like a triplet it actually stands for the pair G and G-T. The number of different orders in which any three pairs of letters can be written is factorial three. In other words, 3 multiplied by 2 multiplied by 1, which is 6. And if we divide the number we've already got by 6, we get…"

She broke off to use the calculator.

"…64,570,081. Therefore, the probability that the letters that Ahmad wrote down were *not* the initials of the three people he was about to meet is about one in 65 million. In other words, it's 65 million times more likely that that's what they were than something else, including the Bedouins' switch."

"Sixty-five million to one? *Sixty-five million?* Is that possible?"

"You've just seen it with your own puffy eyes."

"There's no need to be offensive while you're at it, Dr Cameron."

"You've been drinking too much D 'n' S since getting back from Stockholm, Giles. I can see it in your face."

Fiona reached across to prise the glass from his hand.

"Actually, I think you're right, Fiona. It's this damn business."

"Therefore, I think what must have happened goes something like this. Soon after Ahmad arrived in Sorrento, Steve called to tell him of the arrangements for the meeting. Ahmad wrote down their initials on the back of one of the *Achilles* reports he'd taken with him, and then later by accident he gave that one to Steve. When Steve saw what was on it, he jumped to the conclusion that the Bedouin secret had fallen into his lap. He created a DNA insertion with the same base sequence in cultured cells, checked it could activate *Achilles*, found that it did, and made up a story about how he got to it using a special computer programme—all in the knowledge that Ahmad was dead, and that MECCAR could not identify *Deidamia* publicly because of its pledge to the Bedouins. Not only were the letters nothing to do with the Bedouins' DNA, they were also nothing to do with DNA at all. Rashid Yamani's assumption that Ahmad was given the details of an artificial switch in Sorrento was completely wrong. It was what I've just shown you. Steve just got lucky. By pure chance, that particular sequence happened to work."

Giles got up to walk to the sideboard and poured himself a dry sherry.

"Am I permitted a small one?"

Fiona shrugged her shoulders.

"For you, too?"

"Yes, please, but large and sweet."

Giles did as requested before sitting on the sofa and patting the cushion to invite her over.

"But surely," he resumed, "Ahmad would have noticed that what he had written looked like a base sequence. He was a geneticist. The four letters A, C, G and T are as deeply embedded in every geneticist's nut as trilobites in a chunk of granite."

"So what? He would have found it curious, amusing even, but that's about all. He was hardly going to run around telling everyone about it, was he?"

"So, you really believe *Deidamia* was all down to serendipity, a freak accident?"

"Why not? The history of medicine is littered with discoveries that were accidental—the anaesthetic action of nitrous oxide, the antibacterial activity of penicillin, the anti-malarial activity of quinine, the absorption of X-rays by bones. I could go on. The list is longer than your arm. So why not also the anti-cancer activity of *Deidamia*?"

Giles sniffed his sherry a couple of times, before getting up to place the glass on the table and mix himself another D 'n' S.

"Last one today, I promise."

After swirling the glass several times in deep thought, he returned to the sofa.

"I'm sorry, Fiona. I'm full of admiration, but I'm having difficulty accepting it as the explanation. There must be very few pieces of DNA that would function as a switch for *Achilles*. To stumble across one in that way seems so…"

"We don't know there are very few that would work, Giles. That's your assumption. Steve's paper didn't describe any experiments with other strands of DNA, did it?"

"But a piece of DNA like that or close to it must have ended up in that part of the chromosome more than once during the millions of years of our evolution. It would have conferred such a survival advantage, why don't we all have functioning *Achilles* genes?"

"Because, Professor Butterfield, as you know, under normal circumstances mutations of DNA spread throughout a species only when they confer an advantage for reproduction. If a mutation improves the chances of an individual surviving to puberty and beyond, like increasing your resistance to infection as a child or giving you an advantage when competing for food, it will be passed on to greater numbers of offspring. And with each generation, it will become more and more common. But cancer occurs mostly in old codgers like you...who are long past reproductive capacity."

"Hold on! I hope you're not suggesting..."

"I'll tell you in the morning. But seriously, Giles, you know all this. You also know that Bedouins are a special case. Each tribe is a large extended family, with no inter-marrying between tribes. Consequently, when a new mutation develops in a member of one family, it stays within that family."

Giles chewed his lip. This was new territory for him. Like all medical researchers, he had used statistical analysis countless times in his work, and relied upon it faithfully to guide him in the right direction and draw the correct conclusions. It was part of every scientist's toolkit. And yet now, inexplicably, his confidence in it had tumbled. It was as if his gut feeling was suddenly more important than hard facts—the same failing for which he had slammed so many politicians in the past.

"All you say is true, dear, but for some reason, it's going to take more than numbers and statistics to convince me of this one. Dropping the case could have huge consequences—for genetics, for MECCAR, the College, not to mention you and me. To do so on the basis of a single number worries me. I think we need more to go on."

"This doesn't sound like the objective Giles Butterfield I've come to know and love. I wonder if you're being influenced by other issues. Forget about what we've been through. Forget about our preconceived notions. Ignore the fact we might have wasted a lot of time and energy. Forget about how Rashid might react, and the fact that we, and everyone else, might look a wee bit stupid for having jumped to the wrong conclusion. Be as objective as you are in our research. Think of the number of times you've rammed Descartes' Discours de la Méthode down my throat, when my lab results didn't fit my expectations, and when you've been lecturing to the students about scientific method. What did he say?"

Fiona cupped her ear to give him a prompt.

"'When it's not in our power to determine what is the truth, we should act according to what is most likely.'"

"Precisely. So?"

"But there's something you've ignored, isn't there, Fiona? There was more to Ahmad's note than those seven letters. How does your theory explain the number, the 7430 that Steve very reasonably took to be the base number in the chromosome relative to *Achilles* where the DNA must be inserted? If it wasn't that, what was it?"

Fiona reached for another sheet of paper on the table, and turned it over to reveal a photocopy of the last page of the website report.

"I was coming to that. I agree it looks like 7430. But what if the first number isn't a '7' at all, but a '1' written in the European way with a little tail at the top? It would then be '1430.' Perhaps that was the time of their meeting: half past two in the afternoon. Is that possible? You were there."

"Let me think. The Peyton Rous Lecture always starts at 1:30 p.m., and it lasts half an hour. After I'd left the lecture theatre, I spotted Steve with the girls and joined them. A few minutes later, Ahmad arrived and we moved into the bar. After a quick drink, Steve told me it was time to clear off, and they went to the room next door, leaving me to go onto the terrace. So, yes, I suppose it could have been 2:30. But it could also have been any time between say 2:15 and 2:45."

Giles lifted the photocopy from the table to look at Ahmad's note once again.

"But what else could 'insert at -7430 CTGGTAC' mean other than 'insert this sequence at base number 7,430 upstream from the gene'? It's standard genetics terminology. The sort of thing we use every day. It's unambiguous. It can only mean what it says, can't it?"

Fiona shrugged her shoulders.

"I must admit, I don't have an answer for that one."

"You see it's important we don't forget something else Descartes said, Fiona. 'To be plausible a hypothesis must fit all the known facts'— *all* the known facts, not just the ones that happen to be convenient. We can't turn a blind eye to inconvenient truths, can we? You get full marks for what you've done. It's right up there with your successes in The Jefferson. But I can't accept it as the truth, unless it can explain *everything*. Until then, the possibility remains that what Ahmad wrote down was a description of a DNA insertion that someone passed on to him. Isn't that right?"

"True, yes. But statistically, as you've seen, it's far less likely that it was DNA sequence, than…"

"But extremely unlikely things do happen, Fiona. Listen to this. I've been shat on by a pigeon only three times in my entire life, and believe it or not they all happened within ten minutes of each other in Liverpool's Lime Street Station—each time, perfect hits on the head, splat! What were the chances of that?"

He pushed the calculator in her direction.

"I don't know," she giggled. "Perhaps they'd just got word you used to go pheasant shooting. Which reminds me—it's time we ate. I'm off to the kitchen."

When Fiona reappeared holding a steaming bowl of soup, Giles was sitting on the arm of the sofa, her laptop balanced on his knee.

"Come on," she urged, "it's time to fill that paunch."

He put it to one side, and joined her at the table.

"Anyhow," she beamed, "whatever you think of my theory, I hope you'll agree I've got this recipe right."

As she lifted the lid, Giles leant forward to give it a sniff.

"Cock-a-Leekie? Is that your idea of being romantic?"

"I could respond to that. But fortunately for you, I won't!"

"Very kind."

"You know, at times this Steve business may have got on top of you, but it's also done something positive. It's brought back glimpses of the old Giles Butterfield your Liverpudlian friends used to tell me about. Launching yourself into this adventure has been good for you in some ways. But to get back to business, if you think I could be wrong about Ahmad's note, do you have any ideas of your own?"

"Absolutely none, I'm afraid. But I did discover something very curious while you were in the kitchen. I was thinking about that number."

"What the 7430 or 1430, whichever it is?"

"Yes. During my youth in the Middle East, I learnt about the Islamic calendar. It's based on lunar months, and there are websites that convert our years into theirs. That's what I was doing when you came out of the kitchen. I looked to see in which year of the Islamic calendar the Sorrento symposium was held."

"And?"

"It was 1430."

"1430?"

"Yes. As far as Ahmad and the rest of MECCAR were concerned, when he was in Sorrento it was the year 1430."

Fiona offered him a wicker basket of freshly baked bannock.

"What do you make of that?"

Giles adjusted his glasses as he took a slice.

"Looks like a rather sad attempt at something approximating to bread to me. Probably Scottish, at a guess. Is that right?"

"Very funny! I'll have you know, I baked it exactly according to the traditional recipe. Next time, I'll give you a polythene bag of buns from the local supermarket, nice and soft, loaded with bleach and preservatives."

"Actually, it's delicious, thanks. Far better than all the fancy breads you see around, containing cranberries, figs, pecans, whatever."

"Thanks. To get back to that year 1430, do you think it could have any significance?"

"Not that I can think of right now."

Fiona fished around in her soup until she managed to get a piece of celery and one of chicken on the spoon together.

"I hesitate to say this, Giles, but if you go back to the very beginning, to when you set off for Washington in November, we don't seem to have got very far. We might have got it wrong about Steve—perhaps his story to the police was true. We might have got it wrong about *Deidamia*—perhaps she started life as something else, not a piece of DNA. And we might have got it wrong about Ahmad— perhaps he was not a knight in shining armour. It makes me wonder about other things. Is Aram up to something? If so, is he working on his own, or on instructions from MECCAR? Is Rashid Yamani straight? Or did he deliberately send you up the garden path? Is *anything* as it seems?

"And it's been such a grind. So many dead-ends, red herrings, false leads— forwards, backwards, around in circles, up our arses. Now, we've got two more things to keep us awake at night, neither of which might lead anywhere. It's starting to get me a wee bit depressed."

Giles leant across the table to take her hand.

"Cheer up! Sometimes we can't see it, I know, but we *are* making progress all the time—slowly but surely, step by step. And if we keep going, we will get there in the end."

He gestured towards the print of Gauguin's Rocky Sea Coast that had hung over her fireplace since the day she moved into the flat.

"Think of it like that rising tide over there. Each successive wave reaches a little higher, and recedes a little less. The sea's inexorable rise is almost imperceptible. It seems it will never reach you. But it will. And when it does, it might be sudden and from a completely unexpected direction. The truth that we're searching for is the same. We can't see it approaching, but in fact it is. And sooner or later, it will hit us."

He got up to admire the picture, at the same time searching his head for a few apt lines. As usual, it didn't take him very long.

> "'Say not the struggle nought availeth,
> The labour and the wounds are vain......
> For while the tired waves
> Seem here no painful inch to gain,
> Far back through creeks and inlets making,
> Comes, silent, flooding in, the main.'

"Arthur Hugh Clough, Fiona, one of the great undiscovered geniuses of Victorian literature. And a scouser to boot. Never heard of him, I suppose?"

She dropped her spoon to look at him in admiration.

"No, I haven't…but then I don't have your special qualities, Giles. You're such an amazing person—scientist, historian, polyglot, fighter for truth and justice, a walking anthology of English verse…"

As he returned to his chair, she stretched across the table to grasp his hands.

"Solid and unyielding, like those rocks over there; yet like that sea, also ever- changing to reveal so many different aspects of a wonderful character."

He smiled benignly as he looked over his glasses.

"Aye, that's me—Lear today, Donne tomorrow."

Chapter Nine

By the time he was stepping onto the garden path into a stiff northerly breeze, closing the front door carefully so as not to awaken Fiona upstairs, Giles had spent a difficult night coming to terms with the change in their fortunes. It was still less than a week since his call to Anastasia Kohl had convinced him they had already cracked the case. Rashid's conviction had been the only line to pursue, and Gerhard Goldschmidt-Theissen had seemed the most likely culprit. But now they had two competing theories that were so divergent, so unrelated, that his head was spinning. Who else could have given the information to Ahmad in Sorrento—one of the older professors perhaps, looking for a comfortable retirement, as Rashid had said? Had he noticed anyone hanging around Ahmad, who might have been waiting for an opportunity? Should he get in touch with Ahmad's wife under some pretext, in the hope she would let something slip in conversation? And what could they do to look into Fiona's theory? It was a brilliant piece of work—so typical of her to quietly come up with something like that. But he couldn't accept it until everything about the note had fitted into place. What else could 'insert' have meant other than what it said?

As he made his way down Mansfield Road, keen to make an early start on the mail that would be waiting, the energising effect of the cool air on his face and the singing of the birds in the garden bushes strengthened his conviction that one way or another they would succeed. After all, how many times had they been faced with a conundrum that at first had seemed unfathomable, only to stumble on the answer in the most unexpected way in next to no time? And thank goodness they had Sir Quentin's support. At least that was one thing they didn't have to worry about.

The evening together had been a tonic. Living it up in smart hotels in Paris and Munich had certainly had its positive side, but there was nothing to beat a quiet evening in modest surroundings with a very special person. If Fiona were to follow him to Italy when the big day arrived, as she had promised, he was confident it would be a great success. Perhaps they would start an organic farm together and sell their produce in the local village market. In what spare time was left, they could follow the example of the Marchese, and set up a medical research foundation with the proceeds from his autobiography. The way things were going, it might be worth a mint by the time it was finished.

Upon entering Longwall Street, he reflected on the agreement he and Fiona had reached over their glasses of Gaelic coffee before retiring—that while they'd continue to think about Ahmad's note in the hope of coming up with more ideas, each would also work on something else. Tomorrow evening, once she was back from her shopping expedition to London, Fiona would go through the list of names in the Sorrento programme again, and do some background research on anyone about whom there was the slightest doubt. Over the years, she'd become something of an expert at using search engines to gather information on academics—their grants, publications, lectures, business activities, sponsorships from industry, and so on. For his part, he would look at the hotel records from the symposium, to see if anyone other than Gerhard had stayed for a suspiciously short length of time.

Following the path that skirts the lawn of the College's Longwall Quad, he was alarmed to see the bright colours of Jane's Tiffany lamp through his office window. Presumably she had arrived before sunrise, and forgotten to switch it off when the sun was up. But why was she there at all? Hadn't she said she would be visiting her sister in Chipping Sodbury today?

And why was the door between the two rooms wide open? Normally, she kept it closed on winter mornings, while her electric heater did its job.

He dropped onto one of the wooden benches overlooking the lawn to consider his options. She was bound to suspect where he'd spent the night. How stupid of him not to have gone home to have a shave and change of shirt. As he tidied his hair around his ears and collar, he realised he had also forgotten to put on his tie. Now, he would have to stay where he was for a while in the hope she'd soon leave for her sister's. Resigned to a cold damp wait, he had just buttoned up his jacket when Sir Quentin came into sight on his daily jog with his Jack Russell in tow. There was no way out. He would have to move.

Upon arriving at the office doorstep, he paused to create the loudest sneeze he could muster, followed by much coughing and nose-blowing as he entered. After hanging up his coat and letting out another false sneeze, he closed the door between the two rooms.

"Morning, Jane," he called. "I've shut it to protect you from the most dreadful cold I've developed. Wouldn't want you to catch it. Didn't expect to see you today. Anything I should know about?"

"No, Professor, nothing at all—just the usual letters. There are so many, I thought I'd better get on with them and visit Penelope next week instead. As you'll see, I've put the first lot on your desk already. I'll pop through in a minute to give you some more. Would you like a cup of tea, while I'm at it?"

"Thank you, but I think you'd better stay where you are, Jane. It feels as if this bug is eating my chest away."

"Thank you, Professor. How kind of you. I've often told my neighbours what a considerate man you are. It wouldn't have occurred to most bosses. Perhaps Fiona's also got it. I called the laboratory a few minutes ago, but there was no reply. Were you expecting her to be off today? It's not in my diary."

"I must have forgotten to tell you, sorry. She's going to London today to do some shopping in the sales."

"Do you know when she'll be back?"

"She's staying in her cousin's flat tonight. Should be back tomorrow evening."

"I'll make a note. Did you enjoy your trip?"

"Yes, thanks, very useful."

"Good. So, what shall we do about the letters?"

"Why don't you email the next lot to me as attachments. I'll check them and send them back to you. Then, when you've printed them, push them under the door with their envelopes, and I'll look after them from then on. That way you won't even have to touch them after me."

"Professor Butterfield, you're such an angel! I wouldn't change this job for a million pounds."

As he was going through the first batch of letters, Giles's eyes continually wandered to the *Achilles* website report, lying on the bottom shelf of the rosewood bookcase. From there they would drift to the forlorn-looking bottle of Svaneke Session on the mantelpiece, now completely empty. It was difficult to focus on the chore of routine correspondence with those two on his mind. Perhaps if he broke off and spent a few minutes looking at Ahmad's note once again, he would get some inspiration, or spot a small detail he had overlooked.

Placing the *Achilles* report face down in the centre of the desk, he adjusted the Anglepoise and took the Edwardian magnifying glass from the bookcase. After polishing it on his shirt sleeve, he settled down to scrutinise the green ink of Ahmad's pen above the long meandering trail of tiny letters that was *Achilles'* genetic code. He reflected on the first time he had set eyes on that depiction of what had become the world's most famous gene, when standing in the lobby of Oahu's congress centre. Little did he know where the trail was going to take him.

"Damn!" he uttered, thumping his fist on the desk. "'Insert at.' What the hell could it mean, if it's not…"

"Did you call, Professor?" Jane enquired meekly through the door. "Are those letters all right?"

"Yes, Jane…they are, thank you…perfect, as usual. Sorry to alarm you. I was venting my rage at being unable to understand some of our lab results. Research can be so exasperating at times."

"I must say, I don't know how you scientists cope with all that thinking. Your brains never get a rest."

"Yes, it can be a little taxing. Never mind, it's all part of the job."

After looking through the lens for a minute or so, he reluctantly concluded he was wasting his time. As he stood up to return the report to the bookshelf, he felt compelled to read Ahmad's dedication to Steve on the title page one more time. As he did so, he sensed that part of his brain was trying to tell the rest that there was an unperceived difference between the two pieces of handwriting on the front and back. But what was it? He hadn't noticed anything before. And there was certainly nothing obvious now. He had looked at the report for one reason or another many times during the past few weeks. What was so special this time? Was he imagining it? He scratched his head as he flipped the report over and over again, trying to understand the strange sensation that was running through his head. Was he blind to something that was staring at him in the face?

And then suddenly it jumped at him.

"My God! There it is!" he exclaimed. "So that's what the old grey matter was going on about."

It wasn't much. But it *was* there, no doubt about it. The big question was whether it had any significance. Was it there purely by chance, because Ahmad's style of writing could vary now and then? Or had it been intentional? And if so, what could it mean?

In need of another example of Ahmad's handwriting to take it further, he looked for his wife's book on the Bisistun inscriptions, which he'd bought on Ahmad's recommendation after returning from Sorrento. Finding it on the bookshelf next to Brian Sykes's 'Seven Daughters of Eve', he fanned through its pages hoping to find the scrap of paper on which Ahmad had written the book's details in the congress centre's bar. But it didn't seem to be there. Dangling the book by its covers, he shook it vigorously over his desk. But to his dismay, nothing fell out.

"Jesus! Don't tell me it's gone. Where the hell…?"

He could distinctly remember using it as a bookmark. Had he tossed it away? Had Jane been looking through the book in his absence? He certainly hadn't lent it to anyone. An extraordinary panic came over him, the like of which he hadn't experienced since being separated from his mother as a young child in a busy department store. As he had then rampaged through the shoppers, pushing and shoving, so now he swept aside one volume after another in a frenzy of activity. Not until his feet were buried in books, pamphlets, catalogues, programmes, and journals did he find what he was looking for on the bottom shelf behind a PhD thesis he had examined for Leiden University. With a gasp of relief, he stooped to collect it, before dropping into the gooseneck chair to recover.

"Professor, are you all right?" Jane called. "I was on the phone and heard some noises."

"I'm fine, thanks, Jane. I was reaching for a book, and nearly pulled the entire bookshelf on top of me. Fiona has been warning me for months that it was getting top heavy. I'll have to rearrange them."

"You gave me such a shock," she sighed, appearing at the door with a scarf wrapped around her mouth. "I thought you'd been taken ill. Will you need any help putting them back?"

Giles covered his face with his handkerchief and made sniffing noises.

"No thanks."

"In that case, I'll continue on my way out, if that's all right with you. I've promised to meet Janice from Finance for a cup of tea. Apparently, she has some questions about our accounts."

"No problem, Jane. Come through. I won't help you with your hat and coat. Better keep my distance."

As soon as she had departed, he returned to the scrap of paper to remind himself of what Ahmad had jotted down. He read it out aloud.

"'Sir Henry Rawlinson and the Bisistun Inscriptions by Ra'isa Sharif, Jordanian Academic Press'. Yes, this will do nicely, very nicely indeed. Time to follow Fiona's example, Giles, and get down to some statistics."

After counting the number of times each letter had been used in the note, he returned to the website report to do the same with the words of Ahmad's dedication to Steve, jotting down the numbers on the back of an old university memorandum as he went. After a couple of recounts to be sure he had made no errors, he took his calculator from the desk and did the calculations, fortunately much simpler than the ones Fiona had had to use. His pulse was racing as he repeated them. Yes, there was no doubt about it! The detail that had belatedly caught his eye in the handwriting on the back of the report could not have been a sloppy error or stylistic aberration on Ahmad's part. It was far too unlikely to have been anything like that. It must have been intentional. And if it was intentional, it must have meant something.

Exhilarated by his unexpected progress, he moved to Janes' room, door to reward himself with a pot of Earl Grey and a selection of the Christmas shortbreads Fiona had brought back from Scotland. But by the time the kettle was boiling, his excitement had started to wane. Returning more soberly to his desk with the pot in one hand and a mug with three biscuits balanced on top in the other, he paused to look at himself in the tall mirror that stood by his desk.

"Hold on. Don't get too excited, Giles. Okay, the statistics show it must have been intentional. We now know for sure it doesn't mean what we thought it meant. Rashid's theory is definitely out of the window. But we still don't know what the hell it *means*, do we?

Is Fiona's theory right, or is it something different?"

As he sat down, two of the biscuits fell to the floor, while the third dropped into his mug, painfully splashing hot tea over his thumb. He watched the biscuit slowly disintegrate as the butter within melted and rose to the surface.

"Damn!"

Cleaning up the mess, he decided it was time to give his brain a rest. Jane would not be back for a while, so what better time to attend to the simple matter of looking through the congress centre's hotel guest list, as agreed with Fiona? But first he should get her up to date.

After several calls to Mansfield Road had been unanswered, he tried her mobile, assuming she must have already left for the railway station. After a long delay, a familiar voice answered.

"Aram! What the bloody hell are you doing with Fiona's mobile?"

"Is that you, Professor Butterfield?"

"Yes, it is. Sorry for the language, but what's going on?"

"Fiona is not in the lab, sir. I heard the phone ringing. It was on the floor, under one of the benches, and so I thought I should pick it up. I don't know where she is. She must have dropped it yesterday, and not realised."

"Are you sure that's how you got your hands on it?"

"Yes, sir."

"Is it password protected?"

"I don't know. I haven't tried. Why should…"

"But you answered it."

"You don't need the password to answer a…"

"Yes, that's right. Sorry, I was just…oh, never mind. That's a pity. She'll be mortified when she finds it's not in her bag. Okay Aram, please bring it across, and give it to Jane for safekeeping. I'm sure Fiona would appreciate it."

The fact that Fiona was about to spend a night in London alone at an unknown address without her phone was going to make it very difficult for Giles to concentrate on anything. Not so long ago, it would have been merely an inconvenience. Now he felt as if he had lost not only an arm and a leg, but also half his brain. He reckoned the best thing would be to make a start on those hotel records. Hopefully, she would call as soon as she realised her phone was missing.

The computer printout sitting at the bottom of his "Sorrento" box had been unopened since the cashier at the Splendido Palace Hotel had presented it to him on checking out. He removed the elastic bands and unrolled it across the desk, holding down the top with a book, and letting the rest trail onto his lap as he sat. For each of the guests, the record gave the time and date of checking in, and the same for checking out, or the intended date of departure in the case of those who had not yet left. As commonly practised during scientific meetings, the room rate for each person, to be billed to the sponsors, was the same whatever the category of room. Giles ran his eye from top to bottom.

The list confirmed that Gerhard Goldschmidt-Theissen had departed on the first day of the symposium, checking out at 8:37 a.m. Several had extended their stay by the permitted two or three days. All had arrived either on the day before the symposium or very early in the morning of the first day. With the sole exception of Gerhard, none had left before the symposium had finished. Rashid's conviction that whoever had approached Ahmad would have left early did not point a finger at any new suspects.

"Well, that's that," he muttered. "No progress there."

While rolling up the printout and replacing the bands, he admired the picture on the front of the symposium's programme lying in the box, a glossy photograph of the entrance to the congress centre's main auditorium, where most of the lectures had been delivered, including Ahmad's. He recalled how impressed he had been on first entering the room. The 'Sala Morgagni', named in honour of Giovanni Morgagni, was a large oval room with a domed ceiling, whose walls were adorned with oil paintings of Italy's most celebrated medical men throughout history. It was much more than a lecture theatre. It was a celebration of the country's great, but oft-forgotten, early contributions to the sciences of anatomy, physiology, and pathology—centuries of scholarship that had laid the foundations of modern medicine. He pictured with pleasure how, as Ahmad had hurried to the rostrum, the ceiling lights had slowly dimmed, leaving each painting softly illuminated by a small wall lamp. The effect had been stunning. It was as if all those great men were silently looking on, eager to learn what progress had been made since their own pioneering work had so enlightened the world.

The ceiling had a central window, reminiscent of the roof of the Pantheon in Rome, while the double doors of the main entrance were scaled-down replicas of the Pantheon's own giants. Placing the programme in front of him, Giles took up his magnifying glass again to admire the workmanship of the woodcarvers, who had copied the originals in such extraordinary detail. He was reminded how above the doors there was a brass plaque bearing an inscription, now clearly legible in the photograph.

IN MEMORY OF THE FATHER

OF ANATOMICAL PATHOLOGY

Giovanni Batttista Morgagni

(1682-1771)

He recalled how the exterior of the auditorium had been girdled by a marble-tiled corridor illuminated by Venetian chandeliers, off which doors led to the bar, washrooms, cloakroom, and several meeting rooms of different sizes. Above the door of each meeting room was a plaque similar in design to the one of the Sala Morgagni, but much smaller and made of stainless steel. During the hustle and bustle of the symposium, he had not stopped to read any of them. But now, quite unexpectedly, they were of interest to him, very great interest indeed.

"I wonder," he thought, chewing on his lip. "Could that possibly be it? The answer to it all?"

In an impulse he would long remember, his eyes instinctively searched the blue sky above the rooftops of Longwall Street. But no moon was visible on this occasion, either waning or waxing. In fact, there was no moon at all.

Moving to consult Jane's diary, lying open on her desk, he saw it was a new moon that day. He turned towards the Marchese's ever-present gaze.

"She's turned her back on us this time, sir. No messages. No signals."

There was only one option. Returning to his own desk, he went to the Expedia website, only to learn it was too late for a direct flight. He would have to go with Alitalia from London City airport via Milan, departing at 5:25 p.m., arriving Naples at 10:35 p.m. He looked at his watch—12:14 p.m.

"I suppose I could just about make it—leave a note for Jane, nip home to collect a few things, cab to the station, train to Paddington, then tube and Docklands Light Railway. That would be enough for today. Then overnight in Naples and take the Circumvesuviana to Sorrento first thing. Okay, here goes!"

Chapter Ten

The taxi from Sorrento's railway station entered the familiar driveway of the Splendido Palace Hotel a little after 2:00 p.m., rather later than Giles had planned owing to a leisurely breakfast with the Corriere della Sera. Whatever the circumstances, arriving in Italy always had the effect of pleasantly slowing him down. This time, he could feel it the moment he was drawing back the Hotel Miramare's heavy velvet curtains to let the Neapolitan sunlight stream into the room. Despite his eagerness to test his hunch in the congress centre, the previous day's hectic journey and late arrival had left him in no mood to push himself to the limit. Who knows what surprises and challenges might be around the corner? There had been another factor also in his slow start. He had noticed over the past few weeks that whenever he had reached a crucial step, a defining moment that would dictate the future course of events, he had a natural tendency to pause to prepare himself mentally and physically for the moment, rather than dive straight into it. It wasn't something he did consciously. It just happened. And there could not be any greater defining moment than this one.

Bracing himself for what lay ahead, he entered the Splendido Palace's lobby to find it occupied with what looked like a buffet reception for a commercial event. His heart sank when, after fighting his way through the throng, he came face to face with a large poster hanging from one of the columns. In several languages it announced that the congress centre was hosting an international conference on medical and dental plastics. Being out of the tourist season, he had been assuming the hotel would have plenty of empty rooms. But now he was fearful it might not have any.

The receptionist, a lively middle-aged lady from Salford in the North of England, who had married an Italian musician at an early age, recognised him at once.

"My goodness! It's Professor Butterfield, isn't it? I remember you from that genetics meeting we had here, the one during which that Arab scientist....you know."

"It is indeed, Carol. How are you?"

"I'm very well, thank you. And you?

"Can't complain."

"This is a nice surprise—especially now you're so famous. The manager will be very pleased. Nothing like a celebrity to attract business, he always says. What brings you here this time, the plastics meeting?"

"No, just a winter break…a last-minute decision to get some sunshine. Rather foolishly, looking around, I didn't book a room. Do you have one?"

"You didn't! Oh dear, that could be a problem, Professor, a big problem. This lot arrived yesterday from the four corners of the globe."

As she studied the computer screen, her expression left no doubt about the answer.

"Just as I feared. I'm afraid we're chock-a-block. All that's left is the Presidential Suite…the one where it happened. No surprises there. It's been empty ever since you were here. Not a single booking. The rich and famous aren't interested in it anymore, after all that publicity. Mind you, I can't blame them. Just thinking about that poor man lying in the pool gives me goose bumps. Imagine trying to sleep there, knowing what had happened a few feet away!"

"That sort of thing doesn't fuss me, Carol. I'm not the squeamish type. But I'm sure it would be far too expensive for my small academic pockets. Stupid of me not to have called ahead. Never mind. Hopefully someone else in town will be able to fix me up. Could I use your phone?"

"Hold on a sec, Professor," she said with a twinkle in her eye. "I've got an idea."

A few minutes later, she returned clapping her hands with a triumphant smile.

"Signor Patrono, the manager, said that since it's the illustrious Professor Giles Butterfield of Oxford University, his very words, you can have the Presidential Suite for —wait for it—half the price of a standard room. On top of which, the restaurant, bar and room service will all be complimentary. He'll be out in a minute to shake your hand."

"Carol, I could kiss you."

"Ooh, Professor!" she winked playfully. "I think we'd better leave that till later."

As he completed the registration form, a beaming Signor Patrono skirted the reception desk to embrace him.

"Professore," he boomed, "welcome back to our beautiful little town, and thank you so much for choosing our hotel. It is such a great pleasure to see you again. It will be a privilege to serve you."

Giles shook his hand firmly.

"Thank you so much, sir. I'm overwhelmed by your generosity. I hardly know what to say."

"There is no need to say anything, Professore. It is an honour to have you stay with us. I have just instructed Housekeeping to put a bottle of our best Verdicchio on ice in the suite. Its temperature should be perfect by the time you have unpacked. I will also tell Giovanni, the chef of our Michelin starred restaurant, to send you his VIP Menu so you can choose one of his special dishes in advance. He is from Verona. His 'Frutti di mare misti alla griglia' is fit for Neptune's table, and I also strongly recommend his 'Fegato alla Veneziania.'"

"I'll certainly give them a try. I'm sure they're delicious."

"Now, before I return to my work, Professore, there is just one thing I would like to ask you. As a very special favour, would you permit me to ask one of the local newspapers to take a few photographs of you in the hotel while you are here? Nothing private, of course—just casual snaps, as I think you say, in the bar or lobby, or on the terrace."

"Er…yes, I think so. Why not? I suppose it's the least I could do in return for your kindness."

Signor Patrono hugged him again, this time with several affectionate pats on the back.

"Thank you so much. Now that you are such a celebrity, it would be very good publicity for us, especially with you being in the Presidential Suite. When people learn that the great Professore Giles Butterfield has stayed there, I have no doubt that business will pick up."

"I understand, even if my celebrity status is, to say the least, rather reluctant. I'd be delighted to help. After all, if it hadn't been for my society's symposium, you wouldn't have had the problem in the first place, would you? How did you get on with Dr Sharif's wife by the way? I heard she was a little upset about something."

Signor Patrono blushed, as he gave a synthetic smile that spoke only of pain.

"Thank you for asking, Professore. It is still going through the courts. That can take a very long time in my country."

"I see. I'm sorry to hear that. Well, let's hope the pictures of me do you some good. Do you have any idea when the photographers might turn up?"

"None at all, I'm afraid. It could be any time. They're always very busy."

"Never mind, not a problem. I'll make myself available whenever."

"Thank you so much, Professore. You are most kind. Enjoy your stay. If there's anything you need, I am at your service. Here is my card, with my direct line."

"Thank you."

As Signor Patrono returned to his office, Carol collected the keys of the suite from a locked drawer.

"Now, you did say you're not very squeamish, didn't you, Professor Butterfield?"

"That's right, Carol. Why?"

She dangled three keys on a gold chain in front of his nose.

"In that case, I can tell you about these. They're the very

ones that were in that Arab doctor's trouser pocket, when they pulled him out."

She looked at him inquisitively over her half-moon glasses.

"Does that trouble you?"

"Not at all. After all, they're only chunks of metal, aren't they?"

"That's true. We don't use those electronic key cards for the Presidential Suite.

Signor Patrono says they're not as secure as ordinary keys. Computer geeks have been known to hack into them. And he reckons celebrities prefer old-fashioned keys to cheap pieces of plastic anyway.

"So, here you are. This big fancy one's for the entrance. It also fits the door to the terrace. The medium-sized one is for the cupboard on the terrace, where they keep the recliners, chairs, tables, and so on. And then there's this small one for the mini-bar— more like a 'maxi-bar' from what I've heard."

"Thank you, Carol."

Giles took the key ring, before she offered him a small card with an alphanumeric code printed on it.

"Finally, you'll need this, Professor, unless that is you like walking up flights of stairs. It's the password to the suite's private elevator, the one with the brass door on the other side of the lobby. And that's just about everything. So, I hope you enjoy your stay. How long will you be with us?"

"I don't know, actually. It depends on a few things back home. But before I go off to wallow in unaccustomed opulence, I have one quick question."

"What's that?"

"How do I register for the conference? I shouldn't miss the opportunity while I'm here."

"I thought you were supposed to be on a holiday! You scientists! No problem though. I can do it for you now."

Giles found the suite to be even more luxurious than he had imagined. Upon entering the reception, modelled on the living room of a Tuscan palazzo, he dropped his suitcase to marvel at the frescoed ceiling with its scenes of rural Campania, softly illuminated by a bronze Etruscan-style lamp. Pale green walls decorated with gold-framed watercolours of Italian hill towns provided a backdrop to a rattan sofa and two easy chairs with taupe linen cushions, each bearing the hotel's unique insignia. A broad window, almost the entire width of the room, overhung by a mature wisteria, looked onto the suite's personal terrace with the Bay of Naples beyond.

After taking a close look at the paintings, he moved to the dining room looking forward to finding more of the same. To his surprise, however, it was furnished with a Chinese Chippendale suite in solid ebony, whose oval ebony table and six chairs, upholstered in Siena red silk, sat before a French window to one side of which stood a bougainvillea in a white porcelain pot. What seemed to be a Qing dynasty cabinet against the far wall, proved on closer examination to be a lavishly stocked frigobar.

Not knowing what to expect from the bedroom, he entered it with his eyes closed, opening them only upon feeling the linen bed cover brush against his leg. To his disappointment, it was American colonial-style in burnished cherry, complete with a four-poster, pleasing enough but not what he was hoping for. A small window offered a glimpse of the terrace's fountain, its water sparkling in the afternoon sun. After opening it to enjoy the cool salty breeze, he ventured into the only remaining room, the adjacent study-library, all seventeenth century Spanish with floor-to-ceiling oak panelling and a rough limestone floor. He stooped to look more closely at what appeared to be an authentic mediaeval stonemason's mark. Simply furnished with nothing more than a walnut armchair upholstered in plum and mustard bargello, a rectangular mahogany trestle desk under the window, damask silk curtains in red and gold, and a heavy oak court cupboard, modified internally to accommodate a fax machine and a printer, it was a room where Giles felt he could read and write for many hours.

They had tried to please everyone, and it was a creation of which the management could be proud. Some would consider it a masterpiece. But in Giles's view, it was not a success. Although imaginatively conceived and finished with commendable craftmanship, the contrast in styles was too great for his liking.

It was only after he had unpacked the few things he had brought along that he overcame his reluctance to follow Ahmad's footsteps onto the terrace. Consciously ignoring the pool, he first did a tour of several marble statues of domestic and wild animals, replicas of ones he recognised from visits to the Vatican Museum. After admiring their detail, he turned to the travertine fountain outside the bedroom window to wet his fingers and stroke the lichen and liverworts clinging to the stone. From there, he moved to the small herb garden to sniff the rosemary, thyme, and oregano. After studying the numerals inscribed in the garden's sundial, his eye followed its long shadow to the dark surface of the swimming pool. Broken only by a few floating leaves of evergreen honeysuckle, it evoked in his mind an image of a waiting grave. He tried not to picture the tragic scene the unfortunate maid from nearby Cepano had witnessed. Noting the raised tiles around its perimeter, he wondered at which point Ahmad had tripped.

But *had* he tripped? Had it really been that simple? As he turned to look through the French windows into the dining room, his eyes settled on a crystal ice bucket and bottle of white wine the maid had placed on the table in his absence, his mind's eye replacing it with the empty bottle of Svaneke Session pilsner that had been there that fateful morning. Not until that puzzle had been solved would he be comfortable with Captain Cortese's interpretation of events.

In spite of his late morning start in Naples, he was already feeling the effect of yesterday's journey. Under normal circumstances, he would take a shower now, put on a change of clothing, and relax with some music and a glass of wine. He knew from Conrad that when it came to Verdicchio, Villa Bucci DOCG was one of the very best. It was tempting, but he knew his mind would not rest until he had answered the question that had brought him there. There was no point delaying any longer. Either he was right or he was wrong. And the sooner he knew the answer, the better. The sensible course of action would be to go to the congress centre now and get it over with.

The entrance to the congress centre from the hotel lobby led directly into the marble corridor that encircled the Sala Morgagni. When Giles saw that his hunch about the purpose of the plaques over the doors to the small satellite meeting rooms had been correct, he could feel his heart starting to pound. Like the much larger brass plaque over the entrance to the auditorium, each carried a tribute to an Italian physician who had made an important early contribution to medical science. He recalled that the room in which Ahmad had met with Steve and the girls had been on the far side. He couldn't picture its exact location, but he did know it was immediately next to the bar. That was enough to go on.

Before setting off, he paused to prepare for the worst. Should it turn out that his theory had been wrong, he would remind himself that at least he would have eliminated one possibility. As he'd said to Fiona, that's the way it had to be—a step-by-step process, during which errors were inevitable. So why get uptight if the trip were to end in disappointment? They would simply consider their next move, perhaps during a walk in The Fellows' Garden or over a drink in The Turf. And by then, Fiona's enquiries into the background of everyone who'd attended the symposium might have pointed them in the right direction. If not, they were bound to come up with something else. After all, they always had done, hadn't they?

Thus reassured, he set off slowly down the corridor, doing his best to look casual among the throng of chattering business people as he stopped at the first door to read its plaque. It celebrated a man familiar to every medical student for his anatomical dissections of the tiny hearing and balancing mechanisms inside the middle ear, after whom the narrow tube that connects it to the throat was named.

> In memory of Bartolomeo Eustachi
> (1510-1574)
> Father of Human Anatomy

The next room was dedicated to a pioneer of embryology and teacher of William Harvey, the English physician who discovered the circulation of the blood.

> In memory of Girolamo Fabrici
> (1537-1619)
> Father of Embryology

After that came a Bolognese born exactly two hundred years later, whose name is now more familiar to electricians than it is to doctors and geneticists.

> In memory of Luigi Galvani
> (1737-1798)
> Discoverer of electricity in nerves and muscles

"Odd, isn't it," he mused, "that the word galvanometer should have been given to something we now use to measure currents in wires, when he experimented with frog's legs. I wonder how that came about."

Although he was aware that such pondering was merely a way of reducing his rate of progress, at the same time diverting his mind from its real purpose, the urge to do was so irrepressible.

As it looked as if the names were in alphabetical order, he decided to play a game by guessing who would be the next one in line. After some deliberation, he plumbed for the Italian neurologist who had shared the Nobel Prize with the Spaniard Santiago Cajal. And he was right.

In memory of Camillo Golgi
(1843-1926)
Inventor of silver staining of nerves

Despite his best efforts to remain calm, his pulse was getting faster and his forehead clammier with every step. It wasn't just the approaching answer to his question that was giving him stress. It was also the ever-present possibility, however remote, of being recognised by someone. The only person he had ever known in the medical plastics industry was a neighbour in Liverpool. Fortunately, as Mick O'Dwyer had been in marketing, the chances of his attending such a hi-tech meeting were remote. But over the years, he had known several academics who had moved into senior positions in industry. Heaven forbid he would be unlucky enough to bump into one of them!

To avoid any possibility of making eye contact, he had been fixing his gaze on the marble floor when moving from one door to the next. Having by now bumped into several people as a consequence, he decided instead to put on the sunglasses he'd brought along for some sightseeing. Having done so, however, he found that he couldn't read the next plaque in the soft lighting from the chandeliers. Irritated and more than a little embarrassed, he pushed them to the end of his nose and peered over the top, only to find that the words were now out of focus. When standing on his toes failed to make much difference, he reverted to his normal glasses, and wormed his way back to the centre of the corridor. A frustrating minute followed, while he waited for a projectionist with a ladder to stop talking to an official. Only then could he see the plaque clearly.

In memory of Marcello Malpighi FRS
(1638-1694)
Father of Microscopic Anatomy

"Ah, now there was a clever man, if ever there was one! Elected to Fellowship of the Royal Society after dedicating his treatise on silkworms to it. Wish I'd dreamt up a clever rouse like that. Might not have had to wait until I was nearly on crutches."

Reasoning there could be only one or two more doors before reaching his target, he looked nervously down the corridor, straining his neck to follow its curvature.

"Wouldn't like to know what my blood pressure is right now," he thought, feeling his pulse as he arrived at the next one.

"Now, there's a coincidence!"

In memory of Scipione Riva-Rocci
(1863-1937)
Inventor of the mercury sphygmomanometer

"So that's who came up with the contraption we used to use for measuring blood pressure. Good job they didn't know mercury was poisonous in those days. Perhaps it would never have happened."

As the sound of conversation and laughter emanating from the next room told him it was the bar, he paused to prepare himself for the door that was to follow it. One thing was certain. It was quite definitely the one Ahmad, Steve, and the girls had used for their meeting.

After loosening his collar and taking a deep breath, he worked his way through the crowd jostling into and out of the bar, and then continued ever more slowly until the next door came into view. As he paused to pick up the courage to raise his eyes, a painfully familiar voice roared from behind.

"Well, dog bite me! That takes the biscuit!"

Giles froze. It was the nightmare scenario. Slowly turning, he came face to face with the spotty Celtic complexion of the last person on the face of the earth he wanted to see at that moment.

"Of all people," he boomed, grasping Giles's hand with crushing force, "my old kid on the block—the super sleuth of Stockholm, noble nailer of naughty Nobel Laureates. Didn't know you were into medical plastics, Giles, apart from a Saturday night, of course—wink, wink, nudge, nudge!"

Yes, it was Mick O'Dwyer.

In next to no time, Giles had been press-ganged into the bar by Mick's companions, one of whom pushed an unwanted pint of Guinness into his hand. After being told how his triumph in Sweden had become folklore on Merseyside, he was subjected to a barrage that made the Little Compton experience seem like child's play.

"Quite a shot of you in that Swedish bus stop!" Mick scoffed, bursting into heehaws of laughter. "Front page of The Sun no less—did you hear that, everyone?—next to another one with his arm around some Scottish bird in a posh restaurant. Nice bit of crackling though, Giles, I must say. Where did you dig her up?"

He would remember the next half hour as one of the most excruciating of his life. Rarely had he felt so out of place, so disinterested in those around him, and yet so obliged to appear as others remembered him—the jovial Giles Butterfield of old. When the bell sounded to announce the start of the afternoon session, it could not have been too soon. Once the handshakes, farewells, and promises to keep in touch had abated, he remained where he was while the bar emptied, his Guinness untouched, before regaining the energy to return to the next doorway.

And there on the small plaque above it was the answer to his question.

In memory of Enrico Sertoli
(1842-1910)
Discoverer of the Sertoli cells of the testis

Giles stepped back to support himself against the opposite wall, almost knocking over a young waitress carrying a tray in the process.

"I was right!" he gasped, no longer caring about those around him. "That's it! It must be. I can't have been anything else."

As he stared at the plaque in near disbelief, his emotions were unexpectedly mixed. There was certainly a huge sense of achievement, and equally one of relief. But while he was jubilant that Fiona's theory had clearly been correct, how would Steve and his attorney react to the news? Perhaps they would now claim there had been no theft of intellectual property after all. And if so, would they seek compensation for the devastating effect on his life, his loss of status and income, the stress, the embarrassment, the rumoured split with his wife?

With his autobiography in mind, he took several photographs of the plaque, before cautiously opening the door and peering inside. Finding the room empty, he entered to sit down and collect his thoughts. He looked at his watch and wondered if Fiona might be back from London by now. There was a chance—a small one admittedly, but a chance nevertheless. If she'd found the necklace she was looking for this morning, she might have caught the first train back to Oxford. They were pretty frequent after all, and the journey took only an hour or so.

He started by calling her flat, but there was no answer. Next, he tried her mobile, but only got the answering service. Next in line was the laboratory. Aram answered to say he had not seen her. Finally, he called Jane's desk. She answered.

"Hello, Professor. What a coincidence! Fiona walked through the door only a few minutes ago. I've given her the phone, and she was just showing me a beautiful silver necklace she's bought. Here she is."

"Hello, Giles. I've just got back. I can't believe Aram had my phone yesterday. Somehow, I hadn't noticed it was missing. He said he found it in the lab, but I'm not sure I believe him. I don't remember taking it out when was last there. I certainly didn't make a call."

"Perhaps you put it on the bench, when you were looking for something in your handbag, and it fell to the floor."

Fiona glanced at Jane, now rummaging in a drawer, before lowering her voice.

"Perhaps, but I'm pretty suspicious. You know what I'm on about?"

"Yes, of course, but when I tried to call you, he answered. Surely, if he'd taken it from your bag when you weren't looking, he wouldn't have been so dumb as to have answered knowing it was me."

"Where were you calling from?"

"The one on my desk."

"In which case he wouldn't have known it was you, would he? College extensions don't do Caller ID, do they?"

"That's true. Anyhow, let's talk about it tomorrow."

"Why not today?"

"Because I'm in Sorrento."

"Sorrento! Why on earth?"

"I've got some very good news. After you'd left yesterday, I made some important progress, but of course couldn't let you know. Nor could I tell you I needed to visit the congress centre here to see if my hunch was correct. So, I just got on with it. I dashed to City Airport, caught a flight to Naples via Milan, stayed there overnight, and got here this afternoon."

"What hunch are you talking about? Wait a minute, while I take my coat off, and transfer the call from Jane's to yours."

After a minute or so, Fiona appeared on the line again.

"Right, I'm now reclining in your lovely gooseneck, feet on the desk, admiring the view. I didn't realise it was so comfy. Okay, fill me in."

"Well, once again you can be proud of yourself, Fiona. You were absolutely right. You hit the nail right on the head. Ahmad's note *was* about the arrangements for their meeting. At this moment, I'm in the very room where they met. What looked like 'insert' in Ahmad's note was nothing of the sort. It was actually two words, 'in' and 'Sert,' the second bit beginning with a capital letter. Each meeting room here is dedicated to a different Italian scientist. There's a Galvani room, a Golgi room, and so on. This one is named after Enrico Sertoli. Ahmad's 'in Sert' was shorthand for 'in the Enrico Sertoli Room.'"

"What! Brilliant! There you are. I knew it had to be right. But hold on…bollocks!"

"Very appropriate. But what's your problem?"

"Why appropriate?"

"Sertoli discovered a type of cell that nourishes developing sperms."

"Really? No, what I meant is 'bollocks' as in 'damn.' I'd started to hope I was wrong, given how stupid we're going to look."

"There's nothing to feel stupid about. Steve made the same error, remember, and he was the one who arranged the meeting in the first place. If anyone should have spotted it, it's him. We're the ones who got to the truth. And once again it's thanks to you."

"Thanks, but it wasn't all me. My flash of genius wouldn't have been any use without yours. But you haven't told me yet how you got onto it. I'm fascinated. How did it happen?

"Hold on, Jane's just brought me a cup of tea. Thanks, Jane, just what I needed. Okay, Giles, carry on."

"Yesterday morning, using the magnifying glass from my bookcase, I examined Ahmad's writing on the back of the report very carefully. And for the first time, I noticed that the 'n' and the 's' in 'insert' are not joined together. There's a small gap between them. It's not obvious to the naked eye, but when you use a lens, it's clear. In contrast, all the other letters in each word are joined together. So I began to wonder if it actually represented two words. I then turned the report over to look closely at what he'd written on the front."

"Wait a tick, Giles. Is the report here, or do you have it with you?"

"It's with me, but there should be a photocopy in my Sorrento box, on the floor."

Fiona returned, panting with excitement.

"Okay, got it. I see what you mean. Go on."

"As you can see, his exact words on the front were, 'To Dr Stephen Salomon, with thanks, Ahmad C Sharif, Sorrento.' You can also see that the four uppercase 'S' letters differ in shape from the single lowercase one. The big ones are a bit like what you get with an Arial font in Microsoft Word, while the other one is rather like the Edwardian Script font. Now, if you go to the back page, you'll see that the 's' in 'insert' is not at all like the one in 'thanks.'

It's a smaller version of his four uppercase ones on the front page. This made me wonder if it was actually a capital 'S.' However, as the 's' in 'thanks' is the only lowercase one on the front page, it was possible he was in the habit of using two different versions of a lowercase 's.' Most people don't vary their letters much, of course, but some do. I've noticed your lowercase 'f' has three different versions, for example. So I found a note Ahmad had given me in Sorrento about a book his wife had published. I've got it with me. It reads, 'Sir Henry Rawlinson and the Bisistun Inscriptions, by Ra'isa Sharif, Jordanian Academic Press,' except he abbreviated the last part to 'Jord Acad Pr.'"

"The what inscriptions?"

"Bisistun. It's the true story of a Victorian army officer, who scaled a sheer cliff in the Zagros mountains in what's now Iran to decipher an inscription put there by King Darius of Persia more than two thousand years ago. It was written in three languages: Old Persian, Elamite, and Akkadian. I'll lend you the book sometime. It's fascinating.

"Anyhow, the point is I now had two more examples of Ahmad's capital 'S,' bringing the total to six: in 'Stephen Salomon,' 'Sharif,' 'Sorrento,' 'Sir,' and 'Sharif' again. And I had another six examples of his lowercase ones, giving me seven in all: one in each of 'thanks,' 'Rawlinson,' and 'Ra'isa,' and two in each of 'Bisistun' and 'Inscriptions.'

"I found that the uppercase ones were invariably of the Arial font type, and the small ones always of the Edwardian Script type. Taking a feather out of your cap, I calculated the statistical probability that Ahmad would write all thirteen of them the way he did, if he actually uses the two types as alternatives completely at random."

"And the answer was?"

"One in 8,192."

"Sure?"

"Yes. As there would be a fifty-fifty chance of his using one or the other each time, the answer is 0.5 to the power of thirteen, or in other words 0.5 multiplied by itself twelve times."

"Full marks! So you then did what our old friend Descartes would have done. You concluded that what we'd assumed was a lower case 's' in 'insert' was actually an upper case one.'"

"Precisely. Then, I asked myself what 'in Sert' could have meant. As he'd abbreviated the name of his wife's publisher, I wondered if 'Sert' might also be short for something. And as it started with a capital letter, I reasoned it could be someone's name or the name of a place. I then recalled that each of the meeting rooms here has a small plaque over the door. I didn't know what they were about, as I hadn't looked at them closely, but I did know that a much bigger one over the auditorium's double doors carried a dedication to Giovanni Morgagni. Putting two and two together, I guessed that the room that Steve had booked for the meeting with Ahmad might have honoured someone whose name began with 'Sert.'"

"And so you decided to go and have a look. Fantastic! Giles, this is awesome. So, let me get this right. You're saying it's all over? That we've finished? It's all behind us? It's history? We can start living again?"

"That's about it."

"Wonderful! So what now?"

"Well, you've been telling me how tired and stressed out I've been looking lately, haven't you?"

"For weeks."

"And how I've been taking life too seriously?"

"For months."

"And how I need to look after myself?"

"For years. Come on, get on with it!"

"So I think I'll go and sun myself on the terrace for the rest of the afternoon, have dinner in the Pesce Spada, and then find a lovely Latin lady with whom to spend the evening. I think I've earned it, don't you?"

"If you mean a black eye, yes! When it comes to unfaithful men, you do know we Scots have something in common with Neapolitans, don't you?"

"Go on."

"The only difference is we use malt whisky, instead of aceto balsamico."

"What for?"

"Pickling their nuts."

"Ouch!"

"So instead of risking a fate worse than death, why don't you get on with the stuff I need for the students' next practical class. It's getting urgent."

"Yes, you're right. It is, isn't it? I'll prepare it during the journey home. Promise."

"When will that be?"

"I think the day after tomorrow. I really need a break. Okay with you?"

"Of course. Make the most of it—up to a point."

"Thanks. Ciao."

Before making his way to the terrace, Giles returned to the bar for a nostalgic glass of prosecco at the same table he had shared with Ahmad, Steve, and the girls. With the congress' afternoon session well underway, he reckoned it should be empty. What better way to celebrate the end of the saga?

To his delight, he found that the table, recognisable by a deep scratch in its polished top, was still there. Luigi, the same young barman he had met during the symposium, mixed his drink with his usual attention to detail, before fetching a complimentary bowl of Sicilian cassata ice-cream.

"My, how the world has changed since those days," Giles mused. "Here I am, exactly where I was one year and four months ago. Same table, same Luigi—but now Ahmad's dead, Steve's in a mess…and I'm a celebrity. You never know, do you?"

He took a spoonful of ice cream, taking care to ensure it included several pieces of candied fruit, and sipped his drink.

"Now the pressure's off," he continued, taking another spoonful, "this celebrity status might not be such a bad thing after all. Although the attention and publicity are too much at times, there are undoubtedly advantages. Not many people could get complimentary wine and ice-cream in a place like this, not to mention the bargain room rate. The incident with Mick and his friends was an extreme case—bad luck more than anything. These things are bound to happen every now and then. But all those stories about no privacy, paparazzi around every corner, how it can ruin your private life, and so on are probably gross exaggerations. It's really just a question of how you organise your life, how you manage people and situations. That's all. Prudent living's the secret. As long as you keep your nose clean, don't mix with the wrong company, and avoid risky situations, it's yours to enjoy. Of course, that doesn't mean..."

His ruminating was suddenly interrupted by the arrival of a group of excited photographers, who had entered through the door behind him from the garden. Blinded by camera flashes from all sides, by the time his eyes had recovered the invaders had run off down the corridor.

Luigi appeared from behind one of the marble columns with a broad grin on his Tuscan face.

"You see how famous you are now, Professore. You're a real celebrity. And wasn't the lady beautiful? I wish I could have been as close to her as you."

"Wasn't who beautiful?"

"You didn't see her? Oh, what a pity! You missed a real Neapolitan treat. Signor Patrono's new secretary was posing right behind you. She's last year's Signorina Monte Vesuvio. Una ragazza estremamente bella, molto ben sviluppato."

With sweeping motions of his hands, Luigi left Giles in no doubt about what he had missed.

"Signor Patrono will be very pleased, Professore. The pictures are sure to be everywhere, certainly in tonight's edition of Il Centro, and on the hotel's website— probably also in the newspapers in Naples tomorrow, and perhaps even in magazines soon. He has many contacts in the media. Aren't you happy?"

"Er...yes...of course. Why not?"

Chapter Eleven

After a late night walking the streets of Sorrento, Giles was awoken at 7:30 a.m. by the suite's alarm radio, still tuned into Jordan's JRTV channel. After taking the opportunity to listen to the news in Arabic while getting dressed, his first instinct was to call Rashid Yamani to get him up to date.

"Giles!" Rashid boomed with delight. "How are you? What brings you to the phone, my dear English friend?"

"Good morning, Rashid. I'm calling because we've just solved the riddle of *Deidamia*, and thought you'd like to know."

"What, already? Fantastic! I knew you were the man for the job. Who was the culprit?"

"There wasn't one."

"What do you mean?"

"Ahmad didn't get a DNA sequence from anyone in Sorrento."

"But he must have done. As I told you..."

"No, he didn't, Rashid. I hope you're ready for this. It came as something of a shock to me. You see, what Ahmad wrote on the back of that report was nothing to do with *Achilles*. It was nothing to do with any gene."

"What do you mean?"

"It was actually a note written in shorthand to remind him of the details of a private meeting he was due to have with Steve Salomon and three young research workers during the symposium. Steve had asked Ahmad to give two of his staff some advice about their projects, and invited a German who'd worked with Steve in the past to join them. Their names were Carina Taricani, Gerhard Goldschmidt–Theissen and Amandine

Coupe, and the CT, GGT, and AC were their initials. They were to meet in the congress centre's Enrico Sertoli Room… that's what the 'insert' was all about…at half past two in the afternoon. What Steve and everyone else since, including you and me, thought was the insertion site, base 7,430 upstream from the gene, was nothing of the sort. It was the time, 14:30 written with a European number one. *Deidamia* was the result of pure serendipity, Rashid, nothing else."

"It's almost incredible! How do you know all this, Giles? Can you prove it?"

"Yes, I've done so, with statistics. As I tell my students, we should always follow the advice of Descartes, and accept whatever is most likely. Forget about your biases, preconceived notions, and gut feelings, I say to them. It doesn't matter if it doesn't fit with your latest theory, or goes against the grain, is inconvenient, or means you've wasted a lot of time and effort. It's only statistics that matter—statistics, statistics, statistics. Of course, I don't need to tell *you* that."

"Of course. But what sort of statistics? What numbers did you use?"

"It's a little complicated to explain on the phone, but I can try if you wish."

"Please. I'm intrigued."

"Well, it was like this…."

Giles has just finished relating the story, from Fiona's presentation of her ideas in her apartment to his dash to Sorrento and visit to the congress centre, when the chime of the doorbell announced the arrival of his breakfast.

"So there it is, Rashid. There's no doubt about it. I'll send you the evidence, if you like, so you can see for yourself. But I must rush off now, sorry. Next time you're in the UK, let me know. We'll have dinner in the Magdalen's Great Hall. Laila tiaba."

Luigi entered pushing a trolley laden with brioches, rolls, fruit, yoghurts, juices, conserves, and coffee.

"Buon giorno, Professore," he said, bowing respectfully. "I hope you'll enjoy this. I prepared the fruit salad myself. The chef has been teaching me. The brioches and the bread rolls are freshly baked, of course, and the coffee beans were ground this morning. And oh yes, the marmalade was made from the best Sicilian 'blood' oranges."

"Thank you, Luigi. It looks delicious. A breakfast fit for a setting of this opulence."

"I am so glad you like the suite, sir. It is beautiful, yes?"

"It is indeed. I've never experienced such luxury. Now I know what it's like to be a king."

"You are more than a king, Professore. After all, what is a king? You are far more important."

"You're very kind."

Luigi walked to the French windows to admire the terrace.

"Do you know you are the first person to sleep here, since… what happened?"

Giles nodded sorrowfully.

"Rich people don't want it now. They go to the Excelsior Vittoria, or the Grand Hotel Cocumella. It is such a pity. It is so elegant, so comfortable—the best suite south of Torino, I've been told. I remember how disappointed that American scientist was, the one who organised your symposium here. He told me he was entitled to have it, but he gave it to the Arab doctor to make sure he was comfortable. That was very kind of him, wasn't it? He must be a very nice person."

"Dr Stephen Salomon? Oh, yes, he is…as nice as they come, Luigi. He'd been entitled to it as the symposium's chairperson. Not many people would have made such a sacrifice. But I'm sure he was comfortable enough in one of your standard rooms. I didn't hear him complain. I was certainly very happy with mine."

"A standard room? Oh no, he was not in a standard room, Professore. He was in our only other suite, the Capo di Monte. I took room service to him. It's also very nice, but smaller than this—no dining room, no terrace, no fax machine, scanner, and so on. But it is a beautiful suite nevertheless. Anyhow, I'd better stop talking and let you enjoy your breakfast."

"Thank you, Luigi. I'll see you again before I leave. Have a good day."

As he poured his coffee, Giles threw his mind back to the chat he had had with Steve in the hotel lobby upon arriving for the symposium. There was no doubt in his mind about what Steve had said. He could almost hear him now. "The Presidential Suite had been reserved for me, but instead I took a standard room," and "I hope you'll remember what a martyr I was when you're voting for the society's next president." Probably not those exact words, but pretty close.

"He must have said the same to everyone," Giles fumed, "and all the time, he was in the Capo di Monte, pulling the wool over our eyes to get the top job. What a rotter!"

By the time he was dressed and ready to go out for the day, Giles could see that a thunderstorm was approaching from the north. Undaunted, he made his way downstairs, and collected the largest and brightest umbrella he could find in the concierge's collection. Rain or not, he would make the most of it, starting with a brisk walk to the Piazza Torquato Tasso, and then along the coast for a mile or two.

On his way past a newsagents he collected a copy of Il Centro to see if it had one of the photographs of him in the bar. But it did not.

"Thank God for that!" he gasped. "Hopefully, they were not good enough."

His mood was lifted further when he saw that the clouds had changed direction, and were now heading east towards Castellammare di Stabia. It would have been near perfect strolling along the clifftop, if it had not been for the revelation that Steve had lied to his closest colleagues to improve his chances in the upcoming election.

Upon returning to the town, he idled away an hour in the Piazza della Vittoria, chatting to a few of the locals and befriending a stray cat before dropping into L'Antica Trattoria for a plate of seafood risotto. From there, it was back to the hotel.

Tired after the uphill trek, but generally pleased with his day, he packed in preparation for the next day's journey, before settling down with a glass of D 'n' S by the terrace's herb garden. But the pleasure was ruined by recurring thoughts of Ahmad's demise. For all his bravado when checking in, he had come to realise that the wealthy and VIPs had been wise to avoid the Presidential Suite. There was no way of putting out of your mind the fact that something so dreadful had happened so recently. Even the occasional whiff of chlorine, as the evening breeze wafted across the terrace from the pool, was disturbing. The best thing the hotel could do, he thought, would be to replace the pool with a sundeck and pergola. In fact, he would suggest it to Signor Patrono in the morning.

Chapter Twelve

When the taxi dropped Giles at Naples' Capodichino airport, he found it was crowded with northern Italians returning home after spending the first days of the New Year with their relations. Expecting they would soon disperse, he looked for an empty seat where he could wait for it to happen. Finding one next to a dark-haired girl engrossed in a women's magazine, he dropped into it and placed his briefcase between them. She raised her eyes to greet him with a warm smile.

"Hello, busy isn't it."

"You can say that again! How did you know I was English?"

"Your address...on the luggage label."

"Very observant of you. I've just had the most terrifying cab journey in my life. I now know that road signs that mean 'no entry' everywhere else in Europe mean 'put your foot down and go like hell' around here."

"You get used to it after a while," she replied with a giggle.

"I suppose so...if you survive. And I don't think I want to hear another word of 'O sole mio' for the rest of my life!"

Standing up to remove his jacket, he dropped it over the back of the chair. As he did so, a small transparent plastic bag containing a cigarette butt fell from the top pocket.

"Oops! That must have been a *very* good cigarette!" she joked, bending down to pick it up. "Here you are, sir."

"Grazie mille. Lei e molto gentile."

"It's a pleasure. You don't like my English?"

"Sorry, I didn't mean to imply that. It's very good. But when I'm in Italy, I like to use my Italian."

"I'd rather carry on in English, if you don't mind. I'm on my way to Bristol to study to become a dietician, and I need to practice."

"Bristol? Expect you'll be on the same plane as me then. Between now and then, I'll speak only my best posh English for your benefit."

"Thank you. I like your accent. But to get back to that little plastic bag—if you don't mind me asking, why do you keep that cigarette end in it? Is it a very special one for some reason?"

"You'd think so, wouldn't you? But in fact, I don't smoke. I picked it up to give to my assistant when I get home. I'm a geneticist in Oxford, you see, and she'll use it for my students' next laboratory class. They'll study genes that are in it."

"Genes in a cigarette? You mean genes of tobacco plants?"

"No, the genes of the person who smoked it. She'll extract them from the dried saliva, and then make what are called DNA fingerprints, which are unique to every one of us, apart from identical twins. Between now and getting to London, I have to prepare my instructions for her. No rest for the wicked!"

"Isaiah 48:22."

"Pardon?"

"What you said. It's from the bible. I used to go to a convent school in Cremona."

"Ah, I see. Very clever!"

"Not really. We were fed that sort of thing every day. What you do is *really* clever. I'd better let you get on with it."

"Thank you."

Giles took out a soft drink and a bag of bread rolls, which he'd bought during an early morning trip to a local supermarket.

"I hope you don't mind my having a snack. Unfortunately, I had no time for breakfast."

Her eyes reappeared from behind the magazine.

"Please do. I see you've got my favourite drink, Chinotto."

"You like it, do you? I've never tasted the stuff, actually. A friend from Jordan recommended it to me during a scientific meeting in Sorrento more than a year ago, and I've been intending to give it a try ever since. Today's the big day."

"He's right. It's delicious."

"Here goes. Down the hatch!"

Giles took a cautious first mouthful, swirling it around as if he were a wine taster, before taking a second with visibly greater confidence.

"Mmm...I must say, I agree with you. Not bad at all."

"We Italians don't just make the best wine," she grinned. "We make the best soft drinks too. But for some reason, you don't see them much in England."

"For a soft drink, it certainly does have lots of character," he enthused, followed by another mouthful.

"It's also good for you," she continued. "It contains the juice of a particular type of bitter orange, and is full of herbs—gentian, thyme, tamarind, cinchona, and a few others I've forgotten. You should also try Cedrata and Rabarbara next time you're here."

"I certainly shall. When it comes to life's pleasures, you Italians certainly know a secret or two. It must be in your genes."

She stroked her thighs to smoothen the creases out of her Levis, and winked playfully.

"That's where we keep all our best secrets—in our jeans."

"Ha! Er...yes, well...right, so if you'll excuse me, I think I'll move to a seat by the window now to make a few notes for my assistant in Oxford. I need more light, you see."

"Certainly. Enjoy the rest of your drink. Ciao!"

Having already shown the students how DNA fingerprinting can be used to settle paternity disputes, this time Fiona was to show them how it can also be used solve crimes, using specks of blood, cigarette ends, hairs, sealed envelopes, licked postage stamps, and the like. He would provide her with several such items, supposedly collected from a crime scene. She would recover a tiny amount of DNA from each one, and digest it into hundreds of fragments of different sizes with enzymes. Finally, she would separate the fragments in a gel by exposing them to an electric current, producing a banded pattern similar to a supermarket bar code, the DNA fingerprint. The students would then be asked to identify the murderer using the fingerprints as the only evidence.

After taking another mouthful of Chinotto, he scribbled his notes.

"One copy to each student please, Fiona.

> Police were called to a flat where the owner had been found dead. He had blonde hair, was 29 years old, and was a non-smoker. He'd been shot in head, but no evidence of struggle, and no gun was found. The police collected four specimens for analysis at the scene:
>
> A. Grey hairs found on the victim's jacket
> B. Cigarette butt from the fireplace
> C. Envelope (sealed and reopened), found on the floor
> D. Picture postcard from friends, found in his pocket
>
> Two weeks later, police arrested two suspects, both in their 60s. Each had his thumb pricked by police, and blood spotted onto tissue paper (specimens E and F).
>
> So, there are 6 specimens in total, A to F. Using these, Dr Cameron will show you how DNA can be extracted from hairs, spots of blood, and dried saliva (on the cigarette end, envelope, and stamps). She'll then show you how the DNA obtained from each one can be used to make a DNA fingerprint. Your job is to use the 6 fingerprints to work out which of the suspects was the murderer, and say how you came to your conclusion.
>
> Fiona, the incriminating evidence will be that the DNA fingerprint from specimen E (blood

from one of suspects) will match that from A (grey hairs from victim's jacket). I'll collect both from me. B will be a cigarette butt that I've already picked up in Italy. We'll put specimens C, D, and F together in Magdalen. I'm assuming you'll agree to provide the second blood spot (F), by the way!"

To finish off, he wrote a large letter "B" with his ballpoint pen on the bag containing the cigarette butt.

Once the aircraft was on its way, he would dictate it into his phone for Fiona to type, and that would be that.

Coming after a late night, the warmth of the Mediterranean sun through the window was making him feel very sleepy. Realising the bag drop for his flight would soon be closing, he resisted the urge to take a nap and headed off in that direction, before making his way to the gate.

After bidding goodbye to the Italian girl at the entrance to the aircraft, he squeezed past a well-padded elderly German lady to get to his seat, almost sitting on her lap in the process.

"Careful!" she blurted. "It's very annoying when passengers with window seats are so slow to get on board. If you have a window ticket, you should make sure you're in here first. Most inconsiderate!"

"Madam, I'm very sorry about that little accident, but if there's one thing I'm not, it's inconsiderate," he snapped uncharacteristically. "Where I come from, Magdalen College Oxford, one of the few ancient buildings in my country your lot didn't bomb to smithereens not so long ago, men are gentlemen. As it happens, I'm feeling very tired, very sleepy, and not particularly well."

He flopped into his seat and undid his collar, assuming he would hear no more from her.

"You sound drunk!" she snarled, leaning away from him. "Nothing contagious, I hope?"

"Contagious inebriation! Now that would be something. Or perhaps you meant sleeping sickness, did you? Let me think. No, I don't recall dropping into Africa on the way to Naples from London, getting bitten by a tsetse fly, and putting a few of her mates in my pockets for the ride. No, it's just mental and physical exhaustion I'm afraid, plain and simple. Scientists like me live with our work in our heads day and night. We don't clock off at five like most people, or is it four where you come from? And what's more, we do it for a pittance."

"Ah, you're an academic!" she sighed, her face now buried in a book. "My husband was just as foolish. What's the point of slaving in smelly laboratories and dusty libraries, I used to tell him, when they pay you peanuts? We certainly couldn't have bought our villa in Capri on his salary. Thank goodness my father had more sense."

"A villa in Capri? How nice!"

"Nice? It was a nightmare. I sold it yesterday."

"Why?"

She flashed her eyes around the cabin.

"This lot."

"Really? I've met some very nice Italians. In fact, just a few minutes ago, I was chatting to a lovely…"

"You don't need to tell me. I was watching you. And I know what you were up to. No doubt hoping you might show her around Oxford…and then who knows what? But she had more sense. I'm afraid you came a very poor second to her copy of *Vogue*. Ha! Fortunately for you, I'm not your wife."

"It is indeed most fortunate, madam. Perhaps there is a God after all."

"You're an atheist too? I might have guessed."

Once they were airborne, he was searching for an excuse to move to another seat, when a stewardess arrived with the menus. As soon as his neighbour had made her choice, he seized his opportunity.

"You're having the insalata di arragosta followed by the scaloppa di vitello? Never eat either myself. Don't believe in boiling animals alive, or slaughtering them as mere babes. It'll upset me just to watch. And as I've also got some dictating to do, if you don't mind, I'll get up and…"

"Please do," she retorted. "You're far too sensitive. We have to eat, don't we? And anyway, animals don't feel real pain. Their brains are different."

"Really? You're an expert on such matters, are you? I'd love to learn more, but I really must go, before someone else grabs that seat over there."

The next thing Giles was aware of was the same woman scowling menacingly over him, after being woken up by a painful prod in his ribs.

"Come on, Herr Professor, we've arrived," she hissed. "Wake up! We've landed, and you're the last one. Too many gin and tonics, no doubt. I saw you asleep over your Chicken Kiev. At least my lobster didn't die for nothing!"

"How dare you, madam," he growled, struggling to wrench her walking stick from her hand. "Who the hell are you?"

"What do you mean, you silly man? Have you forgotten already?"

Seeing the commotion, a stewardess came running down the aisle.

"Please!" she exclaimed, coming between them "What's going on?"

"I don't know what's got into him. He was behaving very oddly when he was sitting next to me—thick speech, saying all sorts of nonsense, very aggressive. And now he claims he can't remember me. He's all yours. Good luck!"

"What nonsense!" Giles howled. "I've never set eyes on her before. And this is the only seat I've had. She was attacking me."

"Everything's okay, sir." the stewardess replied softly, trying to calm him down.

"We're in London. You've been asleep. Let me undo your belt, and help you up."

Once in the arrivals lounge, Giles made himself comfortable in the nearest row of empty seats, and promptly fell asleep again. On awakening, aroused by a baby's crying, he had no idea where he was. He was totally bewildered. In fact, he was more than bewildered; he was terrified. He had not experienced anything like it since waking up in a hotel bedroom in pitch darkness after a non-stop flight from Paris to Singapore several years ago. But this was different. It was broad daylight. It was inexplicable. And why was the side of his chest so sore?

He could see he was in an airport. But which one? He looked around for clues.

"Heathrow!" he gasped on seeing a sign to the Heathrow Express railway station. "Good God!"

After fumbling in his pockets, he found his boarding pass.

"Flight BA2607, Naples to London, departure twelve o'clock, arrival one-fifty. Jesus!"

He couldn't remember a second of the flight. He recalled getting up in the morning, checking out of the hotel, doing a little shopping in Sorrento, taking the taxi to the airport, chatting to the Italian girl, and writing his notes by the window—but nothing after that, absolutely nothing.

He looked at the wall clock in front of him—8:05 p.m. And then at his boarding pass again. More than six hours since he'd arrived! Was that possible? When his watch provided the unwelcome answer, he could feel himself starting to panic. Ever since watching his father succumb to Alzheimer's disease, he had been terrified that one day he would recognise the first signs in himself. He recalled vividly the day his father had woken up from an afternoon snooze in his cottage in the English Lake District to be astounded by his garden's lush green grass and roses, believing he was still in Khartoum.

"Oh God, not that, please!" he muttered, bursting into a cold sweat. Grabbing his things, he made his way out of the terminal, and found a coach that was about to leave for Oxford. As soon as he had called Fiona to let her know he was on his way, he picked up the courage to give himself a few memory tests. First, he counted the coins in his trouser pocket with his fingers, wrote down the number, and five minutes later tried to remember how many there were. Next, he tried to memorise the registration numbers of passing vehicles. Two taxis, a Porsche, and a police car later, he moved onto other challenges—the cricket scoreboards in a discarded copy of The Times, and his credit card numbers.

Buoyed up by a reassuring, if not flawless, performance, he persuaded himself that his lapse in the airport had been due to emotional exhaustion, and settled down to read the rest of the newspaper. Unhappily, as the coach turned to enter Oxford's Gloucester Green bus station, and he was folding up the newspaper, his peace of mind was shattered by the realisation that he could not remember where he'd put his glasses.

As usual, Fiona's red Honda Civic was waiting in the bus station, and they were soon on their way to Mansfield Road. But Giles had noticed that her mood was distinctly cold. Rather than bubbling over with excitement and new plans, as he'd expected, she seemed quiet and disinterested. Even her welcoming embrace had been uncharacteristically limp, with no more than the lightest peck on the cheek.

"Are you okay?" he asked apprehensively.

Clearly not wanting to chat, she kept her eyes on the road and flicked her fingernails.

"Yes, thank you, Giles. I'm perfectly okay."

"Everything ready for this evening?"

"Oh, yes, everything. I've even bought a bottle of pure malt whisky for the occasion."

"Nice thought, dear, but don't you think champagne would be more appropriate for a celebration of this importance? There's a bottle in my kitchen. Why don't we drop by and pick it up?"

"Celebration? I think *you've* already celebrated, haven't you? What I have in mind is more of a ritual than a celebration."

Giles gaped at her in confusion.

"The malt is not to *drink*, Giles. No, no, no! It's for a very different purpose. You haven't forgotten what I said on the phone, I trust? You know, about Sicilians using aceto balsamico, but us Scots doing it in our own traditional way?"

Giles burst into hoots of laughter.

"Ha…ha! You could still do it in style though, Fiona, and use bubbly instead."

Fiona's expression remained as it was.

"Have you noticed I'm not laughing, Giles? Did you enjoy yourself the other night?"

"What are you talking about?"

"The lovely Neapolitan lady you promised yourself."

"What? Oh, come on, Fiona, surely you know I was pulling your leg? I promise you I had a meal on my own, went for a walk, and watched television…still alone."

"Really? So how do you explain the photo on the Splendido Palace's website?"

"What photo?"

"You haven't seen it?"

"No. What photo?"

"Last night, I tried to call your mobile, but it was switched off. Can't imagine why! So I went to the hotel's website to get their number. And what did I see right in the middle of the home page, but a photo of 'Il famoso Professore Butterfield con una bellissima amica,' grinning with glass in hand against a backdrop of long peroxide blonde hair, bright red lips, and the biggest cleavage south of the Dolomites."

"Oh my God! I promise you, Fiona, I had no idea she was there. After calling you, I was sitting in the bar alone, when out of the blue I was swamped by a bunch of paparazzi. She was an extra. I didn't even know she was behind me. The barman said she was the manager's new secretary and a local beauty queen, Miss Mount Vesuvius."

"Ha! Miss Silicone Valley would be more appropriate."

"Believe me! It was all a grotesque publicity stunt. I'm a celebrity there, remember. Photos of me in the bar are good for business."

"Whose business? Hers? I can imagine what that is!"

"Look, if you don't believe me, I'll call the hotel now, and get Luigi on the blower."

"Who's he?"

"The barman I mentioned. He saw it all happen."

"For all I know, he could be her pimp."

"Fiona! Okay, I'll give you the number of the hotel, and you can ask to speak to the manager. His name is Patrono."

Giles offered his phone.

"I can't. I'm driving. It's illegal, remember. You're not in Naples now. But okay, I believe you, I suppose. You can put it away."

"Thank God for that! Now let's go and fetch that champagne."

After collecting the bottle, they left the car in the Fellows' car park, and set off on foot for Fiona's flat.

"Have you had time to do the calculations from your last experiment?" he asked hopefully.

Fiona turned to look at him glumly.

"No, sorry. My stats software seems to be corrupted. I asked Aram if I could use his for half an hour, but true to form the sod wouldn't let me."

"Not very helpful of him."

"Nothing new there. He's still so secretive, Giles. I watched him entering a password once. It must have been the complete text of the Qur'an."

"What about our plan in the Grand Café? Have you had a chance to follow up on that?"

"You mean checking to see if any of my files have been altered?"

Giles nodded.

"No, not that either. It's too soon. I've got the software, but haven't picked up the courage to leave my laptop lying around unprotected. I will do so soon. He still acts very oddly. And by the way, listen to this. Yesterday morning, I got to the lab just after five o'clock, because I'd promised to call Craig in Sydney about the project. And lo and behold, who did I find at my desk? When I asked him why he was there, he said he preferred it to his table, because it's a better height."

"I suppose that's true, isn't it?"

"Yes, but that doesn't give him carte blanche to use it. And why was he in the lab at that time of the morning? I don't like his behaviour at all. He's such a loner too. Doesn't seem to have any friends apart from the other Alhazen Fellows. I bumped into Jim Watkins later in the day. He said all the Oxford ones meet in his local pub in Thrupp, The Jolly Boatman, every Sunday, sometimes with one or two visitors, who seem to fly into London Oxford International Airport less than a mile away. They always sit around the same table talking in Arabic or, if the weather's nice, outside by the canal. Recently, one of them dropped a piece of paper on the floor. When Jim picked it up and handed it to him, he saw it was a sketch of what looked like a network of websites and computers.

"It all looks a bit suspicious to me, Giles. Anyhow, to change the subject, I got some bad news yesterday. My big idea about antibody responses to cancer cells was rejected by the Journal of Immunology. The editor said it was too speculative. I'm still recovering."

Having just reached the garden gate, Giles stopped to put a comforting arm around her shoulder.

"Don't take it too seriously, Fiona. After all, peer review is only the opinion of another person—a person who might be prejudiced, not as bright, less knowledgeable, less imaginative, jealous, have an axe to grind, or regard you as a threat? Peer review has been responsible some a lot of blunders in the past. So don't worry."

"What sort of blunders?"

"Every sort imaginable. Not so long ago, a published study found that no less than twelve papers that eventually earned their authors Nobel Prizes had been rejected by at least one top academic journal before being published by another. Howard Florey's grant application to fund his first experiments to see if penicillin could cure mice of a bacterial infection was also rejected by the Medical Research Council. Eventually, it was a pharmaceutical company that put up the money. The same sort of thing's been happening for years. Even Gregor Mendel, the friar whose experiments with sweet peas laid the foundations of genetics, couldn't get his work acknowledged before he died.

"So cheer up! You're in good company."

Fiona snuggled up to him, as a cold wind got up.

"That certainly helps. Thanks."

"I think you should send the paper to another journal first thing. I'll give you a letter to go with it, saying how important I think it is."

She kissed him on the cheek, as she reached to open the gate.

"Thanks, you're a darling. Now, let's go and have a cup of tea and a slice of Dundee cake, while that bottle's on ice."

Once inside the flat, Giles lit the fire, while Fiona went into the kitchen.

"By the way, Giles," she called through the half-open door, "did you remember to dictate the stuff for the students' next practical class? It's getting pretty urgent."

"Damn! No, I didn't, sorry. But I did get as far as jotting down some notes in Naples airport. I was planning to dictate them during the flight, but I'm afraid I slept all the way. As you know, I even fell asleep in Heathrow. I'll do it tomorrow, as soon as I've done that letter for you."

"You're forgiven."

Chapter Thirteen

When Fiona waltzed into Giles's office the next morning to collect his promised letter of support to the Editor of the Journal of Immunology, she was shocked to find him in Jane's room prostrate on the sofa, his face pale, his forehead sweating, his eyes fixed on the ceiling.

"Oh my God!" she shrieked, dropping her coffee. "Giles, what's the matter? Have you had a heart attack?"

"No," he gasped, wiping his brow. "I've just had the most awful shock."

Fiona kneeled beside him to feel his pulse.

"About what?"

"I think I've started with Alzheimer's."

"What! Why on earth…?"

"Because when I switched on my phone just now to dictate the stuff for your practical class from the notes I made in Naples, I found I'd already done it. The entire thing is in there! I've checked the time and date record, and I did it during the flight. But for the life of me, I can't remember doing so. My voice sounds a bit odd too, sort of slightly slurred. But it was definitely during the flight. You can hear the hum of the engines in the background."

"So, you probably did it half asleep after a few glasses. So what?"

"I couldn't have had that many glasses. And there's something else."

"What?"

"You remember I told you I had a nap in Heathrow before getting onto the coach? Well, what I didn't tell you is that when

I woke up, I had absolutely no idea where I was. Not only that, I couldn't remember anything of the flight. It was a complete blank. You know my father had Alzheimer's, don't you? Well, a blood test in Liverpool showed I inherited that apoE4 gene from him, the one that increases your chances of getting it."

"Giles," she said softly, squeezing his hand, "yes, I did know about your father, and I know how painful it was for you. But I don't think for one minute you're developing Alzheimer's. Tell me, can you remember telephoning me in the flat from here this morning?"

"Yes."

"And can you remember why?"

"Yes, to ask if I'd left my wallet on the bedside table."

"That's right. So…that doesn't sound like Alzheimer's, does it?"

"Perhaps not, but I don't think I've banged my head either."

He hauled himself up, feeling his cranium for a bruise.

"We all have occasional lapses of memory, Giles. It's perfectly normal, especially when you're worn out and have a lot on your mind. I forgot where I'd put the chromatography solvents the other day. So stop worrying. Give me the dictation now, and I'll go and type it."

"Okay."

An hour later, Fiona reappeared triumphantly waving an A4 document in the air, which she dropped onto the desk in front of him.

"Here's your copy. All I need now are the specimens for the DNA fingerprints. I suppose the cigarette end you mentioned is in here, is it? Don't get up."

She opened his briefcase, and after some rummaging found three small plastic bags.

"Yes, here's Specimen B, namely one disgusting fag end. Ugh! And I see you've already done Specimens A and E too—a nice big blood spot on a Kleenex tissue, and a few very grey hairs. Perfect! Both from you, I take it?"

Giles's jaw dropped as he stared at the bags.

"Fiona."

"Yes."

"I don't remember collecting those either. The cigarette end, yes. I picked it up in the hotel. But not the other two."

He examined his thumb, and saw the tiny but unmistakable bruise left by a deep pinprick.

"I must have done that during the flight too. Oh God! It must have been pretty painful, and yet..."

"Stop worrying, Giles! You're fine. You were just very tired. I'll take them to the lab. Bye for now."

As she turned to leave, Giles caught her by the arm and pulled her towards him.

"By the way, before you go, dear," he said, softening his voice. "I enjoyed the homecoming treat last night. It was wonderful. "

"So, you *do* remember *that* then?"

"How could I forget it? But I got the impression you weren't too enthusiastic. Is that so?"

"It was okay, I suppose. But I think I've done better."

"What do you mean?"

"I think I left in too long. Your nuts were overdone, weren't they?"

"Ha...ha!" he bellowed. "I've never heard it put that way before."

"What do you mean? Wait a minute, are we on the same wavelength? I'm talking about the Dundee cake. And you?"

"The *cake*? No!"

"What then?"

"In the bedroom, you and me."

"Last night? Are you saying we...?"

"You don't remember?"

Fiona hid her face in embarrassment.

"No... I don't."

"Nothing?"

She shook her head disconsolately.

"No. How awful! Was I awake?"

"Yes, of course. A little heavy-eyed and slower than usual, which I put down to the champagne."

"I don't understand. I'm sorry, but I have to be honest. The last thing I remember was having my shower. Now *I'm* the one who's sounding like an Alzheimer's case."

Neither of them said anything for a couple of minutes, he gazing at the drab grey sky through the window, she propped against the desk, staring into the fireplace.

"Don't worry about it, Fiona. We're both utter wrecks at the moment. You went out like a light afterwards. When I left the flat this morning, you were snoring."

"Snoring? How awful! It gets worse."

"It's all the stress you've been through, coming on top of the College work—the students, your article, the grant application, Aram, the small-minded tittle-tattle going on behind our backs. It would be too much for anyone."

"I suppose you're right. Some people would have cracked up by now, wouldn't they?"

"No doubt about it. I don't know how you've coped."

"I keep saying it, Giles, but it's true. We need a big holiday, somewhere warm and sunny, with gorgeous beaches and delicious food. At the end of the semester, let's do it. Just do it!"

Chapter Fourteen

For the rest of the week, Fiona busied herself preparing for the students' practical class. As she didn't see much of them during the academic year, she treated her occasional forays into their world very seriously. She knew that her laboratory demonstrations, though only a very small part of their medical training, might have a profound influence on their attitude towards research in the future. And that *was* important. Each year there would be one or two with the aptitude and ability to become first-class researchers, and her performance might have a decisive impact on whether those precious few would go on to apply their talents to further medical science. She often wondered how many advances had been delayed with incalculable consequences owing to unimaginative and sloppy teaching.

After a couple of days tidying up the laboratory, polishing the glassware, adjusting the instruments, and preparing the many reagents she would need, she was rehearsing her demonstration to an imaginary audience, when Giles, clearly now in much better spirits, swept into the room, brandishing a needle and syringe in one hand, and a paper bag and an old envelope in the other.

"Herewith, m'lady," he announced, with a deep bow that would have done credit to an Elizabethan courtier, "I delivereth to thy captious mammets the awaited Specimen C, namely one old and forlorn envelope from my desk drawer."

"Thank you, my liege," she giggled, taking the bag with a curtsy.

"Methinks all thou needest now, m'lady, is Specimen D, namely one used postcard, and Specimen F, a second blood. Allow me to consort thee to thy office, where, after thou hast discased, I shall obtain the latter with my argentine butt-shaft here. But be not afeared. I shall be expedient to scotch thy flesh. First, thou must dup thy skirt. Art thou addressed? Dost thou compose?"

"Not likely!"

Giles looked at her aghast.

"How on earth did you understand that lot?"

"Subtle nuances of your courtly body language—such as the way you were drooling at my butt with that weapon quivering in your hand. If you want a blood sample, it'll have to be by pricking my thumb, sorry—perhaps not exactly what you had in mind. And anyway, where did you get all that Old English from?"

"I downloaded a Shakespearean dictionary a while back to help me with the great bard's sonnets, and then decided to memorise it."

"You memorised an entire dictionary?"

"It's only eight pages."

"Nevertheless, I'm impressed. At least it disproves your Alzheimer's theory."

"That occurred to me too—one reason why I am so happy."

"And the other?"

"The sun's shining."

Fiona was all too familiar with the procedure of having blood drawn for their experiments, and had already prepared a box of tissues, several balls of cotton wool, and a bottle of surgical spirit on top of a clean sheet of paper on one of the benches. She made herself comfortable on a stool, offered him a thumb, and closed her eyes.

"Okay, get on with it, Dracula," she sighed, "and no deeper than necessary, please. By the way, you do know that taking blood in the lab is illegal, don't you?"

Giles wetted the cotton wool with spirit, and rubbed her thumb with it.

"Strictly speaking, yes. But I also know there's no danger, if you're as experienced as I am. Such laws are made by moronic bureaucrats with nothing better to do than sit in committee rooms on their ever-expanding arses. I don't need their advice."

"That's not what you said about making tea in the lab. You told me off about that, remember?"

Giles smiled menacingly, as he prepared to prick her thumb.

"Are you rebuking your superior, Dr Cameron?"

"In a way, well, I mean…OUCH!!"

"Sorry, I had a sudden twitch. Be thankful you didn't have to do it to yourself. It's far worse, believe me. Thank goodness I can't remember doing it during the flight…which I must say still worries me a bit.

"Now keep still while I dab this nice big blob of blood onto a Kleenex, before it drips onto the floor. There, that's that. Perfect! Okay, hold onto the cotton wool as usual, while I pop the tissue ever so carefully into this paper bag. Note that I'm not putting it directly into a *plastic* bag this time, because it's still wet. Hopefully, in the aircraft I remembered to let mine dry before putting it away.

"I'll leave it to you to find a postcard. I'm sure there are plenty on your notice board from your many ex-lovers. And look carefully at the stamps. We don't want any of those un-licked self-adhesive types, do we?"

"Do I look like a fool? And how do you know they're *ex-*lovers anyway?"

"No man in his right mind can put up with you for very long."

"Which only goes to prove what I've always suspected about you—that you're bonkers. Take a seat. I'll be back in a tick."

She walked to the far end of the laboratory to put the paper bag and envelope into a box that already contained the other specimens. Upon returning, she sat on Giles's knee and snuggled up like a kitten seeking affection.

"Giles, you know what happened to me the other night, when we were together— not being very interested, not remembering, and so on? There may have been another reason apart from stress and tiredness. I think I may have had a virus."

"Yes?"

"Yes. Because when I eventually got out of bed, I had a splitting headache, and then in the shower I noticed a rash on my chest."

"What sort?"

"Red blotches. It's gone now."

"Itchy?"

"A bit."

"Sore throat, aches and pains?"

"No."

"Temperature?"

"Didn't check, but don't think so."

"Tummy upset, diarrhoea?"

She shook her head.

"Doesn't sound like a virus. More likely an allergy, I'd say. Ever had anything like it before?"

"Don't think so—oh, wait a minute, something a bit like it once as a student. I'd been taking some pills before an exam. But I haven't taken anything like that for ages. So that's not the answer."

"Any unusual foods?"

"Only what we had together—champagne, Dundee cake, and so on—nothing special. There *was* just one other thing. I tried what was left in the fridge of that Italian drink you brought back from Sorrento for me to taste. I almost finished it while I was loading the dishwasher. What's it made of?"

"The juice of a bitter orange apparently, plus lots of herbs. Maybe you're allergic to one of them."

"Perhaps that's the answer. Not likely to explain the other business though, is it? Anyhow, I'd better get on with my rehearsal."

"Okay. If you need anything, give me a buzz. For the next few days, I'll be buried in other people's grant applications. Wouldn't life be simple, if we could all enjoy the same benefits as MECCAR's scientists, and forget about begging for money to buy the things we need to do the job we're paid to do? I think MECCAR got that one right too, Fiona. Perhaps we should become Muslims and move to Wadi Rum. You certainly wouldn't be short of your beloved sun, sand, and blue skies there."

***

It was exactly one week later, when Fiona strode confidently into Giles's office to report on the outcome of the practical class.

"I've got the results," she announced jubilantly, opening her lab book on his desk to reveal photographs of her six DNA fingerprints, labelled A to F. "And believe it or not, they all got it right. Every single student identified the murderer correctly."

"Wonderful! Congratulations, you must have done a good job."

"Although I say it myself, I think the fingerprints were so good that I made it too easy for them. As you can see, the two most important ones, the DNA from your blood and your hair, were beauties."

"They certainly were. Well done!"

"Thanks. To be fair, I shouldn't claim all the credit. You also deserve a commendation—for fortitude at high altitude. I wonder what the passenger next to you thought, when you sat there pricking yourself with a pin, and pulling hairs out of your head? It must have looked very peculiar!"

"Thought I was a masochist, I imagine, and took fright to another seat. I must remember that trick. It might be a good way of hijacking a complete row of seats all to myself on a long-haul flight."

"I'm surprised you had the courage actually," she grinned, stroking his head.

"Perhaps I did it in the washroom, so nobody could see."

"No, what I meant is that if I were you, I'd hang on to every last ageing follicle."

"Cheeky! But seriously, these DNA fingerprints are first class. Full marks to you."

Fiona sat on the edge of his desk, and crossed her arms.

"Thanks again. But now, before I go," she said sternly. "I've a bone to pick. Why didn't you tell me there was a second pair of identical DNA samples there, in addition to the pair from you? I suppose it was to check my results were reproducible, was it? If so, I'm a wee bit disappointed that you didn't trust me."

"But I didn't."

"What! After all these years?"

"I meant I didn't give you a second pair of specimens with identical DNAs. The only two from the same person were the ones you know about: my blood and hair follicles. Sorry, Fiona, I'm afraid you must have made an error. What other two are you talking about? Show me."

Fiona pointed to the results she'd obtained with the DNA from the dried saliva left on the envelope flap, and the DNA from the cigarette end. Giles put on his glasses and compared them.

"Hard to be absolutely sure, but they certainly look the same, I agree. Well, if that's the case, I'm afraid you've very definitely done something wrong."

He opened the top right-hand drawer of his desk to reveal a pile of old envelopes and scraps of paper.

"As I told you, I brought the cigarette butt from Italy. I picked it up when I spotted it, knowing it would remind me to do the dictation. And the envelope came from this drawer. So, something's obviously gone wrong with your procedures— presumably cross-contamination or mislabelling.

"Now, let me ask you a question. Did you include controls to check your methods were working properly? I don't see any."

Fiona looked at him sheepishly.

"Not on this occasion. As you know, for our research I always include some stored blood samples whose DNA fingerprints are already on file, but I didn't think it necessary for the students."

Giles banged his fist on the desk.

"Ah, well, there you are! Fiona, controls are *always* necessary. It doesn't matter what you're doing. You must always, repeat *always*, include controls."

"Oh dear, sorry," she sighed forlornly. "And I thought I'd done so well."

"No use crying over spilt milk. The important thing is to learn from your mistakes.

Did you use up all of each specimen?"

"No, I've still got some of each one. I always keep some in reserve."

"Very good. So you can repeat them, this time with controls?"

"Yes."

"Can you do it before you see the students again?"

"Yes, no problem. I'll start straight away and finish over the weekend."

"Excellent."

***

It was almost two o'clock the following Tuesday afternoon, when Fiona was sitting in the laboratory sticking the last photograph of her new DNA fingerprints into her lab book. Knowing Giles was lunching with Sir Quentin to discuss a new fundraising initiative, which they'd planned to finish on the hour, she tucked the book under her arm and hastened out of the New Building in the hope of catching him before they left the Senior Common Room. As she entered the Cloisters, she spotted him through the arches, leaving the square by way of the Founder's Tower. By the time she had caught up, he was passing by the holly tree in the centre of the St Swithun's lawn, his habitual shortcut to the office.

"Giles," she called, "have you finished already?"

As it was starting to rain, he darted under the holly tree, beckoning her to join him.

"Hello, dear," he sighed, "the answer to your question is yes and no. Just for a change, Sir Q forgot to bring the spreadsheets we were supposed to discuss. So regrettably, not much was achieved. He promised to drop them off in the office within the hour. However, from past experience I think we can forget about that one. No doubt I'll have to collect them from the Lodgings tomorrow."

As the rain got heavier, a loud clap of thunder echoed around the old buildings.

"Let's run for it," he urged, pulling up his collar.

"No, let's stay here, please. I've just had my hair done. It'll probably stop soon. The forecast said sunshine and showers. While we're here, I can show you my new fingerprints. And you'll be very pleased to know I included not just one type of control this time, but three: a commercial DNA sample from Advanced Biotechnologies, the blood sample that I analysed for Prof Fairclough a few weeks ago, and what was left of the sample the Department of Pathology asked us to do."

"Excellent."

Huddling under the branches in an attempt to keep it dry, she opened her book and found the page she needed.

"Now, look here. The Fairclough and Pathology ones gave exactly the same results as before. And the other stuff looks nice too. So, my methods and reagents were okay, weren't they?"

"Looks like it."

"Good. So now you'll believe the other fingerprints must be okay too, yes?"

"Presumably."

Fiona glanced at him oddly, as she turned the page, holding it down against the wind.

"Well, as you can see, just as before, the DNA from the saliva on the envelope matches to a tee the DNA from the cigarette butt. So there's no doubt about it. Those two DNAs were from the same person. Quod erat demonstrandum."

Giles looked aghast, as he took the book to have a closer look.

"That's incredible! I found the cigarette butt on the Presidential Suite's terrace. There's a big cupboard there, where they keep the garden furniture. After I'd been watching TV for an hour or so, I decided to sit on the terrace for a while with a drink. When I opened the cupboard to get a chair, I saw the butt to the floor. Somebody must have tossed it away, and it landed there. The door has big gaps above and below it, like a stable door. So I picked it up with a tissue, and dropped it into one of those small bags from the bathroom."

Unsmiling, Fiona regained possession of the book, firmly prising it from his hand as he tried to look more closely at the other results. Leaning against the trunk of the tree with her arms folded, she held the book tightly to her chest.

"Did you say you were in the Presidential Suite?"

"Yes, that's right. It was the only…"

"My, I hadn't realised it was *Lord* Butterfield already!"

"As I was about to say, it was the only space available. They gave it to me for half the price of a standard room, and what's more…"

"Really? How interesting. Now tell me where the envelope came from."

"Are you feeling okay? You're behaving rather oddly."

"I'm fine, thanks. So, go on…the envelope."

"Fiona, what's got into you?"

"Nothing's got into me. Go on!"

"I showed you where it came from…my desk drawer."

"No, I mean originally. Who gave it to you? There was nothing written on it—no address, no name, nothing."

"I've no idea. It was just an old envelope among all the others. I can't imagine why the DNA on it should match the cigarette's. It's extraordinary, isn't it?"

"Yes, it is, isn't it? And it gets extra-extra-extraordinary."

"What do you mean? Why?"

"Because in addition to the controls I mentioned, I also checked the accuracy of my work in another way. The old postcard that I took from my notice board had *three* stamps on it. For the first lot of analyses last week, I used only one of them. This time around, I analysed both of the other two, to check that I got the same result with each one."

"Excellent. There's no substitute for duplicates."

"Except it turned out they were *not* duplicates, because they'd been licked by different people—one by whoever licked the one I used last week, and the other one by somebody else."

"That was bad luck. Never mind, it was a good idea all the same. Come on, let's dash, or we're going to get soaked. We can finish in the office."

"Wait!" she exclaimed. "Not till I've finished. On Friday, one of the students dropped in to see me, the Chinese boy. He said he'd heard that Forensic Sciences has a new 'Genescanner', the automated fluorescence system that puts the DNA fingerprint results into a computer. He wanted me to demonstrate it to him over the weekend."

"So that's where you were?"

"Yes. And after I'd put all six samples through it, he then asked me to demonstrate the 'Genemapper' software they've also got."

"That's normally used for paternity testing."

"That's right…which happens to have been very fortunate. Fortunate for me, that is…not so fortunate for you."

"What *are* you talking about?"

"Because it told me something *very, very* interesting."

"What?"

"That the two people who licked those stamps were none other than the parents of whoever sealed the envelope."

"What! Have you been dreaming?"

"No, look for yourself."

Fiona opened the book again, unfolded a printout she had fixed to the page with Scotch tape, and held it up in front of his face. After wiping the rain off his glasses with his sleeve, Giles studied it carefully.

"Good grief! What an extraordinary coincidence. Who signed the postcard? Who was it from?"

From the top pocket of her lab coat Fiona withdrew a coffee-stained card bearing a colour photograph of Sydney Opera House. Her hand visibly trembling, she turned it over and held it to his eyes.

"What!" Giles gasped. "The Salomons?"

"That's right—Steve and Marie-Claire, during a trip to Australia ten years ago."

"Wait a minute, Fiona. Let me get this right. You're saying that the envelope that I gave you had been sealed by one of Steve's brood?"

"Yep."

"In that case, I must have brought it back with me from my sabbatical with Steve. But it didn't look that old, nothing like it."

Fiona scowled as she tapped her foot in a puddle that had collected between the roots of the tree, splashing his shoes and trousers with mud.

"But what about the cigarette end that had the very same DNA on it as the envelope. Do you have any theories about how that came to have been smoked by one of Steve's brood, as you put it?"

"I really don't know what to say about that, Fiona. I'm totally confused."

"I'm sorry, Giles, but there's no way out."

"What do you mean?"

Fiona glared at him.

"Don't you have anything else to say?"

"What *are* you talking about?"

"What am I talking about? *What am I talking about?* Giles, my results prove that one of Steve's offspring smoked that cigarette, which you have already admitted came from the terrace of the Presidential Suite in Sorrento."

She supported her chin on her hand in feigned deliberation.

"Now, let me think. I seem to recall you telling me once that during your sabbatical with Steve he had a couple of teenage daughters. Yes?"

"Yes."

"As that was about ten years ago, they'd now be in their twenties."

"Sorry? What's the relevance of that?"

"What's the relevance of that? *What's the relevance of that?* Giles, there's no point pretending to be stupid. You'll have to do much better than that. You were obviously in Sorrento with one of Steve's daughters, weren't you? That's the only possible explanation."

"What! Of course, I wasn't. Don't be ridiculous, Fiona."

"Why is it ridiculous? The evidence speaks for itself."

"Well, it might look like that. But it wasn't the case. I haven't seen either of his daughters since I was there. And even then, it was only from a distance. I didn't actually meet them. I'm completely baffled. What can I say? I suppose one of them must have been on holiday in Sorrento at some time. Either that, or Steve's son, Michael, was on a business trip. He has a leather-goods outlet. He might visit Italy a lot."

"Sorry, Giles! I've checked the sex of the DNA using an amelogenin probe. The smoker was definitely of the female gender."

"Was she? Well, I don't know, Fiona. Maybe one of them was in a nearby room of the hotel at some time, tossed it out of the window, and it landed on the terrace."

"Ha…ha! Giles, you know very well that the Presidential Suite is on the top floor. It's a penthouse, isn't it? It says so on the hotel's website. So either there's been a tornado in the Bay of Naples recently that nobody seems to have noticed, or there's another explanation."

"Fiona, I'm as confused as you. What am I supposed to say?"

"What are you supposed to say? *What are you supposed to say?* How about 'Okay, I give in. It's a fair cop.' Can't you recognise when you're cornered, Giles?"

"A fair cop? Fiona, how can you possibly imagine I was in Sorrento having it off with one of Steve's daughters? It's laughable. As I said, I don't even know them. It's just a coincidence—an astonishing, almost unbelievable one, yes, but…"

Fiona scoffed, almost clipping his nose, as she slammed her lab book closed.

"*An astonishing coincidence*? I wasn't born yesterday, Casanova Butterfield. Now I know who the blonde tart behind you in the bar really was! No wonder you didn't want *me* to accompany you. No room on the plate for a Scottish gooseberry, when a bit of slap and tickle with a Californian peach was on the menu. I wonder which one of them it was. No, wait a minute, perhaps it was both. Yes, that's it. That would certainly have justified the expense of the Presidential

Suite with the nice big four-poster they promote on their website. I hope it had strong springs."

As she turned her back on him defiantly, Giles was almost speechless. He put his hands on her shoulders to turn her, only to receive a sharp elbow in the ribs.

"Ouch! Fiona, for God's sake, snap out of it. This is complete crap, utter fantasy! I've been accused of some crazy things in my life, but nothing quite as crazy as this."

Seeing a couple of students enter the Quad, she about-turned and lowered her voice.

"Crazy? Why is it crazy? For all I know, you might have been in touch with them, in more ways than one, for years."

"Fiona, believe me. I don't know Steve's daughters. I've never spoken to either of them. I can hardly remember what they looked like. Whenever I socialised with the Salomons, it was in a smart restaurant, and his children were at home with a sitter. All I know about his daughters is that they're now marine biologists in San Diego."

Fiona was now rigid, fists clenched. Tears were streaming down her cheeks, taking rivers of mascara with them.

"Giles, just tell me the truth, and have done with. And then we can finish. I'm sure I'll find a job somewhere."

"Okay, that's it! Fiona, let's get this straight. One, I haven't set eyes on either of Steve's daughters since I was there. Two, I'm not interested in anyone but you. Three, I'm not going to listen to any more of this nonsense. There has to be an explanation for what you've found, and it's not the one you're assuming. You either believe me, or you don't. Now, I've work to do. I'm off. Give me a call when you've regained your senses."

With that, he stormed off into the downpour, until at the moment of reaching the border directly in front of Jane's window, he slipped and fell into the gardeners' working compost heap. As he struggled up, brushing the mud and leaves off his flannels, he glanced over his shoulder, hoping to see Fiona running to his aid. But she was not. She was exactly where he had left her, under the holly tree, her head in her hands.

As a squall swept up a maelstrom of leaves from the compost, he resolved to make his way back. He had acted impetuously. There was no point leaving things like that. After buttoning his jacket, he strode across the turf, head bent into the wind. Then inexplicably, about halfway across, he stopped in his tracks. Rooted to the spot, drenched from head to toe, his gaze seemed strangely fixed on the Great Tower. As Fiona wept, her wet hair plastered to her face, her lab book lying in the mud, she watched him between her fingers, and wondered what he was up to. Was he about to beg for forgiveness? Dump her for the other woman? Give her the sack?

Suddenly throwing both arms into the air, he charged towards her, bellowing as he went.

"Fiona, I've got it! I've got it! I've got it!"

He arrived at the tree gasping and panting, perspiration mixed with rain running down his face.

"While you were going on at me, I couldn't think properly. But it's obvious. The two girls who accompanied Steve to Sorrento, Amandine and Carina, must have been his daughters. I remember when they were young; one was fair like Marie-Claire, and the other had dark hair like Steve. It would explain everything: their coyness when I bumped into them after Ahmad's lecture, their inability to speak French or Italian, the accent, the fact that Steve was so tense and edgy—the whole shooting match. That *must* be it! You were right way back, when you suggested they weren't researchers. But they weren't high-class tarts either, as you guessed. They were *Steve's daughters*. They must have accompanied Ahmad to his suite after their dinner together. While they were there, one of them went onto the terrace for a breather and a few puffs on that cigarette."

Fiona collapsed into his arms, planting kisses on both cheeks.

"Yes, that must be it! Oh, thank God for that, Giles," she sobbed, sweeping her hair off her face and looking into his eyes. "I'm sorry, really sorry. I shouldn't have jumped to a stupid conclusion like that. Am I forgiven?"

"Of course."

"So what were they up to?"

"There can be only one explanation, Fiona. Steve must have taken them to Sorrento masquerading as two of his research fellows for the sole purpose of prising MECCAR's secrets out of Ahmad. Getting into the Suite to snoop around was part of the plan. Any information they could find would have been of enormous value for Steve's research. He was desperate to restore his reputation. He arranged the meeting between the girls and Ahmad so they could get to know each other. Then, over dinner in the Pesce Spada, the girls launched a charm offensive. Before Ahmad knew what was happening, they were in his suite. Then, while one of the girls kept him occupied— let's not speculate how—her sister snooped around, looking for anything that might be of interest. It's the oldest trick in the book. They were there as spies, *academic spies*."

"And what about Gerhard what's-his-name from Munich?" Fiona asked. "Where does he fit in? Steve invited him to the meeting too, don't forget."

"Steve was using him. Without knowing it, the poor guy was there as an extra. Remember, Steve arranged the meeting ostensibly so Ahmad could advise the girls on their research projects. Leaving just the three of them together would have been a big risk. As marine biologists, the girls must know something about genes, but probably not very much, and certainly not in relation to cancer. No matter how much Steve might have briefed them, left on their own it would have been obvious to Ahmad that they were amateurs. But with a real geneticist present, they could have deflected any tricky questions in his direction. That's why Steve joined the meeting as a replacement, after learning Gerhard had been taken ill. Crafty bugger! Well, sorry, Steve, not quite crafty enough."

Fiona held his hands and looked at him forlornly as the rain dripped from the leaves overhead.

"Giles, where's this incredible business going to end?"

"As I've said before, dear, with the *truth*—and we'll keep going until we're there."

"Do we have to? Couldn't we just drop it and have done with? Does it really matter what the Salomons were up to? Whatever their motives, we've no evidence they actually succeeded in filching any of MECCAR's secrets, have we? We already know for sure *Deidamia* was not one of them. And even if Steve *was* given the website report by the girls—and we don't know that that's what happened—it was obviously meant for him anyhow…because of what Ahmad had written on the front. So?"

While drying her face with his handkerchief as he mulled it over, he could see she was shivering.

"Why don't we go inside, Fiona, and continue there?"

Shaking her head adamantly, she pulled her white coat tightly around her waist.

"Not just yet. Let's carry on for now."

"If you insist. What you're saying is true, of course. We don't know for certain the girls actually stole anything in Sorrento, whether the website report or anything else. But I don't think we can ignore the fact they were there as impostors. Who knows what it might mean, and where it might lead? Perhaps your DNA fingerprints have opened a can of worms. Perhaps the yanks and some other countries get up to this sort of thing on a regular basis. Scientific congresses the world over might be infiltrated with imposters on the lookout for confidential information for their country's biotech industry. You may have put us onto something really big."

"Yes, but don't forget, Giles, we don't even have absolute proof that Carina and Amandine *were* Steve's daughters, do we? It looks pretty certain, but all we could prove in a court of law is that a cigarette smoked by one of them was on the terrace when you returned to Sorrento. That doesn't prove she was there during the symposium, or that she was Amandine or Carina."

"Yes, you're quite right. In reality, there can't be any other explanation. But proving it is a different matter."

Giles flopped back against the tree and slid down the wet trunk to sit on the grass. Fiona joined him on her haunches.

"Wait a minute!" he exclaimed. "Hold it! Of course, how could I have been so bloody stupid?"

"What?"

"With you going on about what that fag end was supposed to say about my fidelity, we lost sight of the envelope. It's just occurred to me where it may have come from."

"Where?"

"Do you have anything of it left? I don't mean the flap from which you extracted the DNA—the rest of it. Or did you throw it away?"

"I threw it away."

"Shit! Why?"

"I had no use for it, and you're always telling me not to accumulate rubbish in the lab. So?"

"Where did you throw it? And when?"

"I was using it as a bookmark in this lab book. After I'd shown you my first lot of results before the weekend, I dropped it into the trash can by your desk."

"Damn! The maid cleaned the office yesterday. Sometimes she empties it, sometimes she doesn't. I didn't notice. Cross your fingers, hold your breath, and pray all at once. Let's go!"

"Won't Jane be there?"

"I heard the door slam a few minutes ago. She has a dental appointment."

"But first, tell me where you think it came from."

"We'll know in a minute."

After struggling to their feet, they ran hand in hand across the sodden turf, Fiona losing a shoe in the process.

Once inside the office, she grabbed the trash can, and tipped it upside down.

"There it is!" she cried triumphantly, stooping to hand him a crumpled ball of paper. "What are you going to do with it?"

Giles slit it open all around with his penknife, unfolded it so it was a single sheet of paper, and held it in front of the desk lamp.

"Yes! Yes! Yes! There it is, Fiona, just what I thought. See there?"

He pointed to a watermark of a seahorse with two words below it.

"Can you read what it says?"

Fiona took it from him and peered at the letters.

"Splen-di-do Pal-ace. It says Splendido Palace!"

"Exactly. It's one of the hotel's envelopes. When I was in the bar with Steve, Ahmad, and the girls, we exchanged telephone numbers before we broke up. Amandine wrote hers and Carina's on a paper napkin, which she then popped into an envelope for safekeeping. This *has* to be that envelope. It couldn't be anything else. The salivary DNA you analysed from the flap was Amandine's, Fiona. And at some time or other, she was in Ahmad's suite."

"Oh my God, Giles, what a relief! I don't know how many more of these emotional ups and downs I can take. But now I must get these clothes off. I'm sorry, but I'm soaked to the skin and starting to shake all over. You should do the same, including those trousers. Otherwise you'll catch your death."

By the time she had dropped her lab coat to the floor, kicked off the remaining shoe, and taken off her skirt, Giles was standing in nothing but his shirt and underpants.

"Let's go next door and make a pot of tea," she suggested. "It's usually warmer in there. What will it be—Earl Grey, Taylor's, or Jane's green stuff from the market?"

"Taylor's, please. And make it strong."

"Okay. First, I'd better draw the curtains to make sure nobody sees us."

While Fiona filled the kettle, Giles collected the Mojave blanket from the rattan chair, and draped it over her shoulders.

"I think you'd better take the rest of the day off, Fiona. You were drenched even more than me. No arguments. While you're doing that, I'll get the tray ready. Jane bought some new crockery the other day. Said she was tired of drinking out of cracked mugs. So we can have afternoon tea in style."

As Giles was rinsing the cups and saucers, Fiona, clad only in briefs and the blanket, crept up behind him. Wrapping her cold, wet tights around his neck, she dragged him from the sink.

"First, we've reason to celebrate," she giggled. "We were almost divorced a few minutes ago. Now look at us."

Laughing uncontrollably as the blanket dropped to the floor, she pulled him onto the sofa and threw herself on top of him. Unbuttoning his shirt, she gave his paunch a two-handed tweak.

"Fiona, you cheeky…What's got into you? Wait till I get…"

As he struggled to escape, she wrapped her legs around him, pinning him down helplessly.

"Okay, now I've got you where I want you, I'm going to tickle your ribs."

As she did her best, he wriggled and yelped and begged for mercy. His struggles being to no avail, his solution was to give her the tightest bear hug he could muster. As he did so, her head dropped over his shoulder, allowing him to see the door the behind her.

"Oh my God!" he muttered, suddenly going completely limp.

"What's the matter, Giles? Have I injured you?"

Silently, he raised his head again to stare over her shoulder.

"Oh no, don't tell me!" she whispered, burying her head in his chest, as she struggled to cover her bottom with one hand. "There's someone there, isn't there? Please don't say it's Jane."

"No, it isn't Jane. It's even worse."

Giles closed his eyes, as his head dropped back onto the cushion again. Not daring to look behind, Fiona reached for the blanket on the floor, and tried to pull it over them.

"So sorry to disturb," came an all-too-familiar voice, "but the entrance door from the passageway had been left open, you see."

The door from the office creaked, as the intruder slowly advanced.

"It is you, Giles, isn't it…lying there…underneath Fiona?"

Sir Quentin chuckled, as he mischievously tickled the toes of a protruding male foot.

"Ah, yes, so it is! I can see you now. Always wondered why you had this nice comfy sofa here. As promised, I've brought the spreadsheets I forgot to take with me to lunch. I'll leave them on your desk. Don't get up. I'll close the door on my way out.

"Tweedle bye."

As soon as Sir Quentin's heavy footsteps had faded away in the direction of the New Library, Fiona got to her feet, wrapped the blanket around her, and went into the office to lock the door. After sliding the bolt across for good measure, she looked through the window to make sure he was not on his way back, having forgotten to mention something, as so often the case.

Upon returning, she found Giles where she had left him prostrate on the sofa. Passing in silence, she sat at Jane's desk and switched on the Tiffany lamp.

"Can you imagine anything more embarrassing than that?" she groaned. "It'll be all over the College in next to no time. I hope Jane isn't the next one to walk through that door. I couldn't survive another dose."

"No chance of that," Giles assured her. "She's gone for the first stage of an implant. It's a big job."

Feeling a little easier, Fiona finished making the tea, and poured him a cup.

"Do you have any strength left to talk?" she ventured.

Giles gave her a reassuring nod, before rising to collect the pink plastic raincoat Jane always kept in the bottom drawer of her desk. Putting it over his shoulders, with the hood over his head, he tied the sleeves around his neck and returned to the sofa.

"You look like Little Red Riding Hood," she sighed, putting on a brave smile.

Giles sipped his tea, while she continued to stir her own, every now and then filling the spoon and dribbling it back into the cup.

"It's a good brew, thanks, Fiona. If you look on the shelf

over the sink, you'll see a biscuit tin. There should be some of those shortbreads of yours in there. Shall we indulge?"

Leaving her cup on the desk, Fiona collected the tin and squeezed herself beside him.

"Don't look so glum, dear. It's not a tragedy. We'll survive."

"It's not that, Giles. It's something else. I'm concerned at the way I'm not coping with all the stress. It makes me worry about the future. What happened outside under the holly tree was shattering. It wasn't just that it was our first real spat, or the feeling of guilt I have that I didn't trust you or believe you, or the fact that I completely lost control of myself. It's what it says about my state of mind. It's not like me to behave like that, is it? I can certainly fly off the handle every now and then. My mother says I inherited an Irish paddy from her father's side. But that's different. I've never exploded in a blind rage before, and gone to pieces.

"Since you got back from Stockholm, it's been one thing after another. You've been off to Paris, to Munich, to Sorrento, always at the drop of a hat. Nothing's been constant. One day it's been one thing, the next day another. If this business had been limited to just Steve and *Deidamia*, it would have been bad enough, but there's been so much more—Rashid wasting your time on a non-existent gene peddler, your panic about getting Alzheimer's, Aram's suspicious behaviour. And now we've got those girls being Steve's daughters in disguise. So many questions all at once. It's bewildering. I'm worried we won't be able to stop chasing them; that it'll become an obsession; and we won't be able to cope—so that eventually it destroys us and our relationship.

"It's interfering with my work. My nerves are permanently on edge. I'm getting headaches, indigestion, palpitations. And from what happened the other night, it wouldn't surprise me if it's upsetting my hormones too. I'm even wondering if those blotches on my chest were a nervous rash."

Giles put his arm around her in preparation for a pep talk.

"I'm glad you've raised this, Fiona, and not bottled it up.

If only for that reason, what happened out there was probably a good thing. You shouldn't be surprised by your reaction. Your lifetime experience hasn't prepared you for this. It was dropped on you. So it's only natural it's affected you. It hasn't had the same effect on me, because I have an advantage. I've never mentioned it before as there was no reason, but I've been through some very tough situations in my life. In Liverpool a colleague jealous of my success made false allegations of financial impropriety. I proved my innocence, but it took a long time, because the bastard had fabricated evidence. It was a huge ordeal, which I wouldn't have survived if I hadn't changed my approach to life. I realised that the secret was not to toughen up and reinforce my resistance to the pressure, but to change my attitude completely so there was no sense of pressure in the first place. That was the key, and I think the same principle applies to you and me now."

"Sounds simple, but how do I go about it?"

"The tricks that worked for me then wouldn't be appropriate now. In this case, I think the first thing is to remember that nobody is forcing us to do this. It's our choice. We have no contracts with anyone but ourselves, and therefore nobody has the right to expect anything from us. So we should treat it almost as a game, a serious game, but a game nevertheless. Secondly, we should avoid getting frustrated when things go wrong. I've said this before, I know, but it's worth repeating. Take the view that everything is progress, even the setbacks and time-wasters. This is not a delusion. It's the truth. In research we go from one question to another, following a trail of clues, this way and that, sometimes going up blind alleys, sometimes retracing our steps. It's normal, it's what we expect, and because of that it doesn't rankle. As you know, negative scientific papers can be just as important as positive ones, even if they are difficult to get published. This is the same, but with an important difference. In science, however hard we train, however fast we run, however many hurdles we jump, none of us will ever get to the finishing line. It's like that mechanical hare they use in greyhound racing. No matter how fast the dogs chase it, or for how long, they'll never catch it. The best you can hope for in a life of science is to get a few laps under your belt, before you pass the baton to someone else. You know there'll come a day when you'll have to leave it to others, when reluctantly you'll have to step off the track, and wave them off as they continue the journey of discovery without you. But in this business, you and I *can* get to the finishing line. We don't know what path we will follow, or how long it will take, but as long as we adopt the right mental approach, and take our time, we will finish it. There's no reason why *it* should finish *us*."

Fiona paused, eyes closed, while she ran through it all in her head.

"I think you're right, Giles. In fact, I'm sure you are. From now on, I'm going to follow Giles Butterfield's 'four pillars of wisdom.' One, we don't have a contract with anyone but ourselves. Two, treat it as a game, a serious game, but a game nevertheless. Three, everything is progress, even when we go backwards. Four, take our time. I'm going to say that to my four fingers of toast every morning, as I dip them into my boiled egg. I already feel better."

Fiona turned her head to peer at him out of one eye.

"But I still might get a few pills from the GP as a sort of backup, just in case. Okay?"

Without waiting for his reaction, she got up to peer between the curtains, collecting her tea in the process and gulping it down.

"It's stopped raining, and there's even a big piece of cloudless sky overhead. It must be a good omen. How about we face up to the prospect of those cold and sodden clothes, squelch to our respective abodes, and then meet at Pierre Victoire at around seven for three courses, and bottle of red?"

"Splendid idea!"

Chapter Fifteen

After such a hectic day of roller-coasting emotions, the calm ambience and unpretentious décor of Pierre Victoire on Little Clarendon Street was just what they needed. As usual, Giles arrived a few minutes before the agreed hour, and was standing under the bistro's blue and white awning, sheltering from a return of the wind and rain, when Fiona stepped out of her taxi. He was pleased to see how much better she looked after her afternoon nap. The colour had returned to her cheeks, the sparkle to her eyes. Even the natural beauty spot on her left cheek seemed to glow in the soft light from the bistro's window.

Her powers of recovery had always impressed him. Contrary the public image, academic life was not without its stresses and strains, and over the years she had certainly shown the sort of resilience it takes to get to the top. Given the one essential ingredient of a little good fortune—the right idea at the right time, or an experimental result that shone a new light on an old question—she would surely get there one day. But that was her professional life. The fact that she was also able to pick herself up so quickly in the unfamiliarity of the present circumstances boded well for the future. As he helped her to take off her coat, his spirits were high.

Having reserved a table well away from the window, at the far end near the narrow staircase, they would be able to relax knowing they would not be troubled by waving colleagues, or the stares of passers-by who had seen their photographs in the local press.

"I guess it won't be too long before we return to blissful anonymity," Giles murmured, after the waiter had offered them a spare menu to sign. "Once it's all over, people will soon forget us, thank God!"

"But between now and then, we'll enjoy it, won't we?" Fiona whispered, with a wink. "After all, it's only a game, isn't it?"

Throughout the meal, they kept to their pact of avoiding anything to do with *Deidamia*, or even their work in general, until they had got to the cheese and biscuits. Unfortunately, it proved to be a rather bad idea. For while she was struggling to keep a mental record of everything she would want to talk about on the way home, he was forcing himself to chat about politics, sport, and other matters in which he had little interest. It was a struggle for them both.

Seeing the waiter was approaching with the cheeseboard, Fiona raised her glass.

"At this point, we should congratulate ourselves, Giles. We've survived the ordeal. It's the moment we've been waiting for. It's cheese time. Hoorah!"

She helped herself to several oat cakes and a healthy portion of livarot.

"The big question now is whether I can survive this pong!" she added apprehensively. "You know, I think the French must suffer from some kind of olfactory deficiency to be able to share their homes with cheeses like this one. Imagine what it must have been like before there were refrigerators. Anyhow, as I always like to try new food, here goes! Some for you too?"

"*No thank you!* Some of this crumbly Caerphilly and a chunk of mature Cheddar will do me."

"So now, at last, we can talk about important things, yes?"

"Fire away. Just make sure you don't breathe in my direction!"

"I'll do my best! Well, on the way here, I was thinking about my big idea in October, the one about the White House and CIA having done a deal with Ahmad for information on the Bedouins' switch, and then once they'd got their hands on it, bumping him off as the only credible witness. Remember?"

Giles nodded as he replenished a cracker.

"In those days, of course, there was in fact no reason to suspect foul play. The Carabinieri's conclusion that Ahmad had tripped over the tiles at the edge of the pool when jet-lagged and dazzled by the underwater lights was plausible. But things are different now. We know something fishy was definitely going on. We know the girls were not Steve's research fellows, as he claimed, but his daughters masquerading as such to get an introduction to Ahmad. We know they'd been with Ahmad in the restaurant a few hours before his death. And it's pretty certain they accompanied him to his suite afterwards."

"Go on."

"To get straight to the point, it makes me wonder if the girls pushed Ahmad into the pool. It would have been a simple matter to entice him onto the terrace and then give him a shove. When you think about Steve's state of mind at the time, his resentment of MECCAR's success, the humiliation he had suffered, the bad publicity, the professional, financial, domestic, and other problems heaped upon him, he might have pressured the girls into it. Or it could have been at Ted Crabb's behest. Who knows how low he was prepared to stoop with the prospect of the Nobel Prize for one of the biggest breakthroughs in medicine going to an unknown researcher in Jordan, leaving the National Institutes of Health, the University of California, Harvard, and all the other top American universities in his wake.

"Am I being ridiculous?"

"Not at all. But I can think of two things that go against that scenario. When I bumped into Steve on the terrace during the Sorrento symposium, he was boasting about how he'd persuaded Ahmad to send him some DNA samples from the Bedouins and a few other things for his own research. That doesn't sound like someone who was part of a conspiracy to kill him, does it?"

"But you don't know it was genuine, do you? He might have made it up to put everyone off his scent."

Seeing a young couple enter the restaurant, Giles paused while he waited for them to pass behind Fiona's chair to the only empty table.

"Giles, why did you smile at that girl when they squeezed passed?"

"I didn't. It was her boyfriend. He's a student. Why?"

"She's notoriously loose. Her name's Beverley Eddy. The students have a ditty: 'Beverley Eddy. The Balliol Whore. Always ready. Always wants more.' Apparently, those specs are fake. Supposed to make her look intelligent!"

"Thanks, I'll try to remember. The other thing that goes against your conspiracy theory is the perpetrators would have to have known in advance that Ahmad couldn't swim, wouldn't they? Even the CIA couldn't have known that. So, I think we can count that one out. The girls could very well have been there to rob Ahmad of intellectual property. That seems more than likely. But I think we can forget about murder."

"Yes, you're right. Why didn't I think of that?"

"Shall we go? I'll pay on the way out."

Buttoning up their coats on the doorstep, they agreed to walk home past Keble College and down Parks Road to join Holywell Street at the New Bodleian Library. Despite a fresh wind, it would be a pleasant route past Keble College and the Pitt Rivers Museum, and if they started with a diversion up Banbury Road, they could also take in the University Parks.

After such an eventful day and unexpected progress, Fiona's morale was on a high. Everything around her seemed better than before—the smell of the trees, the sound of the wind through their branches, the warm appeal of the old stone buildings, dimly lit by the Victorian street lamps. Relishing the myriad of sensations, it was not until they were passing Rhodes House that she was ready to return to their conversation, when Giles stopped in his tracks.

"What's the matter?" she asked, thinking he must have left his credit card or gloves in the restaurant.

"I've just had a thought. It's about your latest theory, Fiona. There's no way Steve or anyone else could have known that Ahmad couldn't swim *before* the symposium. But Steve did find out *during* it! That's a fact. Why didn't it occur to me sooner?"

"What do mean? How…?"

"Listen. As the chairperson in Sorrento, Steve had been entitled to have the Presidential Suite, but he'd offered it to Ahmad when he invited him to give the Peyton Rous Lecture. Steve was advertising this all and sundry during the symposium, saying he'd taken a standard room like the rest of us instead. He even went as far as suggesting we remembered his great sacrifice when casting our votes for the Society's next President.

"Well, when I returned to Sorrento, Luigi, the young waiter in the bar, brought my breakfast to the suite. While we were chatting, I learnt that Steve had not been in a standard room at all. He'd been in the hotel's only other suite, the Capo di Monte. It's also very nice, Luigi said, but it doesn't have a pool, a terrace, or any of the other special features, like an office, and so on."

"Hold on, Giles. How come you didn't already know Steve was in the other suite. Wasn't it in the hotel's printout you brought back as the Society's next Secretary?"

"No, it wasn't. As the record was only for the sponsors' benefit, and the hotel charges the same rate for each room during symposia, all it gives for each guest are the dates of arrival and departure, no room numbers."

"I see. Okay, go on."

"Now, the Italian newspaper article that reported Ahmad's death said that when he'd learnt from the receptionist on checking in that the Presidential Suite has its own pool, he asked if he could change to a suite without one, explaining that he couldn't swim and was averse to the smell of chlorine. However, when she called the Capo di Monte to do a swap, the occupant refused to do so, saying it wasn't convenient. Of course, she didn't tell Ahmad who this unhelpful person was."

"How did the newspaper know all this?"

"They'd interviewed Ahmad's wife in Lugano by telephone. Now, when Luigi told me that the occupant of the Capo di Monte had been none other than Steve, I was pretty furious he'd been pulling the wool over our eyes to get votes. And that still seems the most likely explanation. But perhaps it occurred to him later…"

"That keeping Ahmad where there was a nice deep pool, out of sight and out of earshot, might be very useful for another reason?"

"Quite! Perhaps the temptation was too great; he coerced the girls; and the rest is history."

"So when poor Ahmad asked if he could change suites, he might have been putting a noose around his neck? Of course, this assumes the girls would have had the strength to push him in. Is that likely?"

"They looked pretty fit to me. If they'd caught him by surprise, I don't think they'd have had any difficulty at all. And don't forget there was some alcohol in his blood—not much, but enough to work in their favour. On which subject, by the way, have you noticed there's been a beer bottle on my mantelpiece since I got back from Sweden?"

"Yes, I have. Definitely not your taste in booze or vases, I thought. I've been meaning to ask you about it."

"I brought it with me from the Stockholm flight."

"Why?"

"According to the newspaper, an empty bottle of that stuff was sitting on the suite's dining table when the maid found Ahmad in the pool. There was no sign of a glass anywhere, apparently, just the bottle. I was amazed because, as you probably know, Muslims aren't permitted to drink alcohol. And there was no doubt about Ahmad's adherence to the rules. When he'd been in the bar with the rest of us, he'd refused a glass of wine for that very reason. He also abstained from eating some olives because it was Ramadan. And he'd been a little late for his lecture because he'd been praying. Muslims have a strict timetable for their prayers, you see, the precise time of day being determined by the date and where they happen to be in the world. For these reasons, I've always found it difficult to believe he'd been drinking beer. But as the Carabinieri had found alcohol in his blood, there seemed to be no doubt about it. I didn't think much about it again, until I was flying home, when the stewardess offered me a bottle of beer from her trolley.

When I saw the label, I realised it was the same brand as the one mentioned in the newspaper. Never having come across it before, I gave it a try. As I did so, I tried to picture Ahmad in his last moments drinking from such a bottle. But for the life of me I couldn't. It just wasn't him. The picture wouldn't come together in my mind. It was as if I were an artist, and every time I put some paint on the canvas, paint of a different colour somewhere else disappeared. Ahmad seemed too polished, to cultured, to drink from a bottle. It seemed utterly impossible."

Giles raised his collar as he turned his back to the wind and sat down on the low wall that borders the museum's lawn, beckoning Fiona to join him.

"So…what's the answer?" she asked, tightening her belt and cuddling up.

"I don't know. But I have a feeling that that bottle holds the key to something very important. It's as if it's a beacon, alerting us to the fact that the story isn't finished."

"No messages from the moon this time, Giles," Fiona smiled knowingly, having spotted him scan the sky, "only clouds. Do you know if the Carabinieri had the bottle tested for fingerprints…of either type?"

Giles shook his head.

"I imagine they didn't, given they were so convinced it was an accident. I certainly haven't seen anything in the press."

"Nevertheless, why don't we do a Google search to see if there's anything out there. We've both been so busy, we could have missed it. Of course, a murderer would have to be pretty stupid to drink out of a bottle, then leave it at the scene of the crime."

"You might think so, but it's not impossible. Years ago, I did a course in forensic pathology. You'd be surprised at what criminals can do in the heat of the moment. They can get confused, panic, rush from the scene. And things like intelligence and education don't come into it. Don't forget most murderers are novices, first-timers doing a one-off. That's where the police have an advantage."

"Okay, so why don't we check it out?"
"Your place or mine?"
"Mine. I forgot to turn the heating down."

Chapter Sixteen

"Wow! More than nine million hits in 0.12 seconds. Do you think Google makes up these numbers, Giles? I mean, how is it possible for anything to work that fast? I feel so ignorant."

After arriving in her flat, Fiona had wasted no time in the hope of learning more about the Carabinieri's investigations into Ahmad Sharif's death, if indeed there had been any.

"I've absolutely no idea how a search engine works, do you?"

"No. Or a steam engine, or an internal combustion engine, for that matter," Giles answered from the fireside, where he was about to start a crossword puzzle. "Or even a sewing machine. And when it comes to anything electronic, I don't know where to start. I mean, how does software enable us to use the same computer in hundreds of different ways? What *is* software? All I know is it's something to do with electrons. And yet in a few years, just about everything we humans do will be under their control—the entire world controlled by invisible particles zooming around invisible circuits. It's scary."

Fiona kept her eyes on the screen.

"I've now added 'Sorrento,' 'beer,' and finally 'fingerprint' to what was already there. And the number of hits came down to a measly 226. I'm now clicking on a link to a page of the newspaper you read in Sorrento, www.ilmattino.it, which I thought might be a good bet. Ah, yes! Brilliant! It's taken me to an article about Ahmad. Let me see how good my fledgling Italian is."

Giles continued with his crossword puzzle, while Fiona worked on her translation at the dining table. Once she had finished, she quietly moved to his side.

"Cosmonaut!" she bellowed.

"Jesus! You gave me a fright. What are you talking about?"

"Six across, nine letters: The clue is 'He zeros in from outer space.' Get it? *Cosmos* plus *nought*."

"How is anyone expected to figure that one out?"

"I did. Now, if you don't mind switching to this, I think you'll be very interested. It's an article that appeared six weeks after the symposium. Where were you then? Can you remember?"

"Let me think…on holiday, motoring through the French countryside."

"Ah yes! Which is presumably why you missed it. It's mostly to do with Mrs Sharif's case against the hotel. But it also gives an update on the forensic stuff. It turns out the Carabinieri did get around to checking that bottle. And, believe it or not, they found absolutely nothing: neither ordinary prints, nor DNA."

"No DNA *anywhere*, not even at the top?"

"No. As the only glasses in the suite were unused ones in a drawer below the frigobar, they said he must have held it in a handkerchief or something with it having come straight from the fridge. But it couldn't have been that cold, surely? And even if *his* prints weren't on it, there should have been somebody else's. It didn't get there on a magic carpet, did it?"

"And how do they explain the absence of DNA where his mouth would have been?"

"They think he must have just opened his mouth and poured it down. Some people do, you know."

"Yes, so I've noticed. But I can't imagine Ahmad doing that. Not for a second. What else does it say?"

"Only that Mrs Sharif's case against the hotel rests on the fact that the bulb of one of the lamps over the terrace was missing."

"How much was she suing them for?"

"A hundred million dollars."

"Now I know what Rashid Yamani meant when he said she's a gold-digger."

"I wish we could find some gold when we dig. The more we dig, all we seem to get are more questions. In spite of my new approach to life, Giles, I still feel the need for something to calm me down. If you've no objection, I think I'll go to the GP in the morning for some tablets."

"If you really feel the need. But I've got another idea. Tomorrow's Wednesday. As I've got nothing on between now and the weekend, why don't we down tools and go to the cottage for a few days? It'll do us a power of good."

"Yes, please!"

"First thing in the morning then, I'll go through Sir Q's spreadsheets. It shouldn't take me more than an hour. Then, I'll nip to the Lodgings to show him what I've done. Should be finished by eleven, I imagine. And then we can be off."

"Wonderful! And while you're doing that, I'll go to the Beaumont Street Clinic. Where's your car at the moment?"

"Fellow's Car Park…as usual."

"Could you unlock it, so if I'm back before you, I can wait inside?"

"Of course."

Chapter Seventeen

"'No ifs and butts,' he said. 'What's the bottom line?' Then it was 'Don't get your knickers in a twist.' Every blasted minute, one snide remark after another," Giles chuntered as he slammed the door of the Austin Healey. "What a squirt that man is, Fiona. He took every opportunity to get in a dig, imagining he'd caught us in flagrante delicto. When I pointed out the many errors in his spreadsheets, his only response was 'Sorry about all those cock-ups, Giles. Or is it cocks-up? I'm never quite sure. You should know, don't you?' Then, before I left, he gave me a glass of that ghastly cheap sherry he always dishes out. 'Bottoms up!' he squeaked with a wink. "Can you believe it? We're talking about the President of Magdalen College for God's sake. And all the time with a silly little grin on that rodentine face of his. I could have rung his scrawny little neck."

"Calm down, Giles. That's what Dr Turnbull's just told me to do. 'Be more philosophical about life,' he said. At moments like this, you should do the same. Look at yourself in the mirror. Your face is red. You're sweating. Your blood pressure must be going through the roof. You can't even fasten your seat belt your hands are trembling so much. Here, let me do it."

Fiona leant across to buckle him up.

"You should be pleased he's pulling your leg. You're always complaining he has no sense of humour. Now you know you were wrong. And it could be much worse. Many in his shoes would be disciplining you by now for gross sexual misconduct on College premises."

"Disciplining *me*? What, for being the victim? Don't forget you were on top, not the other way around. And anyway, the little shrimp's not pulling my leg. He's twisting it as hard as his skinny little rodentine arms can manage. The runt's enjoying every second of it. It's sadism."

"Well, let him. It doesn't do us any harm, does it? Dr Turnbull also told me to try to see the funny side of situations. So, picture the feast that met his eyes, as he entered the room. You've often bemoaned the fact that the two of you don't have anything in common. Well, now you do."

"In common with *him*? Me and that little runt? In what way?"

"You're the only two Oxford dons who've ever seen my bum…this month…in Jane's office. It'll give you something to talk about the next time he forgets his spreadsheets for one of your meetings."

"Over his rump steak, I suppose. And by the way, you're beginning to sound like Jane. It's *my reading room*, remember, not *Jane's office*. She just borrows it. The Marchese didn't give the College more than a million euros so an old maid could have an office to herself."

"All right then, you're the only two who've seen my bum in your reading…"

"Okay, okay! Which reminds me by the way, what on earth were you doing in briefs like that in January? It wouldn't have been so bad, if you hadn't looked like a porno star."

"They're the latest bikini style from Victoria's Secret, if you really want to know—a limited edition, available only on mail order."

"Was that mail order, or *male* order?"

"If you'd rather I'd been in granny-style drawers, I'll remember next time you're up for a nice cup of cocoa. Which would you prefer—tartan plaid or Harris Tweed?"

"I think we'd better change the subject. Did your GP give you anything?"

"He thought I should try to live without 'chemical crutches,' as he put it. 'Try calming herbal teas first,' he said, 'like chamomile, valerian, and kava,' the last of which I'd never heard of. So on the way here, I popped into the Covered Market, and bought all three. That's all I'm going to drink while we're away—two mugs of each every day."

"Sounds like an exciting short break in store for me. When you're not floating around like a zombie, you'll be on the loo peeing. And anyhow, why are those teas any different from pills? They're just as much 'chemical crutches,' aren't they?"

"They're natural."

"What difference does that make? So are botulinum toxin and Amanita toadstools. He didn't give you a proper sedative?"

"He said he didn't want to, but I squeezed a prescription out of him by promising I'd use it only as a last resort. Here it is."

She zipped open her handbag to hand Giles a carefully folded piece of paper.

"Mogadon, ten milligrams at night," he read. "That's a sleeping tablet."

"That's right. So it would be early to bed for me, but not early to rise for you. Sorry about that! Let's hope the teas work. Shall we go? I've been shivering in this old banger for long enough. I'm so looking forward to a few days in that cosy little cottage. Hopefully, by the time we're back, the tittle-tattle emanating from the Lodgings will have settled down."

"Some hope!"

"And before we set off, Giles, there's no such word as rodentine, by the way. It's another one of your specials that I looked up once. His face is *rodent-like*."

"Pah! If there are equine, canine, and feline ones, why not rodentine?"

"There just aren't. That's all. Sorry! Let's go."

Once they were on their way, Fiona was itching to get on with some stocktaking. Whether professionally or in her private life, she had always found it essential to have a clear picture in her mind of where she was up to in any project, and of the route that lay ahead—or at least the first few steps and the alternatives that lay beyond. After making some notes following Giles's departure the previous evening, she had taken them to the GP to read in the waiting room, and was now eager to get started.

"Giles," she ventured, while he was negotiating a roundabout outside Woodstock, a few miles north of Oxford, "is now a good time to do what we said, or is it a bit tricky in this traffic?"

"No problem. I can cope. Fire away."

Fiona made herself as comfortable as she could manage in the patched-up 1960s leather seat.

"By the way, my eyes will be closed while I'm doing this, so I can concentrate. Don't forget to look out for speed cameras. Remember, Woodstock's a notorious hot spot."

"You can rest. I've done this journey so many times I don't have to tell my foot when to slacken off anymore. It just happens."

"Good. Okay, now before you left last night, we agreed that the first thing I'd do would be to summarise where we're up to. Then it'll be your turn to fill in anything I've missed, yes?"

"Yes."

"After that, if there's any time left, we'll discuss the next move. If not, we'll do it this evening?"

"Yes. Always assuming you're not grogged out on herbal teas by then."

"Yipes! Did you see that woman? Or was it just good luck you missed her by an inch?"

"Of course, I saw her!"

"What colour was her coat?"

"Blue."

"Light blue or dark?"

"Fiona! I was driving a car before you'd sat on a tricycle, and I've never killed anyone yet…apart from a few backseat drivers, that is. I brushed that fool of a woman deliberately— high-precision steering to give her an experience to remember. I've probably added years to her life."

"Ha! You expect me to believe that?"

"Of course."

After polishing the windscreen with her handkerchief, Fiona settled into her seat again.

"I'll be talking in sort of third person. Is that okay? That's how I've been rehearsing it."

"Fair enough."

"And you won't mind if I also throw in a theatrical flavour, I hope? It helps me to cope, if I think of it all as fantasy. Okay?"

"Whatever."

"Right then, here goes. Daa-da-da-daaa, 'The Butterfield-Cameron...' Hold on, you've spotted those traffic lights, have you?"

Giles turned his head left and right.

"Which traffic lights?"

"What! Those straight ahead on the brow of..."

"Only joking. I thought you were going to have your eyes closed."

"I've chickened out. I'll start with one closed, and see how it goes."

"Ha! Well, let me warn you, Dr Cameron. If you make one more comment about my driving, I'm going to do a U-turn and go straight back. Right?"

"Yes. Okay, I'll start again. Daa-da-da-daaa, 'The Butterfield-Cameron Adventures, Act I, Part 1, *Achilles* gets his mate.' After being plucked from under the King of Sweden's nose by the police, Dr Stephen Salomon admitted that the brilliant work of his onetime friend, Detective Inspector Giles Butterfield of Oxford Yard, had been right on target. His famous paper in Science had indeed been fraudulent. However, his motive had been only altruistic. When he saw during his journey home from Italy what Dr Ahmad Sharif had written on the back of the copy of the *Achilles* report that he'd given to him, he took it to be the details of the Bedouin tribe's secret DNA switch for the gene. Being a really nice guy, he felt he had a duty to share it with the world. But he couldn't tell the truth about how he came by it, because when the news eventually reached the Bedouins by camel-mail, they would assume that MECCAR's

Director, the urbane and suave Dr Rashid Yamani, had broken his pledge never to go public with anything unique about their genes. And that would have been a PR disaster, destroying any possibility of future cooperation from the tribe...or for that matter from any other group of superstitious people who have sex with their cousins in the proximity of a leaking nuclear reactor...in a desert...with goats watching. *Hold it!*"

As Giles slammed on the brakes, the car swerved and screeched to a halt.

"Jesus, Fiona! What was that for?"

He turned in his seat to see what he'd missed, but there was nothing but an empty road.

"What the hell was that about?"

Fiona hid her face in her hands.

"Oops, sorry! I'd just had a thought, that's all."

"Which was?"

"If all that radioactivity created mutations in tribes of incestuous Bedouins, as claimed by MECCAR, why hasn't it done the same to their herds of incestuous goats? Those billies must be at it all the time— cousins, aunts, sisters, nieces. Someone should study those animals' genes. We might learn something. Perhaps their DNA is protected in some way, or has a better repair mechanism than ours. What do you think?"

Giles was now leaning on the steering wheel, his eyes fixed on the car's bonnet.

"I'm thinking about that U-turn I threatened to make."

"Sorry again. It was stupid of me, I agree. And the goats?"

"It's an interesting thought. We should talk about it sometime. But for now, carry on."

"Where was I? Ah, yes, so to get himself out of this pickle, Dr Salomon fabricated a story about how in a flash of pure Newtonian genius...and with a little help from a computer programme he'd already written, but told nobody about... he'd conceived the beautiful *Deidamia*, potential saviour of mankind, thanks to her unique talent of being able to tickle *Achilles* in places other bits of DNA cannot reach.

"Now it's quite possible that Dr Salomon's story was true. Perhaps he really is the world's first angel-scientist of 'Geek' mythology. On the other hand, he might also be an evil lying bastard, whose only motive was to dig his reputation out of the depths of the shit-bog into which it had sunk…and pocket a million dollars in Swedish crowns in the process. No doubt an army of hard-working Manhattan attorneys is mulling over the issue this very minute."

"Unlikely."

"Why?"

"It's about six in the morning there."

"So? I said they were hard working. Don't interrupt. Remember, you're supposed to be driving—or at least something approaching it.

"Now, as Director of the National Institutes of Health, of which Dr Salomon's National Cancer Institute is but one teeny-weeny bit, it was inevitable that Dr Henry Weinberg, better known among the NIH mafia as 'Hank the Wank,' also walked the plank into the abyss of scientific oblivion. As he sank into the depths, he denied knowing anything about Dr Salomon's naughtiness. But he would, wouldn't he? Detective Inspector Butterfield certainly has his doubts about both Hank and his moll. Their strange antics over chopsticks and Chinese muffins at their home in Chevy Chase were highly suspicious. But again, those Manhattan attorneys will decide…assuming, of course, that everything is paid for well in advance. End of Act I, Part 1.

"OK so far?"

Giles nodded.

"It'll do. How about an intermission? We'll be in Chipping Norton soon."

"Good idea. You can choose the pub, Giles. It'll be on me—my punishment for giving you such a fright before. Three mince pies and a large glass of mulled red wine will do me nicely. And for you a glass of fizzy mineral water…yes…driver?"

Once they were settled into a cosy corner of the Crown and Cushion in the centre of the town, Fiona wasted no time returning to her theatre, while Giles did his best to enjoy his San Pellegrino and two slices of lemon.

"Mmm, this wine's just perfect," she swooned, holding it under his nose. "Just sniff that spicy aroma. But sorry, that's all you get, I'm afraid, driver—just a sniff. I'll make some for you tonight by the fire, I promise."

After two mouthfuls, she resumed where she had left off.

"So here we ago with Act I, Part 2: 'De code deciphered.' Thanks to the cracking code-cracking skills of the ravishing Detective Constable Fiona Cameron, we now know that the letters and numbers that Dr Sharif scribbled on the *Achilles* gene report were *not* the secret details of the Bedouins' DNA switch at all. No, they were merely a shorthand memo about a meeting he was to have with two girls and a German in Sorrento, which Dr Salomon had personally arranged. Like a few other giant strides in medicine, the fact that *Deidamia* worked as an artificial stand-in for the Bedouins' natural switch was entirely serendipot...serendit..."

"Serendipitous."

"Thanks. This wine must be strong. Thus, whether Dr Salomon was guilty of genuine intellectual property theft, or merely guilty of thinking that that's what he was doing, is a moot point. Another one for those overworked and underpaid attorneys to sort out."

She opened her eyes to see that Giles's cheeks were bulging, and two mince pies were missing from the wicker basket.

"Good heavens! Have you got through two already?"

"They're very small," he sputtered. "Each one is less than a mouthful."

"I thought you said last night you were on a diet."

"As I said, they're very small."

"Only by your standards. It's a good job the barman brought several more than he charged us for. Good old Ros!"

"What's it got to with Ros?"

"She taught me her behaviour code in pubs—first the leg show, then the wink. Never wear jeans. And always give the impression you live locally. Of course, she has the advantage of better pegs than mine...doesn't she?"

"Does she?"

"You're pretending you haven't noticed?"

"Well, I've noticed they're okay, but nothing..."

"What! You were positively drooling when you were waiting for us in Scissors the other day. You couldn't take your eyes off them. I was watching you."

"Ah well, there you are, you see. That's what happens when you jump to conclusions, something a scientist should never do. It was what she was *wearing* that interested me. I was thinking of buying you a pair as a surprise gift."

"Were you? Sorry! Now you've made me feel really guilty."

"So you should."

She leant across to kiss him lightly on the cheek.

"I agree," she whispered. "Those fishnet tights she bought in Florence are beautiful. All those fancy patterns."

"They were stockings actually. But if you..."

"Gotcha! So you noticed they were *stockings*? I wonder how you managed that. It wasn't when you dropped your hat on the floor, I don't suppose?"

"Don't be ridiculous! That was..."

"Don't bother," Fiona scoffed, "it's too painful to watch you wriggling like a worm on a hook. Instead, I'm going to keep you to your word. Monday lunch, we'll be off to the Clarendon Centre, where you can help me choose a few pairs, and perhaps a pair of shoes to go with them. I'll make you pay dearly for those roving eyes, Detective Butterfield!

"Okay, let's move on to Act II, Part 1: 'All is revealed.' Thanks to DC Cameron's amazing DNA fingerprints, we've learnt that the two girls in Sorrento were in fact not Dr Salomon's research fellows, as he'd claimed. Nor were they high-class ladies of the night hired for Dr Sharif's pleasure in part payment for the Bedouins' secret, as DC Cameron had postulated. No, lo and behold, they were none other than Dr Salomon's very own daughters, pretending to be cancer researchers. Being marine biologists in sunny San Diego, they were just about able to pull it off. And that, Detectives Cameron and Butterfield suspect, may not have been the only thing they pulled off in Dr Sharif's company. Why? Because, thanks to DC Cameron's DNA fingerprints, we know that at least one of them was almost certainly in his suite. What could they have been there for but to spy on behalf of daddy for MECCAR's secrets? There are two ways in which they could have stolen such information: from Dr Sharif's lips or, much more likely, by searching the suite while his lips were busy in other ways.

"But what about Dr Sharif's death? Could the dastardly duo also have been behind that? Had the Carabinieri got it wrong, when they concluded it was an accident? Might he have been murdered by the sisters Salomon to prevent MECCAR from getting a Nobel Prize and eliminate daddy's biggest competitor all in one go? For the next episode, folks, hang around for Act II, Part 2.

"I guess that'll do for now. Did I leave anything out?"

"Not that I noticed," Giles smirked, "apart from good English."

Fiona gave him a dig in the ribs with her elbow.

"Which we don't talk about anymore, *do we?*"

"No, we don't. Sorry, I was only joking. Let's carry on after we've done some shopping. There's a Sainsbury's supermarket down the road. Finish your wine. I've left you a mince pie."

***

They were well on their way down the A44 towards Moreton-in-Marsh, the car boot packed with groceries, when Fiona was ready to complete her account.

"How long before we get there?" she asked, looking at her watch.

"About ten minutes."

"Good! My bum's getting sore in this seat. People must have had different shapes in those days. Right, okay, Act II, Part 2: 'All adrift in the Sea of Lies.' Thanks to his razor-sharp intellect, Butterfield has discovered that Salomon told other fibs in Sorrento. In fact, one begins to wonder if anything he said was not a porky. Not only was his bit about the girls being his latest research fellows untrue, so also was the claim that he'd checked into an ordinary standard room during the Sorrento symposium so that Ahmad Sharif could have the Presidential Suite. The scoundrel was actually in the hotel's only other suite, the very plush Capo di Monte, and was hiding the fact as a ploy to get votes during the Society's next presidential election. Furthermore, when Dr Sharif asked the receptionist if he could swap suites, owing to the fact he could not swim and disliked the smell of chlorine, Salomon refused to do so, presumably because he didn't want to risk losing those votes. But did he then decide to take advantage of the fact that his Public Enemy Number One could be eliminated by the mere wave of a maiden's hand?"

Fiona rubbed her eyes, as she sat up to look around.

"Phew! That's as much as I can manage for now. Over to you. What's that village over there?"

"Salford. That wasn't a bad summary, Fiona. Not delivered precisely in the manner I'd expected, but none the worse for that. It's an odd situation, isn't it? On the one hand, we might be on the verge of one of the biggest stories in the history of medicine, bigger even than Steve's arrest in Stockholm. An 'all-American' family conspires to steal information from the richest research centre in the world, Islam's jewel of medical scholarship, and while they're at it also to murder the first Muslim Nobel Prize winner-to-be in medicine. And yet on the other hand, we might get no further, the whole thing fizzling out as if it had never happened.

"One point you didn't stress, which surprised me as you've done so before, is that while it seems very likely the girls were on a spying mission, we don't have *proof* of that, do we? Not only do we not have a shred of evidence that they actually stole any information, we also don't have any that they *tried*. Even if they were there with that intention, they might have failed or chickened out at the last minute. Nothing we've got would actually stand up in a court of law."

"That's true. And we don't even have *proof* they were in the suite. All we know is a cigarette butt smoked by one of them was on the terrace. It's not impossible Steve visited Ahmad for a chat, found it inside his own briefcase, and tossed it across the terrace."

"And on top of that there's the beer bottle, isn't there? It occurred to me last night, Fiona, the big question there is not 'Why was none of Ahmad's DNA on the rim?', but 'Why was there *no DNA on it at all*?' Beer must contain millions of DNA fragments of its own, left behind from the yeast cells used to brew it, not to mention contaminating bacteria, like lactobacilli. If I remember correctly, every yeast cell has four sets of sixteen chromosomes. Huge numbers must die during the fermentation process. That's the real issue here—the complete absence of *any* DNA. How can a beer bottle that's been used not have even a trace of its own DNA on its rim? There can be only one answer to that. Somebody must have given it a *really* good clean before leaving the suite. That's why there were no ordinary fingerprints on it too. The Carabinieri got it wrong, Fiona. Their presumption that Ahmad poured it down his gullet is utter piffle. Somebody did a very thorough clean-up job. And to do that, there must have been a very good reason.

"Ahmad Sharif *was* murdered. There can be no other explanation. We don't know how or by whom. And we don't know why. But murdered he was."

Fiona threw back her head and wound down her window to inhale the damp heavy air from a passing farm field.

"Smell those cows, Giles. Listen to those crows. Feel the cool air on your face. I have a feeling we're going to remember this moment for a long, long time."

After they'd turned into the lane off the A44 that leads to the village of Little Compton, Giles stopped the car at the top of the drive that his cottage shared with two others.

"Before we get out, Giles," Fiona urged, "let's see if you're right about beer being loaded with DNA. Can I borrow your phone? Mine's at the bottom of my bag."

A minute later, she was patting Giles on the back.

"Well done, Einstein! You're spot on. There's even a bunch of people who are preparing DNA libraries on hundreds of different types of beer. Okay, so is there anything else to talk about?"

"Yes, there is actually—something that occurred to me last night. It's to do with your DNA fingerprints."

"What was wrong with them?"

"Nothing. It's to do with our interpretation. When you think about it, we don't have proof that it was Steve and his wife who licked those stamps, do we? We're assuming they did, because they'd signed the card. In most people's book that would be enough. But as I've said before, lawyers love to pick holes in DNA evidence, and they can do it very effectively."

Fiona groaned as she slumped back into her seat.

"Ugh! You're right, of course. But those signatures do make it 99 per cent certain, don't they?"

"Yes, but defence lawyers don't use the approach we do as scientists. They don't think like Descartes. In a courtroom, it's not a question of accepting what's most likely. It's a different emphasis. Getting something wrong in science can lead to loss of time and money, delays in progress, and so on. All of that's important. But eventually further research sorts it out, and everyone gets back on track. In a murder trial, what's most important is not to find an innocent person guilty. And defence lawyers can be very smart. Don't forget that jury members are rarely experts in law, medicine, genetics, or statistics. They're chosen at random from the community. All a lawyer has to do is to put sufficient doubt in their minds. That's not too difficult, when you're talking to a group of postmen, plumbers, waitresses, and shop assistants on molecular genetics, laboratory technology, and the finer points of criminal law in a posh accent with a silly wig on your head."

Fiona smiled.

"But in the USA they don't have posh accents or wigs, do they? So hopefully we'll be okay. Sorry! I can see your point, Giles. And it's a good one."

As Giles moved to open the car door, Fiona grabbed his arm.

"Wait! There's something else, Giles. Why should someone who had drunk out of that bottle and then murdered Ahmad have gone to the trouble of cleaning it before leaving it behind, when they could simply have taken it with them? It doesn't make sense."

Giles stared at the grey sky through the grimy windscreen as a few spots of rain began to fall.

"You're right, of course, Fiona. It doesn't make sense. How do we get around that one?"

Fiona propped her head against her window.

"Oh, Giles! I wish the way ahead was as straightforward as negotiating those potholes in your drive. I can't see how we can take it any further on our own. I'm sure you're as reluctant as I am to bring anyone else into it. It would feel like giving our baby away. But I don't see any alternative. That's the harsh truth, isn't it?"

"Perhaps. But who do you think we should talk to?"

"Difficult. I don't think Rashid Yamani would be interested. Why should he care if the Carabinieri got it wrong? There's nothing in it for him. On the contrary, a murder investigation wouldn't be good for MECCAR's image. So far, Ahmad's death has brought them only sympathy. Why rock the boat? Once the possibility of a murder leaked out, people would begin to wonder what sort of place it is. Its many enemies would take advantage. Rumours would abound. 'The place is so secretive,' they'd say, 'what could be going on there? Are they into crime? Are jealousies, power politics, rivalries, or racial differences causing internal warfare?' Rashid's bound to think about such things. No, he's definitely a non-starter."

"So, who are we left with?"

"As far as I can see, Giles, there's only the Carabinieri. We have no choice but to go to Sorrento, and give them the low-down."

Giles shook his head.

"I think it's too soon for that. All we'd get is a polite smile, a weak handshake, and the door. Even if deep down they took our suspicions seriously, they'd use the chinks in the evidence as an excuse to bury it. Better that than the possibility of the world learning they'd overlooked something crucial that was later spotted by a couple of amateurs. The Carabinieri are extremely proud of their reputation and history. Have you ever seen them strutting around the Galleria in Milan, like peacocks with their bums on their heads?"

"So, what do we do?"

Heavy rain was now drumming on the roof and a strong wind buffeting the car. Fiona wound up her window and gestured to Giles to do the same. She looked at him anxiously. It was as if the weather was sending a message that difficult times lay ahead.

"There *is* one thing we could do, Fiona."

"What's that?"

"We could check that the DNA on one of those stamps really was Steve's. That would sort that one out. During my sabbatical there, he was in the habit of keeping samples of his own blood and DNA in the freezer to use as controls in his experiments. We could go to Washington and ask the new NIH Director for permission to spend a few days in Steve's lab while you prepare a DNA fingerprint from one of them. If it confirms that the DNA on one of the stamps was Steve's, that would change things. Then we *could* go to the Carabinieri."

"Good idea. But it would be extremely risky. If there *was* a conspiracy involving Steve and the White House, revealing our new evidence to Hank Weinberg's replacement could be disastrous. Don't forget the Director of the NIH is not selected by academics in the way professors are in universities. It's a presidential nomination. Ted Crabb chose him personally.

We could be walking into a lions' den. Who is the new Director anyway?"

"He's a haematologist. He was chosen because he got a reputation for weeding out and punishing research misconduct in Yale. Someone like that might relish the opportunity to show the world that the NIH has turned a new leaf."

"That's one possibility, sure. But another is he could go straight to Ted Crabb, and warn him we're on his trail."

"But you're forgetting. Fiona, that one of the Director's jobs is to protect the NIH from political interference. So if he did that…"

"Oh, come on, Giles! That's a joke, isn't it? The fact that the President chooses the person whose job it is to protect his institute from politicians has to be one of the biggest conflicts of interest in the universe. It stands to reason we can't trust him. We might even put ourselves in personal danger. 'Welcome to my parlour', said the spider to the fly."

"But if anything happened to both of us, it would look pretty suspicious, wouldn't it? And don't forget, we don't have an ounce of evidence for a conspiracy. It's pure conjecture."

"I still don't think it's a risk worth taking. The consequences could be serious. I think we should go straight to Sorrento, and have done with."

Giles started the engine again and took the car to cottage garden.

"Okay, let's agree to disagree for now. There's no great hurry. We've got a few days of peace and quiet in this nice little village to chew it over. I'm sure by the time we're motoring home on Sunday, we'll have come up with something. We always do.

"And by the way, I gave Conrad another call last night. I asked him about that network of computers and websites on the scrap of paper Jim Watkins picked up from the pub floor. He said he knew nothing about it. It was a total mystery."

"Did that surprise him?"

"Yes. After all, as you know, MECCAR gave his company the job of setting up their entire IT system."

"Okay, you take the brolly, Giles, and let's run for it."

Chapter Eighteen

By the time they were on their way back to Oxford, Fiona was thinking it might have been better to stay in the College after all, and just ignore the smirks and raised eyebrows that Sir Quentin's gossip would surely have provoked. It wasn't that they'd been arguing about what to do next. The problem was more one of frustration, a bothersome disappointment that in spite of the circumstances, with time on their hands away from the pressures of work, they had still not been able to agree on the better course of action. As far as Fiona was concerned, the risks of going to Washington remained far too great, while Giles was still entrenched in the conviction it would be an error to go to Sorrento without more evidence. In spite of many hours chatting together during long walks by day, and in the cottage and local pubs of an evening, their opinions on the matter had not budged.

"Why don't we stop somewhere for lunch?" Fiona suggested, as they passed through Over Kiddington. "I'm hungry and I also need warming up. The heater's not working too well, is it?"

"No, it isn't, sorry. I think there must be a leak somewhere. The Duke of Marlborough's coming up. We can drop in there. I've heard they do pretty good roast beef and Yorkshire pud."

"Yes, please!"

Despite the building's great appeal, once they were inside, Fiona was thinking it might not have been the best choice for the final push she'd had in mind after all. Like so many of the pubs in the area, the restaurant was packed with noisy families after a week of tiresome commuting between their country homes and London offices. But just as she was thinking of returning to the car, the sight of an empty table in front of a blazing log fire was irresistible.

After taking their seats, she offered Giles the bread basket before hastily returning to the inevitable topic, whispering out of fear the intrusion of her voice might upset the delicate balance to her left, where a young couple were evidently in the middle of a domestic crisis. The pallor of the husband's drawn face contrasting with the high colour of her cheeks, they had reached the point of not communicating, staring at their half-empty dishes as if waiting for something to move.

"So, as I said when we set off, Giles," Fiona opened, "I'm afraid my opinion hasn't changed. I still think it would be too risky. We didn't learn anything encouraging about the new Director from the Internet yesterday, did we? As far as I could see, his academic achievements are not brilliant, and his involvement in university politics from such an early age definitely puts me off. I'm always suspicious of young politically active academics. There has to be a reason why an intelligent person with an enquiring mind, keen to push forward human knowledge, drops out to become buried in letters, reports, committees, working parties, councils, and all the rest. I think it's because they've realised they're not good enough at the real job. They've found they cannot compete. They've run out of ideas, or haven't got the staying power to keep going. So they see committees and politics as their salvation, with the bonus of providing opportunities for feathering their nests and making friends in high places. By and large, they're mediocrities whose chief interest is to look after themselves. Therefore, he can't be trusted. Hank Weinberg was different. He *was* a good researcher. He wouldn't have given up lab work if it hadn't been for those allergies to chemicals he developed."

Fiona broke off as the waitress arrived with a bottle of red wine.

"Even if our conspiracy theory is pie in the sky, Giles, I'm sure the new guy isn't going to risk upsetting Ted Crabb, which is what a criminal investigation into Steve and his daughters would do. We should go straight to Sorrento, and forget about Washington. And the sooner the better, because this business is getting me down. So far, I've managed to keep those sleeping pills the GP gave me in their bottle. But honestly, I don't think I'll be able to for very much longer."

Playing footsy under the table, she pursed her lips and gave Giles a wink.

"You don't want me to be on sleeping tablets every night, do you, with all the inevitable inconveniences?"

"Ha! Sorry, dear, that one won't work, I'm afraid. Blackmail never did with me. One of the things we haven't touched on is that apart from your tutor from Pozzuoli you don't know southern Italians very well. They're a very proud lot, on top of which so are the Carabinieri. Add to that combination the Latin temperament, and you've got a very tricky, highly combustible mix. They would be more than reluctant to take us seriously, or at least to admit to it. If we're on the right track, they would find it hugely embarrassing. They would either fly into a rage, accusing us of saying they were incompetent, or look for every excuse to rubbish us. I know I've said it a thousand times, but we can't set foot in Sorrento without at the very least solid evidence that Steve licked one of those stamps."

Giles paused as the young woman at the next table tossed her napkin onto the floor and threw the contents of her glass into her companion's face, before marching off in the direction of the cloakroom. Giles's eyes followed her sympathetically.

"I can imagine what that's all about. He's in a boring office all day. She's at home. A secretary flutters her eyelids. And we all know what happens next.

"Okay, back to where we were. I'm sure you're exaggerating the dangers of going to the NIH. As you saw, only last week the new Director gave a lecture in Dubai on 'Honesty and integrity in medical science.' Last month in Toronto it was 'Ethics and morality in clinical research', or something like that. What an opportunity we'd give him to show he means what he says! He could end up as the chairman of an international commission on research ethics, or a special advisor to UNESCO, that sort of thing.

"Hold on. Here come the prawn cocktails."

Fiona waited for the waitress to place two tall glasses and a plate of brown bread and butter on the table.

"But he might not have such grand ambitions, Giles. He's a small-town boy from Oklahoma, don't forget. If he keeps Ted Crabb happy, the sky will be the limit for him in the USA. On the other hand, if he let us into Steve's lab, Crabb could make his life very difficult."

"And if he doesn't, he would know we might go to the Washington Post or New York Times with accusations of a cover-up."

"I'm not saying he would refuse without justification, Giles. I don't think he'd be so stupid. It might be against NIH regulations, for example, to let people work in their labs without an official appointment like the one you had. Or he might claim the labs are closed while Steve's case is still in progress."

Giles smiled to himself as he shook his head in resignation.

"You know, with the best will in the world, Fiona, I don't think we're going to resolve this thorny issue by more talking. It almost ruined our weekend, and now it's threatening to ruin our lunch. I think we both need a breather. I've got a suggestion. I propose that neither of us mentions the subject for the rest of the week…not once. We can think about it as much as we want, but we can't say a single word. Then, we'll go to a pub, make our decision there and then, drink to it, and that will be that."

Fiona spat on her hand and offered it across the table.

"It's a deal."

Fiona's acceptance of Giles's proposal came more from the attraction of having a break from the dispute than anything else. As she continued with her meal, she was uncomfortably aware that similar pacts in the past had always worked to his advantage. He might not talk about the matter, but the old fox had invariably found other ways of bringing her around to his way of thinking. He was a master at it. There again, she was now more self-assured than in the early days, wasn't she? She could handle him better. So at least she would be in with a chance.

After they had finished their meal, Giles proposed that the pub where the great decision would be made should be the Three Bells on St Clements, a stone's throw from the College gates on the other side of the River Cherwell. When she expressed both surprise and displeasure at the choice, he explained.

"As it happens, Fiona, I dislike the place too. It's the most miserable, dull, tatty, smelly pub in Oxford. What's more, the beer tastes like piss, and the barman's a scruffy long-haired git who's never learnt that to mix an authentic D 'n' S it's essential to use Gosling's Black Seal rum, not some rubbish from Guyana or Mexico; and fresh limes, not last month's lemons. That's why I normally never go there. But it's also why I'm suggesting it on this occasion. It's so bloody awful there'll be no chance of hanging around. We'll make a quick decision and then get the hell out of the place to Fisher's, for a plate of the best fried haddock and chips this side of Padstow."

Chapter Nineteen

It was two weeks later when the Delta Airlines Boeing emerged from heavy clouds on its final descent towards the capital. As agreed, Giles and Fiona had settled their difference of opinion amicably in the Three Bells over a shared bottle of Evian mineral water, and had wasted no time getting on with the next stage.

Fiona unbuckled her seat belt and raised herself to lean across Giles and admire the scene below.

"Sorry to squeeze your paunch," she teased, poking him in the stomach. "I'm hoping to get a good view of the Capitol now we're out of that ghastly turbulence."

"No chance of that, dear. Wrong flight path. You'll have to be patient, I'm afraid."

"Pity, I've always thought it such a romantic building—the graceful classical architecture, the smell of history, the drama of international affairs."

"Graceful without a doubt…historic, indisputably…drama, plenty. But romantic? I'm not so sure about that one. Debating halls awash with power and influence, corridors echoing decisions that have shaped the world, the Senate lauding its achievements around the world can all seem very romantic. But behind the scenes, nothing but greed, corruption, backstabbing, dishonesty, betrayal, and skulduggery. Power politics is a nasty business—always has been, always will be."

Seeing a stewardess approaching, Fiona quickly returned to her seat and buckled up.

"Well, as this is my first trip here, Giles, I'm going to make the most of it. By the time I leave, I want to know the place inside out. And you're going to show it to me. Where did you say we're staying?"

"The Westin."

"In the centre of the city?"

"Dead centre."

"Expensive?"

"You bet! From what I've seen on their website, we'll be living in such luxury you won't want to leave. But don't worry. A few days ago, I got an advance for my autobiography. When I got my publishers up to date after Munich, they were so enthralled I decided to play hard ball."

"What did you say?"

"I told them with all this travelling and so on, I was running out of cash from my meagre academic's salary, and I'd have to leave it unfinished unless they could give me a substantial advance without delay. And you know something? Within days, they'd transferred £10,000 into my bank account. This book's going to be a gold mine. They're even talking about a film. I'm beginning to think I owe a lot to Steve and his daughters."

"*And* to my computer work late at night…yes?"

"Absolutely!"

"*And* to my code-breaking skills?"

"Definitely."

"*And* to my DNA fingerprints?"

"And again."

"In fact, Detective Inspector Butterfield," she scoffed, "I'm beginning to wonder if *you've* done very much at all. You don't think Detective Constable Cameron could be in line for promotion, do you?"

"Now you've drawn it to my attention, I do indeed. In fact, I'll go further than that. Hold on."

Giles took his Barmah hat from the small of his back, and pulled it over her head, pushing as many locks inside it as he could manage. After removing his College tie, he passed it through his key ring and knotted it loosely around her neck, the keys dangling on her chest. Finally, he took his red and gold check scarf from his briefcase, and draped it over her shoulders.

"There you are. Now we're ready for the ceremony. Madam, are you Detective Constable Fiona Cameron?"

"I am, sir."

"Fiona Cameron PhD, geneticist of Magdalen College in the ancient city of Oxford?"

"Yes, sir."

"Friend and confidant of the noble Professor Giles Butterfield?"

"Yes, sir."

"Then, in recognition of your services to criminology, it is my great pleasure to hereby bestow upon you the title of Dame Cameron of St Swithun's. Let me be the first to congratulate you."

Giles leant forward to give her a kiss.

"Thank you, kind sir. Do I have to make a speech now?"

"That'll have to wait, I'm afraid. We're about to land."

"Coming down to earth in more ways than one!"

Once they were in the arrivals lounge, Fiona felt the need for a quick snack before setting off for the Westin.

"Would you like to share a hamburger, Giles?" she asked. "I'm famished. That flight was so bumpy, I hardly ate a scrap."

Giles grimaced.

"Thanks, but you should know me by now. I'd have to be starving."

"According to Ros, the burgers here are in a different class from the ones in Oxford."

"As far as I'm concerned, a burger is a burger, whatever its nationality. While you're doing that, I'll call the hotel from the payphone under the big poster of Manhattan over there. I want to make sure they've got a table for dinner this evening. If we don't need to look for a restaurant, we'll have more time to prepare for tomorrow."

***

The following morning, after the now familiar long night of rehearsals and mock questions, Fiona hailed a cab outside the hotel while Giles signed the breakfast bill. After a tense journey through rush hour traffic, they arrived at the imposing building with a few minutes to spare. As they approached the entrance, Giles wondered if he was being unfair to Fiona by asking her to participate in the ordeal. Perhaps he should give her the option of pulling out? It was not too late after all. He was about to raise the issue, when a brave smile and a reassuring wink gave him the answer. Giving her hand a squeeze, he ushered her through the open door.

The reception they received upon entering the lobby left them in no doubt that they had been expected. But as the uniformed concierge chatted good-naturedly while preparing the security badges and the visitors' book, Giles was unsure whether his cordiality was sincere or just a cover for something else. For despite the old man's smiles and jocularity, the atmosphere was strangely cold, made all the more so by the echoing footsteps of unsmiling staff as they crossed the white marble floor. Recalling his telephone call from the airport, Giles wondered if he might have said too much to the secretary about the purpose of their visit, and gossip had been circulating. Perhaps he should have adopted the approach he had used when he'd called Gunnar Eriksson from the Sheraton in Stockholm, and kept the chat to a minimum.

After declining the concierge's offer of a couple of chairs while he made a telephone call, they wandered uneasily around the lobby, stopping every now and then to admire the potted plants, or to feign interest in one of the many notice boards. Fiona had picked up a couple of leaflets from the desk and was pretending to read them, when a young woman in a long black dress and red blouse appeared from an elevator. After a polite but terse introduction, she asked them to follow her to the third floor.

Upon exiting the elevator, the girl led them down a long corridor, during which Giles spotted the washrooms and darted off, whispering his intentions in Fiona's ear. Reaching an anonymous door at the far end, the girl opened it unceremoniously with her foot and wished Fiona good luck. Though not sure whether she should first wait for Giles, she ventured anxiously inside to find it empty.

The room was not at all as she had expected. Surprised by its heavily worn linoleum floor covering, bare walls, and cheap aluminium garden furniture, she placed her coat and handbag on the table. A cobweb on the overhead lampshade implied months of disuse, as did the dust on several wooden chairs arranged along one wall. Apart from the single bulb over the table, the only light was from three small windows, each with a Venetian blind whose blue slats were chaotically disarranged. A plastic bucket containing a brown paper bag served as a trash can. An obsolete dot matrix printer, a stack of paper, and a used Starbuck's coffee cup lay abandoned in one corner.

As she surveyed the scene, she tried to read the mindset of their hosts. What had been the purpose of choosing such a room? She had been expecting at the very least a well-furnished office with an attentive secretary on hand. If their intention had been to give a negative message, they could not have done better. Any optimism Fiona may have had for the outcome had already been dashed. But time would tell.

She moved to one of the windows and raised its blind to get a better idea of where they were. Seeing the busy street scene below made her reflect on how dull she had been finding Oxford of late. If it were not for Giles, there would be little to keep her there. She had changed a lot over the years. Even her trips to congresses abroad, once a cause for great excitement, had become tedious—the same cities, the same faces, the same routine. Fortunately, thanks to Giles's talent for raising money, their research was as rewarding as ever. Nothing could surpass the thrill of being the first person on the face of the earth to discover something new about the natural world. It made all the privations of academic life worthwhile. Many of her student friends were now surely earning much more in industry, but at what price? To be told what research to do, when to do it, how to do it, and worst of all, when to stop doing it, instead of following your own instincts and ideas wherever they led, was too great a sacrifice as far as she was concerned. But that was work. Sooner or later it would end, wouldn't it? They needed to look after their personal lives too. And Magdalen was certainly not the best place for that.

Her daydreaming was broken by the arrival of an energetic middle-aged blonde wearing a pink cashmere suit, stiletto heels, and heavy jewellery. After introducing herself, she wiped one of the chairs with a tissue from her handbag, and sat down.

"I'm an attorney," she spouted. "I suppose you're Dr Cameron, the biologist, are you?"

"Yes, that's right. How do you do?"

"What do I do? I specialise in forensic DNA evidence. They thought I should hear what you have to say. Here's my card. The MSc was in Forensic Genetics, University of North Texas, the PhD in Criminal Justice at John Jay College, New York. We shouldn't wait for the others. I've been asked to get started, if that's okay with you? Is the Professor not coming?"

"He's in the washroom."

"I see. Well while we're waiting, I'll get myself organised."

She had just taken a yellow notepad, silver fountain pen, and reading glasses from her bag, when Giles strode through the door drying his hands on a handkerchief.

"Ugh! No soap, and nothing to wipe…"

"This is Dr Virginia Brandolin," Fiona interrupted. "She's an attorney specialising in DNA. Here's her card. The others will be here soon."

Giles glanced at the card and offered his hand.

"Giles Butterfield. Delighted to meet you."

He took one of the aluminium chairs, and went through the motions of sorting through his notes as he prepared himself mentally for the occasion. During the flight, they had agreed he should open by summarising the entire story, starting with MECCAR's announcement of the discovery of *Achilles* in

Oahu. When he had got as far as Fiona's laboratory class for the students on DNA fingerprints, she would take over to show her findings.

Throughout Giles's presentation, Virginia Brandolin scribbled furiously in her notepad, tearing off one page after another as she listened. Fiona eyed her with apprehension, as she struggled to keep up with Giles's carefully prepared account. Once he had finished, Fiona arranged the photographs of her DNA fingerprints on the table. As she did so, the girl who had escorted them from the lobby reappeared with a pot of coffee and a box of pastries. Giles took the tray from her and did the honours, while Fiona described where each of the six samples of DNA had come from.

After briefly scanning the pictures, Virginia Brandolin announced her verdict.

"Congratulations, Dr Cameron! These prints are quite excellent, and I agree with your conclusions. Whoever smoked that cigarette also sealed the envelope that was in Professor Butterfield's desk drawer, and what's more, that person was most definitely an offspring of whoever licked those stamps. Yes, it certainly looks as if the girls in Sorrento could have been Dr Salomon's daughters."

As she paused to sip her coffee, the door opened and three latecomers entered. After making their apologies, they took their places in the row of wooden chairs.

"But unfortunately, there's a problem," Virginia Brandolin resumed, ignoring the new arrivals. "As the card was signed by Dr and Mrs Salomon, you have fallen into the trap of assuming it was also they who applied the stamps. Although highly probable, this is nevertheless an *assumption*."

She dropped her pen into her handbag and removed her reading glasses.

"I'm very sorry," she sighed. "You have done very well, but not quite well enough. To take this business any further, you will need proof that the DNA on the stamps belonged to the Salomons. Now I must rush. What time is it?"

She drew up her sleeve to look at an outsized gold watch before turning to her compatriots.

"Carlo, se si chiama un taxi ora, sarò in grado di andare alla riunione. Qui puoi usare il mio telefono."

As she offered Carlo her mobile phone, Giles gestured to her to remain seated.

"Mi scusi, Dottoressa... Carlo will not be needing your telephone, as it is unlikely you will want to go to your other meeting when you've heard what else we have to say."

"You speak Italian, Professor?"

"Yes, but unfortunately not quite well enough to give this presentation in your beautiful language, I'm sorry."

"I see. And what else is it that you have to say?"

"It concerns those stamps. As you correctly said, we cannot be certain that the Salomons put them on the card without supporting evidence, and that is why we arrived here in Rome from New York, not London as you may have assumed."

"You flew here from New York?"

"That's right, from JFK to Fiumicino. You see, after Dr Cameron had made her fingerprints, we discussed our next move. She was of the opinion we should take them directly to the Carabinieri in Sorrento. I understood her sense of urgency, but believed it essential to first confirm that one of the two DNA fingerprints from the stamps matched Dr Salomon's. Fortunately, I knew from a period of study leave a few years ago that he was in the habit of using his own DNA as a control to check that his laboratory procedures were working properly, and kept samples of it in a freezer for that purpose. I thought we should go to Washington and ask the new Director of the National Institutes of Health for permission to spend a few days in Dr Salomon's laboratory, more correctly his former laboratory, so that Dr Cameron could prepare a fingerprint from one of the samples. However, she felt this would be too risky. She feared the new Director might not cooperate in order to protect the NIH from further scandal. She also suggested he might warn others about what we are up to, and that we might even be putting ourselves in danger.

"After we had reached an impasse on the matter during a few days in my cottage, we decided to let it rest for a week. Then we would meet in a pub to make our decision. And that's what we did. As it happens, our decision was to go to Washington, and I'm pleased to say we found the Director to be most helpful. His only condition was that a witness should be present whenever Dr Cameron was in the laboratory. Everything went smoothly from then on, but while there we had a change of plan. Fearing that our interest in the case might not be welcomed by the Carabinieri, we decided instead to bring the DNA fingerprints here, the headquarters of the Polizia di Stato in Rome. So now Dr Cameron will show you those results. Fiona…"

Virginia Brandolin nodded approvingly, and made herself comfortable again. The others, all wearing the white-belted two-tone blue uniform of the Rome police, looked on with renewed interest.

Fiona placed the new prints on the table alongside a computer printout. Raising her hand to indicate that no explanation was needed, Virginia Brandolin leaned forward and adjusted her glasses. Her eyes flicked up and down as she compared the columns of black and white bands.

"Your trip to Washington was very worthwhile, Dr Cameron. Yes, there's no doubt that two of the stamps were put there by Dr Salomon, and that he is indeed the father of whoever sealed the envelope and smoked the cigarette. Therefore, I now agree that your suspicion that the girls were masquerading as scientists with the intention of stealing MECCAR's secrets for their father is very reasonable.

"However, I'm afraid there is another problem, which is that you have no evidence that they actually stole anything, do you? We can't have them arrested for pretending to be Dr Salomon's research fellows. The organisers of the symposium and its sponsors might have reason to be unhappy, but that's as far as it goes. That in itself was not illegal. So, I'm sorry, in the absence of evidence that they stole any of MECCAR's intellectual property, there's still nothing we can do."

As she glanced at her watch again and started to collect her belongings, Giles steeled himself for the pronouncement of his life.

"On the contrary, Dottoressa, when you have heard what I am about to say, I think you will agree there is a lot you need to do."

"Oh! Why?"

"Because I'm afraid we're talking about something more serious than mere academic espionage—*much* more serious."

"Such as?"

"Omisido, Dottoressa!" Giles bellowed. "Omisido!"

Virginia Brandolin stared at him expressionless.

"Pardon?"

"Un omisido, Signora, un omisido molto terribile."

She looked towards Fiona in puzzlement, scratching her head.

"I'm sorry, I don't understand."

"He means murder," Fiona explained softly, looking a little embarrassed.

"Oh! You mean omicidio, Professor. Omicidio, pronounced o-mee-chid-ee-o."

"Yes, sorry, of course!"

"Homicide? Are you serious?"

"Most definitely."

"Of whom?"

"Dr Sharif."

"But you said it was an accident. There were no suspicious circumstances, you said. He went for a walk on the terrace late at night after a drink, tripped over, and could not swim. So, what are you talking about?"

"That is what the Carabinieri concluded, yes. But we think they got it wrong. In fact, we know they did. Dr Sharif did not trip into the pool. He was pushed into it."

"By whom?"

"The sisters Salomon."

"Why on earth would they have…?"

"For a very simple reason: to deny Dr Sharif the Nobel Prize that he deserved for discovering the *Achilles* gene. You see, the prize cannot be awarded posthumously. You can't be selected if you're already dead, even if you made the most important medical discovery ever. Alfred Nobel put it in his will. Everyone knew Dr Sharif was in line for the honour. It was just a matter of time. And when it happened, it would have been much more than another embarrassment for Dr Salomon. It would have been humiliating for the entire National Institutes of Health and top American universities, and a disaster for the US President, the blame for which would have fallen on Dr Salomon's shoulders. And having established such a vast lead, Dr Sharif would have been a thorn in Dr Salomon's flesh for years to come, as one breakthrough from this team followed another. On top of all this, the Salomons could have had another motive—vengeance, retribution, call it what you will—as Dr Sharif's discovery had dropped the family into a living hell."

Virginia Brandolin stood up to walk with a sense of urgency to the door. After peering down the corridor, she asked Carlo to stand outside and returned hastily to her chair.

"Okay, I can see it's quite possible the Salomons could have been motivated to murder Dr Sharif. That I accept. But I haven't seen any evidence that he was pushed into the pool, and did not simply fall into it. Do you have any?"

Chewing on her pen, she tilted her chair onto its back legs, and rocked it to-and-fro, as if to stress she would wait as long as it took to get to the bottom of Giles's extraordinary accusation.

"Indeed, we do. It came to me during the week that Dr Cameron and I were discussing whether we should go to Washington or Sorrento. I was working…"

"Excuse me, Professor, but first it's crucial I get the chronology right. The time you're going to talk about now is the period *after* you had returned from your few days in your cottage, but *before* the two of you had gone to the pub to agree on what to do next?"

"Correct."

"Thank you. Please continue."

"I was working alone in Dr Cameron's flat, when I went into her kitchen. Upon opening the fridge, my eyes were drawn to an almost empty bottle of Chinotto, a beverage with which I'm sure you are very familiar. It was one I had taken from the suite's frigobar before checking out of the hotel in Sorrento. Dr Sharif had recommended it to me during the symposium, and I'd been intending to try it ever since, but had never got around to it. I had opened the bottle in the lobby of Naples airport, consumed about half of it, and kept the rest for Dr Cameron to try. Now, standing in the kitchen, it suddenly occurred to me that Dr Sharif had said that his suite's frigobar didn't have any Chinotto. Plenty of champagne, he had joked, but nothing so humble as Chinotto. So I started wondering who could have put it in the frigobar. It seemed unlikely it was Dr Sharif, as the barman in the congress centre had said the hotel had only cans of the stuff. And as the receptionist had told me I was the first person to stay in the suite since Dr Sharif's death, it couldn't have been put there by another guest."

"Wait a minute, Professor! Why had nobody stayed in the suite before you?"

"Apparently, the super-rich didn't like the idea of sleeping where there had been such a recent tragedy."

"Ah, I see. Not surprising, I suppose. Carry on."

"So I wondered if it could have been the girls, who had been staying in a different hotel. I was mulling this over when Dr Cameron entered the kitchen. She'd just been to a pharmacy to get some ointment for a rash, which she thought was due some sleeping tablets she'd been taking since we'd returned from the cottage. On questioning her, I learnt it was similar to one she'd developed the day after my return from Sorrento. On that occasion, she hadn't been taking pills of any kind, but had commented that the rash resembled one she'd had as a student when taking tablets for exam nerves. All of this gave me an idea. I telephoned a colleague who specialises in toxicology to ask if he could do some tests on what remained of the Chinotto. He agreed, and a few days later we had the results.

"Fiona, over to you…"

Fiona swept her DNA fingerprints to one side and placed two laboratory printouts on the table.

"You can ignore the jumble of numbers, Dr Brandolin. Just go to the summaries at the bottom, where you'll see that this particular bottle of Chinotto contained much more than herbs and the juice of a bitter orange. It also contained the drug flunitrazepam and some alcohol. The former is closely related chemically to nitrazepam, the active ingredient in Mogadon, the sleeping tablets my GP had prescribed. And both are related to diazepam, the sedative in Valium, which I took briefly as a student. They're all benzodiazepines.

"Unknown to Professor Butterfield, during the evening of his return from Sorrento, I had drunk most of what was left of the Chinotto. The next morning, I noticed the rash he's referred to. I had no idea what had caused it, but as it went away quite quickly, I put it out of my mind. It didn't return until about three weeks later, after I'd started taking the Mogadon. It's often the case that if you're allergic to one member of a class of drugs, you're allergic to all of them, and this made Professor Butterfield wonder if the Chinotto had been spiked with a benzodiazepine."

Virginia Brandolin picked up one of the printouts to study it more closely.

"Does flunitrazepam have another name?"

"Yes, rohypnol."

"Ah! Sometimes called ropies, roach, or rope? The date rapists' favourite assistant?"

"That's right. It's a rapidly acting brain depressant that also happens to be soluble, tasteless, odourless, and colourless—perfect for dropping into the drink of an intended victim, especially one containing alcohol, which enhances its effect."

"Yes, you said the Chinotto also contained some alcohol, didn't you, which it doesn't normally. I'll come back to that. But for now, let me ask the Professor something."

Virginia Brandolin removed her glasses and pointed them at Giles.

"Professor Butterfield, is that really all it took for you to be suspicious about the contents of the bottle—Dr Cameron's rash? That would have been remarkably astute of you."

"No, actually there was more than that. Two things had been troubling me since my return from Sorrento. I had slept throughout the flight from Naples. Nothing unusual about that. But what *was* unusual was that as soon as I was in the arrivals lounge, I lay down and fell asleep again. When I woke up several hours later, I had no idea where I was and no recollection of the flight. I could remember getting up in the morning, shopping in a supermarket, a hair-raising journey to Naples airport, and chatting to a young lady—but nothing after boarding the aircraft. Then, the next morning, I discovered that during the flight I had dictated some instructions for Dr Cameron and prepared some of the samples for the laboratory class you know about. And yet I couldn't remember any of it.

"The other thing that had been troubling me happened during the evening of my return. Dr Cameron and I were playing a game of dominoes in her flat after dinner."

"Dominoes?" Virginia Brandolin exclaimed. "Not what I'd expect of two molecular geneticists!"

"No? Well, Dr Cameron keeps a few games in a cupboard for when her young niece pays a visit—Scrabble, tiddlywinks, Chinese chequers, that sort of thing. We sometimes play one or the other when we need to relax, and there's been plenty of that that lately."

He loosened his collar before wiping his brow with his handkerchief.

"Well, after a while, she seemed to be losing interest. I found that strange, as normally she's very enthusiastic. She had also become rather slow to respond to my moves. I tried to get her more involved, but it had no effect. And then eventually, she dropped off to sleep, which is most unlike her, and remained that way until I departed the next morning."

Virginia Brandolin raised her eyebrows and smiled facetiously.

"She remained asleep until you *departed the next morning*?"

"Er…yes, that's right. I stayed overnight in case she was ill."

"And was she?"

"Fortunately not."

"I see. You said she's normally *very enthusiastic* about dominoes?"

"Yes."

"Normally, she really enjoys…it?"

Giles wiped his brow again.

"Yes."

"But not this time? She was rather *slow to respond* to your moves?"

"Er…yes."

"Whatever you tried, you couldn't get her interested?"

"That's right."

Turning towards the policemen, Virginia Brandolin winked discreetly.

"Tell me, Professor, what sort of things did you try?"

"What do you mean?"

"What did you do to get her *more involved*, as you put it?"

Giles wiped his brow once again.

"Is that important?"

"It might be…to Dr Cameron. Did you try really hard?"

"I'm not sure where this is leading, but yes I did, as a matter of fact."

"What exactly did you do?"

"FOR GOD'S SAKE, WOMAN!" Giles exploded. "Why are you so interested in such intimate, I mean *intricate*, details?"

Virginia Brandolin burst into laughter.

"Oh, Professor, you English can be so coy! Why don't you just tell the truth? The two of you made love. Normally she's passionate, but this time she was half asleep and disinterested. Correct?"

Giles nodded, feeling very foolish.

"It's much better to be straight, Professor, especially when talking to lawyers. I'm sorry if I've embarrassed you, but there's no reason to be. Dr Cameron is a very attractive young lady."

"Yes…quite…well, if I may continue, Dottoressa, the next day I learnt from Dr Cameron that she could not remember anything of our…activity. It then occurred to me that our two episodes of memory loss had something in common. Each had followed drinking from the bottle of Chinotto. Although drugs are not my specialty, I did know that some sedatives can produce anterograde amnesia—loss of the ability to store new memories while you're under their influence, while leaving memories already there unaffected. This is very different from the type of amnesia that occurs after a head injury, for example, when you cannot remember some things that happened *before* the blow. So, I put two and two together."

"And got five! Fascinating, Professor. I congratulate you. You are clearly a very perceptive man. Now, to change the subject, you said the Chinotto also contained some alcohol. Why did you ask your Oxford colleague to look for that as well? I don't suppose he found it by accident. It's a very different chemical, isn't it?"

"Yes, it is, totally different. For the flunitrazepam he used reverse phase liquid chromatography-tandem mass spectrometry, and for alcohol he used headspace-gas chromatography."

"Forgive me, but I'm not even going to try to write that down!"

"They're a mouthful, aren't they? As you know, the Carabinieri had found alcohol in Dr Sharif's blood. They'd had good reason to look for it, as there had been an empty beer bottle on the suite's table. Once they'd got a positive result, I presume they didn't see any need to go looking for drugs also with complicated expensive assays. It seemed pretty obvious what had happened.

"So when my colleague told me the Chinotto contained rohypnol, I wondered if the alcohol in Dr Sharif's blood might also have come from there, and asked him to take a look. The combination is very potent, which is why it's so popular with date rapists."

"Very interesting, Professor. So you're thinking Dr Sharif was murdered by someone who knew three things: his taste for

Chinotto, his inability to swim, and the properties of rohypnol? This certainly makes the Salomons suspects, I agree. And the empty bottle of beer was left there as a red herring, as I think you English call it?"

"Yes."

Virginia Brandolin closed her eyes for what must have been a full minute before continuing.

"Professor, when you took the bottle of Chinotto from the cabinet, was it full?"

"The bottle?"

"Yes."

"Yes, it was, completely."

"So, clearly it could not have been used to drug Dr Sharif, could it?"

"No."

"Where there any other bottles of Chinotto there?"

"No, just the one."

"Interesting. What do you know about the beer bottle? Did our friends down the coast examine it?"

"Yes. But they didn't find anything on it—no ordinary fingerprints anywhere, no DNA on the rim. Nothing."

"Extraordinary! So how do you put all this together?"

It was time for Fiona to take over again, and it was the part she had been dreading most. After anxiously collecting a few cards from her bag, she took a deep breath.

"Our belief, Avocado, is that when the Salomons flew to Italy…"

She promptly stopped at the sight of Virginia Brandolin giggling behind her hand.

"My apologies, Dr Cameron! Your correctness is laudable, but the word you're looking for is Avvocato. The other one is pear-shaped, thick-skinned, and has a heart of stone. Not like me at all!"

"Sorry…I'm a little nervous."

"Perfectly natural…and again, my apologies… please continue."

"We think that when the Salomons left for Italy, they must have taken a few rohypnol tablets with them. Although they're illegal in the USA, plenty get into the country from Mexico. Their plan was for the girls to accompany Dr Sharif to his suite, and then surreptitiously drop one into whatever he was drinking. When it had taken effect, they would search the suite for information about MECCAR's research, tidy up, wash the glasses, and leave, by which time Dr Sharif would be asleep. When he awoke several hours later, he would have no recollection of what had happened, apart from the period between their entering the suite and the onset of the drug's effect.

"That's what they had *planned* to do. However, soon after arriving in Sorrento, they changed their plan. The catalyst was the discovery by Dr Salomon that Dr Sharif could not swim. They then decided to go a step further. They would entice Dr Sharif onto the suite's terrace and push him into the pool."

Vittoria Brandolin raised a finger.

"Are you working on the *assumption* Dr Salomon discovered that Dr Sharif could not swim, or do you *know* this was the case?"

"We know it was the case, Giles answered. Fiona, could you show Dr Brandolin the article in Il Mattino that reported Dr Sharif's death?"

Relieved that Giles was taking over again, Fiona found the cutting in his briefcase, and placed it on the table. Virginia Brandolin scanned the article before reading the relevant paragraph for her colleagues to hear.

"It says here that 'Dr Sharif's wife, who was on vacation in Lugano but had been in contact with her husband regularly by phone, said he had not known that the suite had a pool until checking in. As he was a non-swimmer and disliked the smell of chlorine, he had asked the receptionist if he could change to an alternative suite. She had contacted the occupant of the only other suite, the Capo di Monte, which does not have a pool, but had been told it would not be convenient.'"

"When I first saw that article," Giles explained, "there was no reason to connect the incident with Dr Salomon, as he had told me when I arrived at the symposium that he was in a standard room. However, during my return visit to Sorrento, one of the waiters told me that he had in fact stayed in the Capo di Monte, a smaller suite with no terrace or pool. I then realised that Dr Salomon must have been the person to whom the receptionist had conveyed Dr Sharif's request to exchange suites. When Dr Salomon told her it would not be convenient, the truth was that having learnt from her that Dr Sharif was a non-swimmer, he preferred to leave him where he was—where there was a very private pool. He then coerced his daughters to take advantage of this unexpected opportunity. And instead of using their rohypnol pills merely to facilitate their search for MECCAR's secrets, they would use them also for a more sinister purpose.

"Later on, when we were in the bar together, Dr Sharif told us how fond he was of Chinotto, and how there was none in the suite's frigobar. Armed with this additional information, the Salomons decided to refine their plan. When they accompanied him to his suite that evening, the girls would take a gift of two bottles of Chinotto already spiked with the drug. Far better that than risk being caught dropping pills into his orange juice or mineral water. They bought them from a local supermarket, added one or two pills to each, and carefully replaced the tops. Very shrewdly, they also added some alcohol, reasoning that if they left an empty beer bottle on the table, the Carabinieri would check his blood for alcohol. Upon finding it, they would take its presence as confirmation that he'd been drinking and assume his death was a tragic accident. Which is exactly what happened."

"Stop there, please," Virginia Brandolin requested. "When did the episode in the bar occur, when Dr Sharif told you about the Chinotto?"

"Sorry, I thought I'd made that clear. Immediately after his lecture, and before his meeting with Dr Salomon and the girls."

"And when did that begin?"

"Their meeting?"

"Yes."

"Around two-thirty."

"And he died the same night?"

"Yes."

"I'm trying to judge whether your theory is plausible. Do you know at what time they met Dr Sharif in the evening?"

"Yes. The three of them had dinner in the hotel's fish restaurant. I was with Dr Salomon at another table. They probably met at around eight o'clock."

"Which means they would have had four or five hours to go to the supermarket and make their preparations?"

Giles and Fiona nodded in unison.

"Enough, I suppose. What would they have used for the alcohol, grappa?"

"Probably not, on account of its taste and aroma," Giles replied. "I think vodka's more likely. It's at least 40 per cent alcohol. So, if they replaced 40 ml of Chinotto with the same volume of vodka, it would contain at least 16 ml of alcohol. That's about the same amount as in a small glass of wine or a bottle of beer. And as a Chinotto bottle is 200 ml, it would not be noticeable. If they'd used a stronger vodka, and they go up to 90 per cent alcohol, they could have used less, of course."

"So, what happened next in this scenario?"

"When they met Dr Sharif for dinner, they took the two bottles of Chinotto with them. Once in his suite, they put them into the frigobar to cool. A little later, they took one out, together with a bottle of beer for the girls to share, and went onto the terrace to enjoy the view. When Dr Sharif was getting drowsy and unsteady on his feet, they pushed him into the pool. Then, they washed the glasses and put them away, cleaned the beer bottle, put it on the table, and departed, taking the empty Chinotto bottle with them. The second bottle was still where they'd put it…in the frigobar. And that's where it remained, until I came across it."

Virginia Brandolin got up to pace around the room, wringing her hands and repeatedly sweeping her hair from her face. Pausing in a corner, she propped herself against the wall and crossed her arms, her eyes flitting between the policemen, Giles, and Fiona.

"There are still some things that require explanation, both of you. The first concerns the beer bottle. The forensic laboratory in Naples will have used the polymerase chain reaction, of course, to amplify any DNA on the rim of the bottle before preparing the DNA fingerprints. As you know, the reaction needs only a few molecules to work on. The only way to ensure there would be none would have been to clean the bottle with…"

"Sodium hypochlorite," Fiona interrupted, "widely used to clean surfaces in genetics laboratories, including our own, and also readily available from supermarkets in the form of bleach. They could have bought a Clorox spray or similar during their visit to the supermarket."

"That's true. But when you saw the girls in the restaurant, Professor, were they carrying handbags?"

"Yes, quite large ones actually."

Satisfied with the answers, Virginia Brandolin returned to her chair.

"Okay, now something else. Academics like you, even the very best, can sometimes get buried in the science and overlook details that take the trained minds of legal and law enforcement professionals to spot."

She glanced at the policemen with a knowing smile as if to prepare them for a development they were likely to enjoy.

"Why do you think they took two bottles of Chinotto to Dr Sharif? One would have been enough, wouldn't it?"

"I assume to have one in reserve," Giles answered, "in case they had an accident and knocked one over. Belt and bracers. Dr Salomon is like that."

"Also, I suppose to have taken only one bottle," Fiona added, "would have looked a little mean."

Virginia Brandolin nodded approvingly.

"Fair enough. And you're suggesting they put both in the frigobar upon arriving?"

"Yes," Fiona answered.

"Then after a while they took one out, and left the other one where it was, with the intention of either using it later, in the unlikely event they needed a second, or taking it away with them when they departed?"

"Exactly."

"But they didn't do either. When they'd finished the job, they left the unused one where they'd put it. And that's the one Professor Butterfield collected during his return visit."

"That's right."

"So, you're saying that despite having the presence of mind to clean the glasses and put them away, clean the beer bottle very carefully, tidy up the suite, collect the used Chinotto bottle, and so on, the girls completely forgot about the other bottle in the frigobar? Is that plausible? It seems extremely unlikely to me."

"No," Giles answered, "that's not what happened."

"No?"

"No. They didn't *forget* about the second bottle. They had no choice but to leave it where it was."

"Why?"

"As the Presidential Suite's very large frigobar is stocked with expensive wines, its door locks automatically when you close it. Then you need a key to open it. When the girls were preparing to leave, the key was in Dr Sharif's trouser pocket, who by then, of course, was at the bottom of the pool."

"How do you know it was in his pocket, Professor?"

"All the keys of the suite, for the entrance door, the French windows to the terrace, and the frigobar, were on the same ring. When I checked into the hotel, the receptionist told me they had been found in Dr Sharif's pocket. She wanted to be sure I would be comfortable with the fact."

"And presumably you were. Good! So that's that one out of the way. Now, the next point is that you don't have incontrovertible evidence that the girls were in the suite *when Dr Sharif drowned*, do you? Perhaps the three of them just went for a walk after dining in the restaurant, not to Dr Sharif's suite. The cigarette butt is not sufficient evidence, because you don't know when or how it got there. A jury might accept it, but equally they might not. If you still had that bottle, it might make all the difference. We could dust it for fingerprints, the usual type, and send digital records of whatever we found to the FBI. The Americans could then compare them with the girls' prints.

"But I suppose your colleague tossed it away with all his other laboratory trash, did he?"

Giles and Fiona glanced at each other knowingly.

"Yes, I'm afraid that's exactly what he did," Giles answered sombrely.

"Well, I'm very sorry, Professor, Dr Cameron, but without that…"

"In fact," Giles continued, now glowing with satisfaction, "that was not the case at all. I'm sorry to have teased you. The truth is that as soon as we saw the results, Dr Cameron had the presence of mind to run to my colleague's laboratory to make sure that that did not happen."

"Brilliant! Where is it then?"

"In my briefcase."

"Plastic?"

"No, leather."

"The bottle, Professor, not your briefcase!"

"Sorry! Glass. It's a glass bottle."

"Excellent, in that case there's a good chance it will still have fingerprints on it."

Beaming from ear to ear, Fiona took a brown paper bag from Giles's briefcase and handed it to her.

"Thank you, Dr Cameron. Do you know happen to know where the girls live?"

"San Diego."

"Both of them?"

"Yes. They're marine biologists."

"I see. So that will be all for today. As soon as I know anything, I'll send you a message. Which hotel are you in?"

"The Westin," Fiona answered.

"Very nice! While you are waiting to hear from me, you should take the opportunity to do some sightseeing. In my view, Rome is the most beautiful city in the world."

"I'm surprised to hear that coming from a Venetian!" Fiona ventured, now brimming with confidence.

"How did you know I am…?"

"Your surname, Brandolin. It doesn't end in a vowel."

"Well, well! I didn't know English girls were so knowledgeable about Italian names."

"Actually, most of them are not," Fiona replied grinning, "Most know about as much as you seem to about Scottish ones!"

"Cameron?"

"Yes."

"Mi dispiace!"

Chapter Twenty

The next few days were Fiona's reward for all the effort of the past weeks. The weather was perfect for her long-awaited introduction to the Eternal City, and as far as she was concerned, Virginia Brandolin's message could take its time. She was as eager as Giles to know the outcome, but as her GP had stressed, there were other things in life apart from work.

Early each morning she would leave the Westin in high spirits to enjoy the sunshine while window shopping in Via Vittorio Veneto, then find a small bar for a cappuccino and an apricot or chocolate brioche, mingling with Romans of all types and ages at every opportunity. Meanwhile Giles, less persuaded that the residents were the city's greatest asset, would take a leisurely breakfast with the morning's issue of La Repubblica. At around nine o'clock, they would meet in the lobby and set off for the day's tour of monuments, museums, and churches, ending with dinner in a carefully chosen trattoria, all planned by Fiona the previous evening.

Apart from her birthday celebration in La Pergola, the highlight was a visit to the Capitoline Hill. Ever since reading Gibbon's 'Decline and Fall of the Roman Empire' as a child in the Isle of Skye, where her parents had tried their hand at running a guesthouse for a few years, she had longed to look down on the ruins of the Forum. During the long winter nights in her bedroom overlooking the River Sligachan, she would turn the pages by the light of a candle and picture the city in its prime, its streets congested with people and animals, the air filled with alien noises and smells. Drifting asleep on warm summer nights, she would imagine the sounds from the restaurant's kitchen below to be the clatter of chariots and carts in the city's cobbled byways.

And so it was with unbridled joy that she raced up the broad staircase of the Cordonata to sprint across the Piazza del Campidoglio towards the equestrian statue at its centre. As she looked into the eyes of the rider, Giles caught up at a more leisurely pace to place an arm around her waist.

"You know, more than once during this saga," he said quietly, "when pondering how Steve and his ilk yearn so much for accolades, I've recalled a few of the words that this great man wrote. 'All is ephemeral,' he said, 'fame and the famous as well.' You wouldn't expect that from a man like him, would you? Marcus Aurelius was a remarkable emperor, and a wise one to boot."

"Until he chose Commodus to be his successor, I suppose!"

"That's true. Which I suppose only goes to prove none of us is perfect."

Fiona's eyes moved from the statue to look into his.

"I think *you* are, Giles, as near as makes no difference. That's why you're here now with me, and not in the university playing politics, hobnobbing with the influential, back-scratching the well-connected, and licking the bottoms of the powerful, like so many at your stage of academic life. That's why in the cause of truth and justice you've risked everything."

She grasped his hand to kiss him on the cheek.

"Thank you, dear, very kind, but I'm only too aware of my many imperfections— which brings me to a point. Truth and justice, you said. Well, yes, that's part of it, certainly. But sometimes I wonder if there's more to it than that, something less palatable—a less virtuous, less noble motive."

"What do you mean?"

"Later…now's not the time. Let's go and look at the Forum."

After asking a German tourist to photograph them with a view of the Curia and Sacra Via behind, they negotiated a safe passage between horn-blowing cars, motorbikes, and scooters across Piazza Venezia before joining the crowd on Via del Corso. Upon reaching Piazza Colonna, they popped into the Caffè di Noto for a much-needed snack. As they waited for their drinks, Giles admired the architecture of the piazza through the bar's expansive windows.

"Just look at those buildings, that column, the fountain—harmony and beauty everywhere. You can understand why so many of our poets came here, can't you? Byron, Keats, Shelley, Browning. The list goes on. There's something very special about this country, the air, the sounds, the light. Whenever I'm in Italy, I feel it's where I belong."

Fiona threw her mind back to the thoughts she'd had about their future, when waiting for the others to arrive in the police station.

"I think Italy's where you do belong, Giles. It has the same effect on me too. We've been here just a few days, and it feels like a lifetime. As soon as we get back to Oxford, we should hand in our resignations, put my flat on the market, and move here—simple as that. Why wait? We've done our bit for science. We need to start living. And what better place to do it in than here?"

She got up and moved to the window to wave to a group of passing teenagers, accompanied by their schoolteacher.

"It's a wonderful country for kids too, you know. A few years ago, a study showed that Italian children are the happiest in Europe."

"I'm sure. It's a measure of the health of the society. Whatever people say about politics here, the corruption, the mafia, and so on, to my way of thinking Italians have just about perfected the art of living. In this wonderful peninsula, it's about as good as gets. And what's more, they've woven the secrets into the fabric of their everyday lives—a tapestry that shimmers but never fades in the Mediterranean sun."

He looked at the cloudless sky above the statue of St. Paul atop the Colonna Antonina.

"The sun also makes a difference to your life, of course. I've tried to analyse what it is about sunlight that makes you feel so good. I came to the conclusion it's something to do with shadows, because you feel uplifted and energised the moment they appear, even if you can't see the sky or see the light falling on you. I don't think warmth has much to do with it, as it has the same psychological effect on cold winter days as on hot humid summer ones, at least it does with me. I think it must be an optical effect that releases feel-good hormones in our brains. Something to do with our evolution and our dependence on the sun for food and security. That's my theory, anyhow. But whatever the explanation, there's no getting away from the fact that sunshine just makes you feel wonderful—in mind, body, and soul. And nowhere more than here in Italy."

As Giles reflected for a few seconds, Fiona guessed what might be coming next. She was right.

> "'To see the sun set, sure he'll rise tomorrow,
> Not through a misty morning, twinkling weak as
> A drunken man's dead eye in maudlin sorrow,
> But with all Heaven to himself…'"

Reaching to place a hand over his mouth, she took over.

> "'I love the language, that soft bastard Latin,
> Which melts like kisses from a female mouth,
> And sounds as if it should be writ on satin.'"

Giles looked at her aghast.

"I thought that might impress you, Professor Butterfield. It's Byron isn't it?"

"How come you…?"

"Alessandro, my Italian tutor, comes out with it every time he's packing for his next trip home."

"Ah…I see…so you've seen him packing, have you?"

"No, it's what he told me, that's all."

"I see, he only *told* you he recites Byron when he's packing all on his own. And yet somehow you know those lines pretty well."

"There's a simple explanation. After he told me about it, I asked him to recite the lines. And I liked them so much, I wrote them down and learnt the lot. So there!"

"Really? Well, I'm still not sure I like the sound of this, Dr Cameron—alone together, and he going on about kisses and women's mouths. I wonder why it was only that poem he told you about. I think I need to keep an eye on him!"

"Don't worry, you can relax. I've tried everything— expensive perfume, really cheap sluttish perfume, miniskirts, tight low-cut sweaters. But never any effect."

"Have you now? In that case, he's either gay or a eunuch."

"Judging by the hairs on his chest, he's certainly not the latter."

Seeing the waiter approaching, they returned to the table.

"Giles, in a less frivolous vein," she whispered, "what did you mean before, about your imperfections and motives? You know, when we were looking at the statue."

"Ah…I didn't think you'd wait very long. But now is as good a time as any, I suppose. It goes like this. During my sabbatical with Steve years ago, one of Hank Weinberg's young staff had an idea about killing cancer cells by knocking out their mitochondrial DNA, thereby starving them of energy. As you know, Hank's an authority on mitochondria. About six months later, exactly the same idea featured in an article Hank had been asked to write for the Journal of Clinical Investigation. He'd published it without the lad's permission or giving him any credit, not even a mention in the acknowledgments section. Poor Martin was devastated. I told him to go to Hank and complain. When he picked up the courage to do so, Hank said he couldn't remember the conversation. The idea had just come into his head, he said. And that was that."

"Let me work this out. So now you're wondering if the real reason you went after Steve was because you knew that if you were right, it wouldn't just be him who suffered, as Steve's superior, Hank would suffer too? You're thinking that subconsciously you wanted to punish Hank through Steve?

That's a ridiculous suggestion, Giles. That wouldn't be you at all."

"No, it's not that. You've got it wrong."

"What is it, then?"

"When Martin told me about Hank's reaction, I should have gone to see Hank, and demanded that he write to the Editor to put the record straight. But I didn't. I did absolutely nothing. If I'd acted responsibly on that occasion, we might not be here now. By letting Hank get away with plagiarism, I let the entire National Institutes of Health off the hook. When those at the top are permitted to crap on those lower down, the rest feel it's okay to do the same. I call it 'trickle-down feconomics.'"

"So, you're thinking your real motive might be to redeem yourself?"

Giles raised his eyes and nodded.

"Giles, you're being stupid! It's okay being self-critical, but you overdo it. You scrutinise your every thought, your every action. It's madness. What happened was an internal matter, nothing to do with you. You were there as a guest, remember. Therefore, officially it was none of your business. And anyhow, that Martin, whoever he was, was quite capable of looking after himself. I assume he was wearing long trousers? He could have written to the Editor himself. It wasn't your responsibility. Forget it."

"I had, more or less, until the damn press started treating me like a saint. Since then, I haven't been able to get it out of my head."

Fiona opened her handbag and took out a folded sheet of paper.

"Well, let me see if this can. Since we're in the epicentre of sartorial elegance, I thought I'd treat you to some new clothes—not big things, just accessories. So yesterday I made myself a list. Here it is."

She unfolded the paper, and placed it on the table.

"Let's start with the tie. I thought a plain green silk one would go nicely with that grey jacket you keep…"

She stopped reading as Giles lifted the corner to take a peek at the other side.

"Hold on, what's this underneath? It's in Arabic."

"Yes, that's what I thought. It's the first page of an old fax I came across in Steve's lab, when I was looking for something to write notes on."

"Where was it?"

"In a drawer below a pile of used paper bags, bus tickets, and other trash. I assumed it had been sent to one of his Alhazen Fellows from somewhere, and took it to be rubbish like the rest."

"You said it was the first page. Where are the rest?"

"In the hotel. This is the only one I didn't use for the lab work."

"Why didn't you show it to me? As it's in Arabic, it might be important."

Fiona smiled and gave him a confident wink.

"The same thought occurred to me at first. But don't worry, it definitely isn't important. It can't be. If you look at the top, you'll see it was received on the ninth of June, the year before last, which was five weeks *before* MECCAR announced its discovery of *Achilles*. That's why I didn't mention it. So you can relax!"

By now Giles had turned the page over, and was scanning it from top to bottom.

"But Fiona, it wasn't received on the ninth of June. We were in the States, remember, where fax machines print the month first, and the day second, not the other way around like ours do. This fax was received three months later than you thought, on the sixth of September. And you know what day that was, don't you?"

Fiona thought for a few a seconds and then held her head in horror.

"Oh, my God! Was it the last day of the Sorrento symposium?"

"Correct. Now look at the telephone number. It was sent from Italy."

He grabbed his phone from his inside pocket, and scrolled through his contacts list.

"Just what I feared. It was sent to Steve's telephone-fax at his home in Chevy Chase."

He scrolled through the list again.

"And the sender's number differs from the Presidential Suite's direct line by just the last digit: a two instead of a one. So, there's not much doubt where it came from, is there? It was received in Steve's home at 5:02 p.m., which would have been 11:02 p.m. in Sorrento."

"I can't believe this! You're saying I've been sitting on a fax that was sent from the Presidential Suite to Steve's home at 11:02 p.m. on the very night Ahmad was murdered?"

Giles nodded.

"Oh my God, what have I done?"

"Too early to know, I'm afraid. But two things are certain. We were right about the girls being on a spying mission. Not much doubt about that. And we also know for sure they were in Ahmad's suite on the night in question."

"That's true. So what does the fax say? Can you understand it?"

Giles studied it as Fiona waited on edge.

"It's rather odd. Looks like the transcript of a talk Ahmad might have been planning to give. He introduces himself, then goes on to say…listen to this…'Why did I ask for this press conference so soon after arriving in London from Sorrento, having first collected my wife and children in Lugano?' After that he says a few things about MECCAR, how wonderful it is… how more breakthroughs are on the way…its unconventional methods…then the last bit on the page says…'For there are two sides to MECCAR, the side you know, and the one you do not know—a side that nobody outside its walls has ever seen, a dark side that lies hidden in the shadows…And that is what has brought me here today.'

"That's as far as this page goes. It looks important, very important. I'm afraid we need to go straight back to the hotel to translate the whole lot. To be on the safe side, I'll pick up a dictionary on the way. Arabic-Italian would do, if that's all they've got."

Leaving some cash on the table, they hastened to a local bookstore, before hastening up Via del Tritone towards Piazza Barberini. When they reached the square's central fountain, Giles stopped to recover his breath.

"Phew! Too many gnocchi," he panted, dropping onto his knees to splash water on his face. "I need a breather. What a struggle! I wonder why Romans can't get out of the damn way when it's obvious you're in a hurry. And why they waste paint on zebra crossings, I can't imagine. They're like honey traps for the amusement of homicidal drivers."

Fiona sat uncomfortably on the low railing that encircles the fountain while waiting for him to recover.

"Giles, I think you mentioned once that the Presidential Suite's study has a photocopier, didn't you?"

Giles grunted with a nod.

"In that case, why do you think the girls faxed documents to Steve, instead of just copying them? After all, he was in Sorrento, not at home."

Giles dried his face on a handkerchief.

"Didn't want to risk being caught red-handed, I suppose. If there'd been a lot of stuff to copy, it might have been difficult conceal it on the way out."

"But faxing will have left a tell-tale record in the machine or the hotel's system, wouldn't it? That wasn't a very smart thing to do from a murder scene."

A tense silence followed, during which several pigeons arrived looking for crumbs. Fiona scattered them with her foot, losing a shoe in the process.

"You don't think we could have got it wrong after all, do you, Giles? If we were right the first time, and the girls were only after MECCAR's intellectual property, nothing more, the fact that the hotel had a record of the faxes wouldn't really have mattered. The sponsors of the symposium footing the bill wouldn't have been interested. I'm sure they wouldn't have considered charging Ahmad for his faxes any more than his telephone calls, drinks, or room service. But if the girls had just murdered him, or were planning to, surely they'd have kept clear of the fax machine."

"If they were thinking rationally, yes. But don't forget they were inexperienced. We're not talking about seasoned criminals or professional spies. They were under huge pressure, quite possibly panicking at that stage."

They stared at the cobbled stones, the water running over the brim of the fountain's shell-like dish scarcely audible above the din of the nearby traffic. After waiting for a couple of pedestrians to pass, Giles revealed other concerns.

"Actually, something else occurred to me on the way. If that fax was sent at two minutes past eleven, presumably Ahmad would have been in the pool by then. But according to that article in Il Mattino, the forensic pathologist put the time of drowning at about three in the morning. That's a difference of four hours."

"Is it possible to place the time of death so accurately?"

Giles shrugged his shoulders.

"Possibly. How long does it take rohypnol to start having its effect? Any idea?"

"I looked it up. Starts in about fifteen minutes, and reaches its peak in an hour or so. But he'd also had some alcohol, which will have enhanced the effect."

Giles had now joined Fiona at the railing.

"Do you think Steve will have had the fax translated, Giles?"

"Being in Arabic, I imagine he would have assumed it was something personal, nothing to do with MECCAR's science, which I think would have been in English. And getting it translated would have been risky anyway. Who could he have asked without giving the game away?"

"Okay, are you ready to continue? Not far to go."

Reaching the hotel a few yards ahead of Giles, Fiona was approached by the concierge as she entered the lobby.

"For you, Signorina," he whispered, pressing a sealed envelope in her hand. "It was delivered by the police. If you need help of any kind, I am at your service."

"Thank you, Maurizio, but I'm sure it's okay."

She turned towards Giles, as he emerged from the rotating door with his jacket and tie on his arm.

"This must be from Virginia," she called, flapping the envelope in the air.

They hurried into the lounge to drop onto the first empty sofa. Fingers trembling, Fiona ripped the envelope open to find a handwritten letter inside. She read it carefully before revealing its content.

"She says the bottle was covered in prints, but none of them matched any of the girls' prints. They also checked Steve's, but again no match. Not a single Salomon print anywhere. She also asked the lab in Naples to test one of Ahmad's frozen blood samples for 7-aminoflunitrazepam, which she says is rohypnol's major metabolite."

"And?"

"It was positive. So she's concluded we must be right about Ahmad being drugged and pushed in, but reckons there's insufficient evidence to accuse the girls of doing it. Now listen to this. 'Further investigations will be necessary. From now on you must leave it to the police. They will keep the Carabinieri fully informed about what has happened. Let me know at once if you have any other information or ideas that might help them in their enquiries. Thank you for all you have done. Have a safe journey back to Oxford. Best wishes, Virginia Brandolin.'"

Sinking into the soft velvet cushions, Fiona gazed at the frescoed ceiling, fanning herself with the envelope.

"Leave it to the police?" she gasped. "Like hell we will! I don't care how many Mogadons and herbal teas it takes, I'm not going to let that brassy cow get the credit for all our hard work."

"That's the spirit! Of course, at the end of the day, we'll have no choice but to leave it to them. But now's definitely not the time. I agree. Now, do you have the energy to go and get the rest of the fax?"

"Aye-aye, sir!"

Fiona was in her long dressing gown and slippers when she stepped out of the elevator carrying several sheets of paper rolled up in an elastic band. After checking that nobody was approaching, she ran across the red carpet to join Giles on the sofa again.

"I hope nobody minds me looking like this," she whispered, wrapping the gown tightly around her waist, and drawing her feet onto the cushion. "I was sweating from head to toe after that dash outside, and took a quick shower. Here you are—ten pages to add to the one you've got. As you'll see, my lab notes are on the other side.

"Now before I disappear again, things keep occurring to me. Perhaps the girls were wearing gloves when they put the Chinotto bottles in the frigobar. That could explain the lack of prints, couldn't it? Did you notice if they had any when they were leaving the restaurant?"

Giles shook his head.

"No, they didn't. And anyhow, it would have looked a little odd, wouldn't it, if they'd put on gloves just to travel upstairs in the elevator."

"That's true. So much for that big idea! Have you had any new thoughts?"

Giles rubbed his chin pensively.

"Yes, I have actually. If their plan had been only to fax information to Steve's home, I'm wondering if the fact that the Capo di Monte doesn't have a fax machine was why he refused to change suites with Ahmad, nothing to do with the pool."

"How do you know the Capo di Monte doesn't have a fax?"

"It's something else that Luigi mentioned when he brought me my breakfast. When Steve booked the Presidential Suite for Ahmad, he'd have known it had a fax machine, because it's mentioned on the hotel's website. And by the time the receptionist called him at Ahmad's request, he'd have seen that the Capo di Monte does not. Perhaps the pool was a red herring, after all. Perhaps we were caught hook, line, and sinker by a fish!"

Ignoring the arrival of some hotel guests at a nearby coffee table, Fiona stood up and walked around the room, now in her bare feet, before returning to kneel behind the sofa.

"So let me get this right," she whispered in his ear, "we're now saying the girls may have gone to Sorrento with the sole intention of searching Ahmad's suite, and faxing anything that looked of interest to Steve's home. We also know that somebody drugged Ahmad and pushed him into the pool. But it was *not* the girls. It was someone else. So what on earth happened? And without drugging Ahmad, how could the girls have searched his suite?"

"I can think of a simple answer to the last question. While one of them was in the study, the other one kept him busy in the bedroom. They were both very attractive young ladies. And with his wife being in Lugano...."

"Yes, of course. When the cat's away, the *rats* can play."

Fiona looked to the ceiling apologetically.

"Sorry Ahmad!"

"Then, after they'd finished the job and departed," Giles continued, "Ahmad had a second visitor, who brought the gift of Chinotto."

"All of which could explain why the time of death was at least four hours after this fax was sent."

"Quite."

"But who could it have been? And for what reason?"

Giles removed the elastic band from the roll, and placed it on his lap.

"Perhaps this fax will give us the answer. Time for me to get on with it, I'm afraid. See you later."

"Yes, good luck!"

Chapter Twenty-One

While waiting for the waiter to bring him a pot of tea, Giles checked that the pages were in the correct order. Then he flattened them as best he could on the coffee table. The first thing that struck him was that much of the text was within quotation marks. As he flicked through the pages, he saw that the impression he'd gained in the Caffè di Noto—that it might be the transcript of a presentation Ahmad had been planning to give at a press conference—seemed to be correct. What was equally intriguing was the fact that the presentation appeared to include a verbatim record of a speech somebody had made in Ahmad's presence in the past.

Aware that a young man at a nearby writing table was taking an unwelcome interest, he gathered the papers, and moved to a desk behind a couple of Norfolk Island Pines in large terracotta pots. Once he had drawn the waiter's attention to his new position, he felt his pockets unsuccessfully for his notebook.

"Damn! Okay, I'll have to make the most of these."

He was referring to a complimentary pad of multicoloured Post-it Notes that had been given to him by the assistant in the bookshop. After painstakingly numbering each one in the bottom right-hand corner, he poured himself a cup of tea, moved a nearby standard lamp to the best position, and launched himself into the task.

The second page of the fax was mostly a description of the event during which the speech in question had been delivered. The speaker had been an elderly Jordanian, born into a poor family of seven children. His father had been a baker, whose meagre income his wife had supplemented by taking in laundry.

As a child, he had had the disadvantage of chronic ill health, the result of a bone infection that had left him with a limp. But he had been an exceptionally bright and industrious child, who in spite of everything had gone on to win an international scholarship at Harvard University.

Thinking that he recognised the speaker's description, but unable to place him, Giles returned to the lobby to consult MECCAR's website on the public computer terminal that was there. Very soon he had confirmation that his hunch was correct. The speaker had been none other than Hassan ibn Sulaymaan al-Mughrabi, MECCAR's venerated founding father.

As he worked his way through the translation, scribbling on his Post-it Notes as he went, Giles became more and more amazed by what he was reading. In fact, at times it seemed too fantastic to be true. So much so that at one point he was on the verge of giving Fiona a call, but then had second thoughts. She was probably already in bed with her book by now, or even asleep. And if she insisted on coming down so as to be on the spot as the translation progressed, her presence might attract unwanted attention. Better carry on alone, he decided.

By the time he had finished the last sentence of the last page, tired and bleary-eyed, it was well past three o'clock. It had been a monumental task. With so many unfamiliar words, he certainly could not have succeeded without the dictionary. As he sat back in the chair to recover from the effort, he studied the hotel's opulent decor, so different from his usual writing places—the chandeliers, the antiques, the silk and velvet curtains, the exotic plants in ornamental vases. He reflected on how difficult he would find it to work creatively in the midst of such luxury. Over the years, he had learnt that to be at his most productive it was better to be in relatively simple surroundings, especially close to nature. His best ideas had almost always popped into his head in such circumstances—alone on a Sunday in his office in the College, plodding up a hillside in the English Lake District, sitting in an abandoned railway station in Nottinghamshire. He wondered why it had been so.

Perhaps it was the lack of sensory input that freed up critical nerve cells in his brain, he thought, allowing them to express themselves in unusual ways. Maybe that's why, in spite of all the time and privileges at their disposal, royals and aristocrats, their brains forever clogged and cluttered with the stimuli of luxury, seem to have been so uncreative down the centuries. Would the likes of Leonardo da Vinci, James Watt, Richard Arkwright, and Michael Faraday have changed the world if they'd been born into untold riches?

Emerging from his musing, he realised he was now completely alone, almost eerily so—no soft music, no muffled conversations, no chinking of wine glasses and coffee cups, just the occasional distant footsteps of the concierge on the marble floor. The fact that the lighting had been dimmed heightened his sense of isolation. It was an odd feeling. He had never been in such circumstances. Parting the fronds of the plants at his side, he saw through the windows that it was now windy and raining outside. He smiled at the coffee table covered haphazardly with Post-it Notes, with several stuck to the legs and one on the tea pot from when he had run out of space.

After looking over his shoulder to check nobody was there, he took out his phone, set the camera's to timer to ten seconds, and propped it against a couple of encyclopaedias on a nearby French sideboard. Henrik Olsson had taught him an important lesson at that snow-covered bus stop in Stockholm. While his first reaction to the now famous picture had been one of embarrassment and annoyance, with his autobiography in mind, the incident had at least taught him the value of recording notable events,. And there was no doubt that this was one, perhaps his biggest yet. For what Fiona had found, long abandoned in Steve's laboratory, was nothing short of sensational.

Sorting out the puzzle of Sorrento had been like unravelling a bowl of spaghetti. How appropriate that the final strand had been drawn in Rome. At last, everything seemed to be clear. But any sense of relief was tempered by the shattering implications of the 'dark side' of MECCAR that Ahmad would have revealed to the world had his escape to London not been thwarted.

Having made his way to the elevator, he stopped at the open door before deciding to use the staircase instead. After the comfort of the upholstered chair for so long, his legs had stiffened and needed some exercise. He also needed a few minutes to prepare himself for Fiona's reaction to the news. There was no way he could delay it until the morning. She would never forgive him.

As soon as she heard the door handle move, Fiona jumped off the bed to greet him. Brandishing a half-empty bottle of vermouth, she closed the door with a deft flick of her foot, and bundled him onto the bed with a swing of the hips.

"My, that took you a long time! I tried to sleep but couldn't. Then I tried to read, but that didn't work. Then I decided to sort out my shopping. But when that didn't work either, I'm afraid I opened this bottle."

Giles watched as she twirled at the foot of the bed in a new nightdress. What do you think of this? It's from La Senza."

"It certainly beats the tweed kilt you bought this time last year. But haven't you had too much to drink?"

"Sorry! It's the only way I could survive. Would you like some?"

"Not just now, thanks."

After helping him to take off his shoes and socks, she sat on the bed beside him.

"Right, so tell me what I've been sitting on. I've been preparing myself for the worst."

"The content of that fax, Fiona, is quite extraordinary. In fact, it's more than extraordinary; it's almost incredible. In a million years, you wouldn't guess what's in that document."

He handed her the Post-it Notes, stuck together in order like a book.

"It's all in there. You can read it for yourself. It's probably the best way. Anything you don't understand, just ask."

"All of them?"

Giles nodded solemnly, while she puffed up her pillow and made herself comfortable.

"Can't you give me a clue of what it's all about first—just a teeny-weeny one?"

"Okay, just a starter to whet your appetite. You remember I mentioned in the bar that it looked like the transcript of a press conference that Ahmad had been planning to give in London after Sorrento? Well, I was right. And what he would have revealed about MECCAR would have stunned the entire scientific world."

"Why?"

"You'll see. What the girls faxed to Steve was the complete text of what Ahmad would have said to the journalists."

"He'd discovered another wonder gene, had he? What did he call it, Ahmadeus?"

"Nice one! No, it's bigger than any gene. It's bigger than a million genes. What you found, Fiona, was the medical scoop of the century—a story so big that I've no doubt some people would do anything to keep it under wraps."

"*Anything?*"

"Anything."

"You mean, like…?"

"Anything. But you'll have to see for yourself, and draw your own conclusion. It's my turn to take it easy."

"How many pages of this tiny scribble are there? I'm going to need a microscope."

"They're numbered. If you're feeling sorry for yourself, think of what I had to endure. You can skip the first few lines. But from then on, read the whole lot…aloud please, but not *too* loud. I have a headache. And prepare yourself for a shock."

Turning onto her side, Fiona adjusted the shade of her bedside lamp.

"Sorry about my derrière. Right, skip the first part you said…take a deep breath…and here goes…

"'Having introduced myself, I shall now come to the point,' it starts. Actually, your scribble is not too difficult to decipher after all, Giles. I feel better now. 'Why did I ask for this press conference so soon after arriving in London from Sorrento, having first collected my wife and children in Lugano? You are all aware that MECCAR is a unique institution. It has many remarkable features—an amazing location in the mountainous desert of Wadi Rum, stunning architecture, vast laboratories packed with the very latest equipment, beautiful gardens. There is nothing like it anywhere. It is the envy of every medical scientist in the West. And it has produced amazing results. The discovery of the *Achilles* gene has brought us close to a cure for cancer, and I can tell you that other breakthroughs are on the horizon. How would you feel if I told you that within a year we could have a vaccine against the AIDS virus?

"'As you know, the details of MECCAR's research are a closely guarded secret. You are probably also familiar with some of its other departures from convention—its refusal to allow other scientists to visit the institute, for example, and the fact that the results of its research are not published in peer review journals in the usual way, but instead are announced on dedicated websites, and then only when a breakthrough has been made. All of this is familiar to you. But there is more to MECCAR's methods than this, much more. For there are two sides to MECCAR, the side you know, and the one you do not know—a side that nobody outside its walls has ever seen, a dark side that lies hidden in the shadows of the mountains of Jebel Khasch and Jebel um Adaami. And that is what has brought me here today.

"'To hide the remarkable truth I am about to reveal, MECCAR goes to the most extraordinary lengths. All employees, even the Director himself, are required to sign an oath of perpetual secrecy about the methods used in their research. Security officers screen all telephone calls, letters, faxes, text messages, and emails. Only in exceptional circumstances are staff, even the most senior ones, permitted to attend international congresses or symposia. The one I have just come from in Italy was my first—a very special privilege.

"'So seriously does MECCAR take secrecy that the penalty for disclosing confidential information to outsiders is the most severe. As a reminder of their oath, every employee is given a small piece of Venetian glass on the anniversary of his or her appointment. The tie pin I am wearing is one. Those of you who are familiar with the history of Venice's ancient glass industry, and the punishment meted out for revealing trade secrets, will understand. Yes, from the moment I leave this room, a scimitar will hang over my head for the rest of my life.

"'What on earth could MECCAR be hiding to explain such behaviour? And why am I prepared to risk my life to let the cat out of the bag, as you English say? The story started many years ago. Long before MECCAR's first stone was laid, I was one of a select group of people who had been invited to the village of Musha in Egypt's province of Asyut to hear what would prove to be a truly historic speech. None of us had been given much information, other than it was to be of great importance for Islam and medical science. Normally, I would have treated such a claim as extravagant nonsense, but when I saw who had signed the letter, I knew it should be taken seriously. The person I am talking about is shown on my first slide. Born in…'"

"You can skip the next two Post-it Notes," Giles interjected. "It's a potted biography of MECCAR's founding father, Hassan ibn Sulaymaan al-Mughrabi."

"Well, that's good news. Okay, let me see…here we are. 'After staying in a guesthouse overnight, I arrived for the event a few minutes early. I showed my invitation to the doorman, and made my way to the back of a dimly lit dusty room. I was still taking stock of the situation, when the great man entered from the right. He walked with slow deliberation, dragging his left leg as if it were pulling a ball and chain—a tall, stooping figure with a meticulously trimmed white beard. One could see at once that this was no ordinary person. Drawn by the power of his persona, I pushed my way towards the front, until I squeezed into the second row. While it was clear many of those around me were also academics, others were politicians, bankers, businessmen, and…'"

"You can skip this bit too," Giles interrupted again. "It's just a description of the audience."

"Okay. Down we go to…here. 'Leaning on his stick, like a shepherd watching his flock, the old man waited for the chatter to settle. There was no smile, no welcoming gesture. He just peered through the haze, looking for familiar faces. After acknowledging a few with nods, he spoke, quietly and slowly, but also confidently. Knowing it would be an important occasion, I had taken a microphone and recorder with me. What I shall read to you now from the pages in front of me is an unedited transcript of his speech:

> "'Friends, thank you for coming here today. I know many of you have travelled great distances, and that you come from many walks of life: science, medicine, politics, education, industry, commerce. I am most privileged to have your trust. After all, none of you yet knows the purpose of my talk.
>
> 'I invited you here today to tell you about an idea that I have been developing for several years. In fact, for me it has become much more than a mere idea. It has become a dream, a dream that I believe could return Islam to the pinnacle of scholarship it once occupied in our ancient cities of Baghdad and Cordoba. Whether or not this dream will become a reality will depend very much on you, and people like you.
>
> 'When I was a postgraduate student in the USA, I would often reflect on its pre-eminence in the sciences, especially medical science. I wondered why this was the case, and how it had come to pass. I thought about the advantages it gives to the country's industries and commerce; how these help its economy; and how this in turn increases its standing and influence in

the world. I would also think of the countless benefits its achievements in science have given to humankind. I would then contrast this success story with the meagre contribution to scientific progress we have made during the past few hundred years. I wondered how this had come to pass, and what I could do to reverse it.

'Let me give you some numbers to illustrate what I am talking about. Many studies of scientific publications—by which I mean articles in specialist journals describing the results of research in universities and research institutes—have shown that of all the nations in the world the USA has made the biggest contributions to science and medicine. By contrast, at the present time, not a single Islamic country appears in the list of the top thirty. Tiny countries like Switzerland, the Netherlands, and Denmark—with few natural resources, small populations, and little land—make our nations look like scientific dwarfs. Alas, when it comes to science, medicine, technology, and engineering, we are almost nothing. If we suddenly did not exist, the scientific world would not even notice.

'The standing of the USA in this regard is reflected in the Nobel Prizes, a nation's record of which is a virtual barometer of its value to the world of science. For many years, the USA has led the world in all three Prizes in the sciences, namely for Physiology or Medicine, Chemistry, and Physics. Since World War II, members of American universities have won about two hundred Prizes in science. Of special moment to us Muslims is the fact that this success story is also very much a Jewish one. For almost half of all those Prizes were awarded to Jews. Indeed, the remarkable record of Jews in Nobel Prizes is not confined to the USA. It is a global phenomenon. A total world population of about twelve million people has won about one hundred. In contrast, we Muslims, who number one and a half billion, to date have been awarded just three—one in Physics, and two in Chemistry. That's one for every 500 million of us, compared with one for about every 1.2 million Americans, one for every 120,000 Jews, and about one for every 60,000 American Jews. The chasm between them and us has a major impact on how the world views us, and consequently how it treats us. Because of our poor recent productivity in science, the average Westerner believes it has always been that way. That is the sad truth.

'So, while the United States and its Jewish citizens currently occupy the summit of science, we are at the bottom looking up. In fact, the truth is we are not even looking, because we are not interested in what's going on up there. What would our forefathers think of this situation— all those great scholars, mathematicians, physicians, surgeons, astronomers, and scientists of our glorious past? Would it not be wonderful, I thought, if we could return to those days, and share that summit—even better, displace the Americans from it. Think of the good it would do for humankind if another one and a half billion human brains started to use their imagination, ideas, and creativity to further scientific progress. And think of the respect we would rightfully earn, how the standing of Islam would rise in the eyes of the world.

'I asked myself time and again. Why is America, and indeed the whole of the Western world, so superior to us in science today? What has changed compared with centuries ago? What are we doing wrong? And why are we doing nothing about it? It is certainly not because our faith rejects science. Lest some of you are under that delusion, let me remind you of some of the words of the Prophet. "That person who shall pursue the path of knowledge, God will direct him to the path of Paradise." "The superiority of a learned man over an ignorant worshipper is like that of the full moon over all the stars." "Seek knowledge from the cradle to the grave." "The pursuit of knowledge is a divine commandment for every Muslim." And "The ink of the scholar is more holy than the blood of the martyr."

'In his book "Ma'lam fi al-tariq", known in English as "Milestones", Sayyid Qutb reminded us that "Muslims have drifted away from…their way of life, and forgotten that Islam…made them responsible for learning all the sciences."

'Perhaps some of you imagine that the explanation of our poor recent performance is because we have a different type of mind—not inferior to others, just different. While we can excel in art, culture, and literature, you might think, we just cannot *do* science. And that's all there is to it. Well, if you think that way, you are obviously ignorant of our ancient history of scholarly achievements, which has shown that as a people we have everything it takes. And it is still that way. In the modern world, outstanding performance in science is born of three things: money to build fine universities and research centres; some highly intelligent creative people; and the will and energy to organize and combine those two resources. Everybody knows we have the wealth, thanks to the oil beneath our feet. If we can use it to create the tallest buildings in the world, the biggest manmade island, and the most luxurious hotels, we can surely use it to build the biggest and best universities. And our history shows that we also have the brains.

'We Muslims were once the giants not just of science, but of all intellectual activities. In those days, Arabic was the language of scholarship in the same way that Latin was for a while in Europe, and English is today. I am referring to the "Golden Age of the Abbasids," a period of more than two hundred years spanning the eighth to the tenth centuries of the Christian calendar, when we were unrivalled in every field of learning—mathematics, chemistry, medicine, engineering, optics, astronomy, agriculture, and more. It was a time when the world's first astronomical observatory was constructed in Baghdad; when we printed the first medical book on paper, complete with beautiful anatomical drawings; when we transported thousands of ancient Greek texts from Constantinople and translated them into Arabic, saving them for posterity; and when our greatest scientific genius, Abu Ali al-Hassan Ibn al-Haytham, whom the West calls Alhazen, laid the foundations of the modern scientific method, in the process writing more than two hundred books on science and mathematics, which centuries later would influence many other European scholars—Isaac Newton, Johannes Kepler, Leonardo da Vinci, and Roger Bacon, to name but a few.

'When our ancestors entered southern Spain from Africa in the Christians' eighth century, they found an intellectual wasteland

and transformed it into a fountain of science, mathematics, medicine, music, and art. We converted the plains of dust, pebbles, and weeds into orchards of oranges and lemons, apricots and peaches, plums, figs, almonds, and pomegranates. We planted the first vineyards in that soil. Fields of artichokes, aubergines, celery, fennel, squash, pumpkins, sugar cane, cotton, and wheat, even bananas and rice, none of which had ever grown there before, flourished year upon year. Such achievements would not have been possible without knowledge of botany and horticulture, and of hydrodynamics and engineering to create irrigation systems. Moorish Spain, as they now call our Al-Andalus, was the jewel of Europe. Its capital, Cordoba, was a magnificent city of two hundred thousand houses, six hundred mosques, almost a thousand public baths, and fifty hospitals. Its paved streets could be followed for fifteen kilometres in any direction with the light of lamps to guide your every step at night. Its library held more than half a million texts on science, engineering, geography, history, meteorology, and music. The city was a showcase of architectural wonders that the Christians later adapted to create the gothic arches, campaniles, and ribbed vaults of their churches, places of worship that now often echo to the flute, harp, and oboe, whose basic designs we also conceived.'"

Fiona gasped in disbelief.

"This is getting too much, Giles! Next, he'll be saying they invented the bagpipes."

"Funny you should say that."

"What's that supposed to mean?"

"Some historians believe the Crusaders brought them back from Palestine."

"Don't be ridiculous!"

"It's true."

"Rubbish! Bagpipes are as Scottish as haggis."

"They'd probably agree."

"Pardon?"

"It's also a myth that haggis is Scottish. It originated in Lancashire, just north of Liverpool."

"What a load of crap!"

"Ha! You can say that again. Which is probably why they left it to you lot."

"I'm ignoring you from now on. Where was I? Ah, yes…

"'We excelled in cartography. We invented the magnetic compass. We perfected the astrolabe. We…'"

"I can't take any more of this, Giles. Where's the next paragraph?"

"But it's all true, Fiona. Their great achievements are unknown to most people today. The origins of many of the things we take for granted have been forgotten. We think the Western world invented everything. It didn't."

"Okay, I'll believe you. Here we go again…

"'And all of this was achieved in a land of such religious tolerance that even its Hebrew writers enjoyed a golden age, at a time when throughout the rest of Europe the Jews were being persecuted. When the Spaniards ousted both of us in 1492, they were astounded by the vast store of supposedly lost Greek and Roman texts they found in our cities. At once, they set about translating them into Latin and transporting them throughout Europe. Without this storehouse of knowledge, they would not have emerged from their Dark Ages for many generations. We taught the Hindu Arabic system of numbers to the Italian Fibonacci, when he visited Bugia in their thirteenth century, from whom it spread throughout Europe, and from there to the entire Western world. Had we not done so, there would be no mathematics as the world knows it today. We gave them the concept of zero. And how many know that the word 'algebra' is derived from the middle part of "Kitab al-Jabr wa-l- Muqabalah", the very first book on the subject?

'In the West you often hear it said that Muslims are "rooted in the Dark Ages." After what I have just said, can you imagine a more absurd assertion? The fools who utter such words do not understand that we did not have any Dark Ages—that it was only European Christians who endured them, and that while they were living in squalor and ignorance, we were creating the glories of Baghdad and Cordoba.

'If we could do all those things then, and with far fewer resources than we have now, there is no doubt we could recover our past greatness in science, medicine, and technology today. There is no reason why we could not create a New Golden Age. All it needs is the self-belief, the will, and the energy to do it. Why not? After all, we are the same people with the same genes as our ancestors of a thousand years ago.

'This is the dream that came to me as I lay awake one hot summer night in Damascus. I saw glittering universities in the cities and deserts. I saw Muslim scientists proudly presenting their discoveries to international audiences aghast at what they were seeing and hearing. I saw Nobel Prize ceremonies in Stockholm packed with Muslims celebrating the latest of a long series of Laureates. I saw the good it was doing for the world in the form of new drugs, vaccines, technologies, chemical processes, electronics, materials, and most important of all, ideas. This is the dream I want you to help me to realise.

'By now, many of you are probably thinking, "He is crazy. How could we possibly achieve that? We have fallen too far behind. How could we succeed to a degree that would enable us to beat the West to the breakthroughs? It would take a thousand years."

'I have thought long and hard about this. It is true we would be starting at the bottom. It would not be easy. But we *could* do it. And we could do it much more quickly than you imagine. How? We would start by building the best research centres in the world, and filling them with the latest equipment. This would send a powerful message about the seriousness of our ambitions. We would recruit Muslim scientists trained in the West, attracted from around the world by fantastic facilities, salaries, and accommodation, and the promise of virtually unlimited research budgets. The first research centre would be in medicine, as medical advances attract greater public interest than those in other sciences. It would focus on two important diseases that, in spite of many millions of dollars of research over many years, the West has not yet conquered: cancer and AIDS. It would be called the Middle East Centre for Cancer and AIDS Research— MECCAR for short. We would pour all our early efforts into conquering these two diseases.

We would protect our work with the highest level of security, keeping all results secret until we are certain that a major breakthrough has been made. Each breakthrough would be announced in a way that could not be hindered by Western scientists. Instead of submitting our findings for publication to Western journals, whose editors and referees would be biased and obstructive, we would announce them on dedicated websites.

'Once we have announced our first breakthrough, we would receive the admiration of the world. The best young brains would come to work with us from far and wide. From then on, a self-perpetuating cycle of achievement, investment, and growth would drive us onwards. History shows this to be the pattern. The countries that produce the best research also attract the best brains from around the world, which further improves the quality and quantity of their research. The expertise and specialist knowledge thus gained benefits national industries, as academic experts are available to advise them on technical matters, give them ideas, update them on the very latest discoveries, and license new patents. Industry responds by pumping money into the research centres and universities. The graduates of the universities go on to develop innovative companies of their own, which then enter into partnerships and collaborations with the universities. One thing leads to another, one benefit generates another, and so it continues.

'This is how the Americans got to where they are now. Their history shows that academic success generates more success by acting as a magnet for talent and money. Since World War II the USA has been the number-one destination for both students and established scientists leaving their native shores. A few years ago, a study by the University of Missouri showed that individuals making exceptional contributions to science in the USA are drawn disproportionately from those who were born and educated in other countries. A quarter of the Nobel Prizes that have gone to the faculty members of US universities were won by immigrants. The country is host to more than half a million students from other countries. These young people are the recipients of a third of all PhDs in the sciences and engineering, every ten of which has been estimated to generate on average about six patents. I have not invented these figures. They are the published results of studies, surveys, and official records, which are available to everyone.

'It is also important for you to understand that the US success story in science was achieved without the benefit of the world's best school education system. The one is not a prerequisite for the other. The American experience demonstrates that national excellence in scientific research has nothing to do with the overall standard of education of the people. American citizens in general are not the best educated in the world. Studies by organizations like the American College Testing Program, the Conference Board, and the National Assessment of Adult Literacy have shown this to be the case. In one study, half of all students applying for university entrance were found to have inadequate skills in reading, writing, and mathematics. In another, almost 70 per cent of college students were determined to be 'not proficient in prose literacy.' Fewer than 40 per cent of adults in Washington DC could read everything on a packet of food. More than 10 per cent of eighteen to twenty-four year-olds could not find the USA on a world map, and almost 70 per cent could not find their special friend Great Britain. Imagine how many could have found Syria, Lebanon, Iraq, Yemen, or Egypt. No, do not worry. We do not have to start with our schools.

'Our greatest challenge will not be to make it happen, but to make it happen speedily. Under normal circumstances, it would take ten or fifteen years to develop world-beating research programs, no matter how much money and how many people were put into them. Even then there could be no guarantee we would start making real breakthroughs in less than another ten years. We need to move faster, much faster. Very soon there will be huge competition from China, which has already started to invest heavily in its universities. Not so long ago, Chinese faces were rarely seen at scientific congresses. No Chinese names appeared on the programmes, and no scientific articles with Chinese co-authors were published in the top journals. But things are changing very quickly. The tide is turning. Then there will be Russia to keep an eye on, for example, which has many excellent scientists. If we do not move swiftly, we will miss our opportunity.

'To achieve our ultimate goal, I have said we must build centres that are capable of research of the very highest quality, with the best laboratories, the highest level of security, and abundant funding. But more than that will be needed. If we are to race ahead within a few years, we will need something very special to give us an advantage.

'So, my friends, what is the solution? It is this. MECCAR and her sister centres would do more than their own research in their own laboratories. They would also house intelligence centres—call them academic espionage centres, if you like—which would continuously gather the latest unpublished findings on a few carefully selected research topics from the top laboratories around the world. As fast as the data arrive from the USA, Europe, Japan, and elsewhere, our scientists would continuously compare, pool, integrate, analyse, and interpret them with the aid of supercomputers. In this way, after doing a few experiments of their own to check their interpretation and conclusions were correct, they would find the answers to some of the really big questions long before any of the individual groups that had produced the data.

'You are no doubt thinking, 'Surely, research teams already share their latest findings at every opportunity—at congresses, over the telephone, by emails, during visits to each other's laboratories, and in the journals? This is normal practice, isn't it? It is going on all the time. Researchers around the world are like one big family, in which every member is regularly updated on everybody else's latest findings, ideas, and activities. The academic world is a vast network, through which information is constantly flowing in all directions.

'Wouldn't that be nice? But unfortunately, it is not quite like that. When I was doing my PhD in biological sciences at Harvard, I observed many academics in many different specialties. I lived among them for four years. And during that time, I learnt how the results of scientific research are processed, stored, analysed, and interpreted before they are eventually shared with other teams around the world. And I learnt many things that outsiders would never imagine.

'It may surprise the non-academics among you that the communication of the results of research between scientists is often very slow. Furthermore, when it eventually happens, it can be very patchy. Paradoxically, the highly competitive nature of science in the West, in which researchers fight for limited funding, for pages in journals, for places in the programmes of congresses, for laboratory facilities and staff in their universities, for grants, for promotions, and for awards and prizes, provides a powerful disincentive for prompt and full disclosure of their latest and most important findings. In spite of all you may have heard about scientists being dedicated and working only for the good of humankind, the reality is often very different. What makes most of them tick is personal ambition. In that respect, they are no different from anyone else. They want their research to succeed because it will help them to succeed professionally, and to have all the things that come with that: security, better jobs, better salaries, status, positions on committees, lecture tours, prizes, consultancies with industry, and so on. As a consequence, Western science is a rat race, in which dog bites dog. I know this is…'"

"Isn't that wonderful?" Giles interrupted. "You can just picture them, can't you? Do you reckon you and I are rats or dogs? But he was absolutely right. I'm sure the average visitor to Oxford imagines we live a life of protected bliss, a world where everyone loves everyone else, and lives only for the pursuit knowledge. They would never imagine the skulduggery, duplicity, deceit, back-scratching, and trickery that can go on behind the scenes in the furtherance of personal ambition."

"You're right, but can I go on?"

"Yes, sorry."

"Thanks. Where was I up to? Ah, yes."

"'I know this is not how the public imagines it. They think it is a world where success, money, power, celebrity status, and politics have no place. But they are wrong. When a scientist makes a really important discovery, he or she is happy for more than one reason. Because it represents progress and will do some good, certainly, but also because it will do *him* or *her* a lot of good. If it is a really massive breakthrough, it is true they might rush into press to try and achieve instant stardom. But such occasions are rare. Generally, science progresses like a series of stepping stones across a river, in which the stones are just under the surface of murky water. At any one time, everyone is looking for the next stone. They are supposed to help each other. But cooperation can be less than perfect. Sometimes, when someone spots the next stone, they will cover it for a time, or just keep quiet, while furtively looking for the one beyond it. And then upon seeing that one, keep quiet again in the hope of spotting the third in line—all with the aim of eventually being able to jump onto the bank on the other side, and announce to the world that they got there first. The worst culprits might even drop a few banana skins behind as they sprint—inaccurate information, incompletely described laboratory methods, missing data, and so on. I've seen it all.

'What I have just described is not uncommon. Don't forget that all the world's scientists do not work in one big room together, looking over each other's shoulders. They are isolated in different offices and laboratories, in different buildings, in different cities, in different countries, in different continents. It is the easiest thing in the world to conceal the fact that you have discovered something you would prefer to keep to yourself for a few months, or even longer. If you know that A does not cause B, like everyone was assuming, but in fact causes C instead, you can then concentrate on C while the others continue to waste their time on B. And then when you find that C does something very important to D, you can go on to study D, while the others are still wasting their efforts on B. While you are speeding down the freeway, they are going up one suburban cul-de-sac after another—getting nowhere, running out of money, running out of ideas, and eventually running out of jobs. This can be very good for the careers of the scientists who have the advantage, but obviously bad for scientific progress. Science needs everyone to be working together, like rowers in a boat.

'Now, ask yourself where all these important research findings are before they are eventually revealed to other scientists by one means or another. They're not just inside the heads of the discoverers. They are sitting in computers, memory sticks, external hard drives, clouds, laboratory notebooks, and so on. And they could be sitting there for a very long time.

'And this is only part of the problem. Also important is the fact that at any one moment all top research teams have a hoard of other unpublished data in those same computers and notebooks. These data may not be of such obvious value. Indeed, they may seem to be of no value at all at the time. But that does not necessarily mean they are not important. Perhaps if a particular team knew what some other teams thousands of miles away had discovered in their experiments, but not understood, they would recognize the significance of those findings and be able to interpret them. It can be difficult to know if a piece belongs to a jigsaw puzzle, when nobody knows what the puzzle is going to look like when it is finished. Seeing a few extra pieces that were not known to exist might make all the difference. Scientists do not have the cardboard box with the picture on the front.

'Eventually, most important research data do appear in the public domain, of course, but it can take even longer than you might imagine from what I have just said. Once researchers have decided to go public with their findings, it can be another year, two years, three years, even longer before scientists everywhere learn about them.

'Why is this the case? It is partly because many research projects simply take a long time to complete. The time between the first experiment and the last in a series might be two or three years. Then the data have to be analysed, and the outcomes of those analyses discussed in internal meetings. The team might then decide to do a few more experiments of a different type to confirm the results. Once conclusions have been reached about what those results mean, the next step might be to present them for discussion at a congress. The chosen congress might be held only once a year. To try and get onto the programme, the team has to submit a brief summary of its findings to an organizing committee several months in advance, and at the same time give a commitment that they will not submit the same results for presentation at any other meeting, or in an article for publication in a journal, until a decision has been reached. The total number of such summaries submitted might be twenty times the number of places in the programme. So only a small proportion can be selected for presentation. If the work is selected, the embargo on public disclosure is extended until the congress has been held and the presentation delivered.

'The next and final stage in the process is publication in a scientific journal, such as Nature, Science, or Lancet. Writing a scientific paper can be a very slow process. Increasingly, many authors in different countries are involved. I have seen papers with more than one hundred authors in ten or more countries. Ten or twelve authors is common. Many decisions have to be agreed upon—what data to include, how to present them, what they mean, how they add to existing knowledge, and so on. The manuscript may go through as many as five or six drafts before all the authors are happy with it. Then, the editor of the chosen journal has to get it reviewed critically by two or three external referees. These are always busy academics, some with heavy teaching, administrative, and other responsibilities, who do this sort of thing as a favour to the journals. Each time a paper arrives on their desks for review, they know it is going to eat into their precious time for their own work. They also know they are not going to be paid for their efforts. It is always voluntary, considered to be an honour. Not surprisingly, most papers received by the reviewers are pushed to one side for a few weeks, even a couple of months, before getting their attention. Some reviewers may even deliberately delay the completion of their report, if the paper they have received is from a competitor whose progress they want to slow down, or if they want to give themselves time to use the new information to advantage in their own research before others get to know about it. Because authors are aware that some reviewers take advantage of their position in this way, they may take defensive measures. They might postpone submitting a paper for several months, for example, or omit a critical piece of information, without which a reviewer would be unable to extend the work.

'Then there is the fact that almost no paper is accepted for publication without first being returned to the authors for revision. They might be asked to check their laboratory methods, repeat experiments or statistical analyses, answer criticisms about the interpretation of the results, extend the work a little, refer to someone else's work, and so on. The paper might have to travel back and forth between the authors, the editor, and reviewers several times before it is accepted, if indeed it is ever accepted. Very often papers are not accepted by the first journal. Some top journals reject about ninety per cent. Even papers that eventually went on to win their authors a Nobel Prize have suffered this fate. I could give you numerous examples. When a paper has been rejected, the authors have to modify and reformat it for submission to another journal.

And so it goes on. Even after being accepted, it might not appear in print for several months, if there is no online version of the journal.

'The way in which academic research is funded can also delay the timely release of important findings. It is not possible for Western scientists to do research without grants from bodies like the National Institutes of Health in the USA, and the Medical Research Council in Britain. Writing a grant application can take months. Then, the time between submitting it and getting the money might be almost a year. If it is not awarded, as is usually the case, the process has to be repeated. As the success rate can be as low as five or ten per cent, every trick in the book is used. The chances of success are greatly enhanced, if an application contains data from the applicant's unpublished work that suggest that the line of investigation being proposed is likely to be successful. So scientists will sometimes delay publication of new data so they can be included as 'preliminary results' in a grant application.

'And finally there is the effect of the commercialisation of academic research. These days, academics are under pressure to patent their discoveries, so their universities can use the patents to generate money. As a general rule, nothing can be patented if it is already in the public domain, in other words, if it has already been published or presented at a congress.

'The cumulative effect of these many causes of delay is that at any particular moment a mountain of unpublished data sits in thousands of computers and laboratory notebooks around the world. Just think about it—all that precious information, sitting there, doing nothing, waiting for its moment, each piece known to only a few people. Now imagine what could be achieved if all that information scattered around the world were to be gathered together, and sent to teams of scientists in specialised centres; if from that day on, all the best new data generated in the best laboratories were to follow on a regular basis; and if our scientists had the time and computing power to sift, pool, analyse, discuss, and interpret them. Imagine then how many breakthroughs they could achieve long before the rest. And imagine how quickly they could announce those breakthroughs by creating special websites for the purpose, instead of submitting them to congresses and journals. For this, my friends, is exactly how I propose our new research centres will function, and in this way make the breakthroughs years before rest.'"

Fiona gasped as she dropped the remaining Notes onto the bed.

"What! Surely, he's not suggesting…"

"Keep going!" Giles urged. "As they say, the best is yet to come."

"What? I can't imagine what it is!"

"'It would be the dawn of another Golden Age of Islamic scholarship to rival those of the Abbasids of Baghdad and the Ummayids of Cordoba. Think of the benefits that would ensue. Would foreign professors and students continue to flock to America's shores to feed its universities with their intelligence, knowledge, creativity, and energy? Of course not! They would come to us instead. Then as one thing led to another, as I have described, we would go from strength to strength, until eventually we did not need to collect all those data from around the world. Our own research programmes would be so well developed and so advanced we would be sailing in the wind, leaving the others in our wake.

'I can see some of you rolling your eyes, others laughing behind your hands. 'How could we poach all those data from under their noses?' you are asking. 'And how could we fool the world into believing the breakthroughs were the products of our own research? Has he gone mad in his old age?

'Let me consider the second point first. Each centre would be built in a remote region of our lands. No visitors would be allowed. To outsiders they would simply look like what they actually are—the greatest research laboratory complexes in the world. They would be packed with the latest equipment. There would be beautiful offices and residential accommodation for the staff. All of this would be publicised at a lavish press conference on the opening day of each centre. From then on, an impression of great activity would prevail. The laboratories would be functioning 24/7, with staff continually coming and going. Many reagents and chemicals would be bought from Western companies as evidence of great activity.

'The job of collecting and sending the data would be done by a worldwide network of research fellows, created to enable young Muslim graduates get experience in the best centres around the world. But they would be doing more than getting the experience that one day would equip them to occupy positions in our own centres and universities. They would also be working as the data gatherers. They would be the peasants in the fields, collecting the seeds so that others in our centres can mill the flour and bake the bread. This network would be called the Alhazen International Research Fellowship Programme. All applicants for a fellowship would be carefully vetted. Then when the list is complete, hundreds of the best universities and research institutes around the world would be invited to host one or more for a period of five years. We would pay all costs and give the hosts generous grants for running expenses and equipment. To research directors, deans, rectors, and professors in Europe, the USA and elsewhere—all of them highly dependent on extramural funding to support their work—the scheme would be irresistible. They would be trampling on each other for a slice of the ka'ak.

'Once installed in their universities overseas, the Alhazen Fellows would start copying the files containing all those unpublished data sitting in their colleagues' computers, going through their laboratory books, and secretly recording confidential internal presentations and discussion groups. Their own laptops would be protected with the very latest security technology. We would set up Internet clouds through which they would route the data, everything encrypted to the most secure level.

'Everyone in our centres, scientists and non-scientists alike, and all the Alhazen Fellows would be required to take oaths of lifetime secrecy. The punishment for breaking the oath would be death. If they were to flee, we would follow them to the end of the earth. No matter how long it took, there would be no escape. Is that too harsh? I do not think so, not when one considers the importance of this programme, and the millions of sick people who would eventually benefit from its discoveries. For its purpose is not just to benefit Islam. Equally, it is to benefit humankind. By speeding up the pace of research in medical science, it will bring forward the development of new drugs and other treatments for disease, new types of immunisation, new procedures for the early diagnosis of diseases, gene therapies, stem cell therapies, unimagined new technologies.

'The programme I have described will, of course, cost much money. I will not give you an estimate of the budget, because it is not necessary to do so today. But I am delighted to tell you that I have found a philanthropic person in our lands, one of the richest men in the world, who shares my vision and has agreed to underwrite at least the first stage. I cannot tell you his name, as he wishes to remain anonymous. With his help, we have all we need to get started. The site on which MECCAR will be built has been chosen, and we are ready to work on its design with a team of architects.

'So my friends, there it is. You have been chosen as the first to learn of this proposal because of your positions and reputations in your respective walks of life. For now, I ask you to treat the information as privileged and strictly confidential. When the time is right, the world will be informed.'"

Having reached the end of the oration, Fiona read aloud the last few words that Ahmad would have said to the assembled journalists.

"'There you have it, ladies and gentlemen. When I heard those words, I was an immediate convert. I recall leaving the room keen to be one of the first scientists to work in MECCAR. Ever since being a student in Damascus, my burning ambition has been to find a cure for cancer. So you can understand why, when I received an invitation to attend for interview, the idea of working in MECCAR was impossible to resist. I can remember my first day very clearly. There was no doubt in my mind that Hassan ibn Sulaymaan al-Mughrabi was right in every way. I embraced his dream and became devoted to it. That is one reason why my team discovered the *Achilles* gene so quickly. We worked day and night to analyse data sent to us by newly appointed Alhazen Fellows in the USA, UK, Japan, France, Germany, and Switzerland. After piecing the evidence together like a giant jigsaw puzzle, we knew that the gene existed, and that it had the potential to kill cancer cells. But it was also clear that it had never functioned since the day it had been created by a simple accident of nature perhaps millions of years ago.

"'For the gene to function as a cancer cell killer, it was obvious that it needed a DNA switch—what we geneticists call an 'enhancer'—which could recognise when the cell has become malignant, and respond by activating the gene. There was nothing new about that idea. All genes have a switch that responds to specific chemical messengers entering the nucleus from other parts of the cell. We did not know how to give *Achilles* an artificial switch, because neither we nor anyone else knew enough about what sort of chemicals cancer cells produce and send to their genes. Consequently, we could not go any further.

"'We were then faced with the problem of how to report our discovery of *Achilles* to the world. How would anyone believe we had done this in such a short space of time without outside help? The solution was to invent a story of a unique group of people, in whom a chance mutation of their DNA had given *Achilles* the switch it needs. That mythical group of people was, of course, the Bedouin tribe that the world knows about. We then realised that to know they were protected against cancer it would be necessary for them to have always lived in an area where there is a high risk of the disease. And that's why we said they lived near a nuclear reactor in the Negev Desert. It was all a fabrication.

"'Not long after MECCAR had announced our success at a press conference in Oahu, I started to have misgivings about my work. As the world poured praise on me, and talked of my getting the Nobel Prize, I felt dishonest, unclean, a traitor to my scientific brothers and sisters in other countries. It was a question of conscience. It came to a head when the Director of MECCAR, Dr Rashid Yamani, said he wanted to give me another project. Alhazen Fellows had already been given instructions, he said, and the data for the project had started to arrive.

"'It was then that I realised I could not continue a life of such deception. The same evening, I discussed it with my wife. Although reluctant at first, she eventually agreed that I should defect at the first opportunity, and tell the truth about MECCAR to the world. Dr Stephen Salomon and his symposium in Sorrento gave me that opportunity.

"'Now you know the truth about MECCAR, and the truth about me. Fortunately, Dr Yamani did not discover my plans before I reached the relative safety of your shores. That's all I have to say. Thank you.'"

Fiona slumped into her pillow, her hands clasped to her face, unable to think of words worthy of the occasion. But Giles could. Raising his hand to forestall any interruption, his eyes tightly closed, he whispered a few lines that welled up from the depths of his soul:

"'In wailful choir the small gnats mourn
Among the river sallows, borne aloft
Or sinking as the light wind lives or dies.
And full-grown lambs loud bleat from hilly bourn;
Hedge-crickets sing; and now with treble soft
The redbreast whistles from a garden-croft
And gathering swallows twitter in the skies.'"

Fiona waited a while to be sure he had finished.

"Are you okay?"

"Perfectly okay, thanks. That was John Keats' ode 'To Autumn', Fiona. We're just a stone's throw from where the poor lad died in a small room overlooking the Spanish Steps. Those lines are some of the most poignant and beautiful in the English language."

"I agree...but what the *hell* have they got to do with this?"

Fiona flailed her arms and legs to toss the Notes hither and thither.

"Absolutely nothing! And that's exactly the point. At times like this, Keats and his like help to keep me sane. Repeating those lines reminds me of how much more there is to life than what I'm so often forced to endure out of MY OWN BLOODY STUPIDITY!"

Fiona jumped as his fists thumped the bed-head. As he turned over, the yellow, brown, green, and orange Notes scattered over the grey and silver bedspread brought to his mind the leaves of sycamore, plain, and oak that had been cavorting on Magdalen's flagstones when he was departing for Heathrow all those months ago. The entire story since that fateful day flashed through his mind.

Fiona started gathering the Notes together, taking care to return them to their correct order.

"I can't believe it, Giles. What these scraps of paper say is almost too much to take in. Just think of it. While Steve's girls were spying on Ahmad in Sorrento, MECCAR was spying on everyone else, including Steve's lot in Bethesda, and I assume us also. How ironic can you get?

"It explains a lot. Now we know what our own Aram Abd al-Jabbaar and his friends have been up to— his sneaky behaviour, my lab results in his computer, that confidential document you saw on his screen, the diagram of a computer network that was dropped onto the floor in the Jolly Boatman. Right from the word go, I didn't trust him, as I kept telling you. He's probably going through my laptop this very minute, if my latest results haven't already been sent to MECCAR by spyware installed by him. And I haven't even looked at them yet."

"Let me have some of that vermouth," Giles groaned. "That's how desperate, I am."

"I can give you something much better than that. Close your eyes again."

While Giles did as instructed, Fiona got up and went to the frigobar. Upon hearing the tinkling of ice cubes, he peered between his heavy eyelids to see a glass of D 'n' S before him, the first since they'd arrived.

"Fiona, you're a darling! How come? I'd given up hope."

"This morning, after breakfast, I risked life and limb scouring the local streets for the three essential ingredients, including some nice fresh Sicilian limes. And believe it or not, I found them all in the same little shop."

"Wonderful! All I need now is a plate of Lancashire hotpot and a couple of Eccles cakes, and I'd be in heaven."

Giles patted the bed to encourage her to return to his side.

"Incredible, isn't it? Hardly anything we've encountered in this saga has been as it seemed—places, people, things, events, the whole damn lot. The Bedouin family doesn't exist. *Deidamia* wasn't Steve's invention. She wasn't anyone's invention. What Ahmad wrote on that report wasn't even a genetic code. Steve's computer programme was a myth. The two girls weren't Steve's research fellows…or even high-class tarts. Rashid sent us up the garden path in pursuit of DNA peddlers. The Alhazen Fellows are academic pirates plundering the fruits of everyone else's work. I'd better tell Henrik Olsson to get a DNA fingerprint done on his girlfriend's baby. It might be Gunnar Eriksson's. The only thing that's not an illusion is *Achilles*. Thank God for that."

As she was listening, Fiona had returned to the job of gathering the Notes.

"No grant applications," she sighed, "no toil and sweat, no late nights, no brainstorming sessions in the lab. All the top cancer labs in the world networked with MECCAR as the nerve centre. While the rest of us thought we were competing with MECCAR, the truth is we were working for them."

"Extraordinary, isn't it?"

"It's more than extraordinary, Giles."

"Dishonourable?"

"Worse than that. Despicable, I'd say. Shameful."

"Loathsome?"

"That too. And what's more, absolutely…"

"BRILLIANT!"

"What?"

"Brilliant. That's what it was, Fiona. We might not like to admit it, but whatever else you might think about it, that's exactly what it was. Brilliant. What Hassan ibn Sulaymaan al-Mughrabi presented that day was a stroke of genius."

"How can you say that?"

"For the simple reason it's the truth. You can't get away from it. To have come up with an idea like that and see it through is utterly mind-boggling. You have to take your hat off to him."

"But, Giles, it was *criminal*. MECCAR was, and presumably still is, exploiting, manipulating, deceiving, and thieving from the rest of us, breaking the trust that exists, or at least is supposed to exist, between scientists the world over."

"I'm not disputing any of that. I'm just saying it was brilliant. The proof is in the pudding. Nobody else thought of it, did they? And he was right. It worked. It was a success. MECCAR got to *Achilles* first. Presumably, the rest of us would have got there eventually, but how long would it have taken—two years, four years, five? Who knows?"

"That's one way of looking at it, I suppose. But it's still all those other things too. And as far as I'm concerned, that's what matters. What's the point of being brilliant, if all you're going to use it for is crime?"

Fiona said no more while she collected the last few Notes, which had found their way into her pillowcase. After placing them on her bedside table, she went to the bathroom.

"What a nightmare!" she called through the half-open door. "In fact, I wish that's all it was. Hold on, perhaps that's what it is! I've never told you this, too embarrassing, but a few a few days after I'd moved to Oxford, I dreamt I was in an old castle. All these strange faces kept appearing from nowhere. It was terrifying. And then I came across you, sitting in chains in a rat-infested dungeon, covered in cobwebs, mosses, fungi, and cockroaches, tucking into a cheeseburger and French fries, with a parrot on your shoulder. It was all so weird that in the dream I actually said to myself, 'This can't be true. It's too crazy. It must be a nightmare. If I just keep calm and wait, eventually I'll wake up.' Then I sat down on an old wooden box that happened to be there, and waited. And guess what?"

"You woke up."

"Yes. I was in bed with my boyfriend. Isn't that amazing?"

"Who was that in those days, may I ask?"

"Hamish Henderson."

"What! 'Hard-boiled' Henderson, that thick zoology student from Eigg? That wasn't amazing. It was disgusting."

"He happens to be very nice...and very good under the sheets, I'll have you know."

"Was he, really? Despite that, it's pretty obvious who you were really lusting after. And it wasn't him."

"Why is that?"

"It's as clear as day from that nightmare. There can be only one interpretation. I was in chains because you assumed I was inaccessible in those days. The dungeon was your mind's reconstruction of Magdalen College. The nasty stuff all over me was your brain's way of saying I was untouchable, out of reach."

"Ha! You've got a very good imagination. What about the parrot then, and that cheeseburger? Where do they fit in?"

"That's a tough one, I have to admit."

Giles rubbed his stubble, as he chewed it over.

"I know. Got it! There's only one type of shoulder on which you'll find such a feathered creature, a pirate's. Pirates are thieves, aren't they? I'd stolen your heart. That's what the cheeseburger was all about too. It was an association of ideas—junk food, cholesterol, heart disease, heartache. There you are, solved. Easy!"

"And what about the rat that was running around?"

"Sir Quentin, of course, our rodentine President—sorry rodent-like."

"You should open a fairground stall with a crystal ball, interpreting dreams. You'd be a real hit."

"I'll think about that. However, I've got a feeling we're not going to wake up from this one. We're both well and truly wide awake. MECCAR is not as it seemed. Ahmad was about to spill the beans. Rashid found out. And MECCAR got him before he had a chance to take the lid off. I can't see any other interpretation."

Fiona reappeared draped in a bath towel, and sat cross-legged on the dressing table stool to massage her feet with a tube of cream from the bathroom.

"You know, Giles, if I'm honest, I have to admit I was always a wee bit uneasy about our murder theory. The girls didn't really fit the picture of evil assassins, did they? After all, if they were as timid as you said they were after Ahmad's lecture, they'd hardly have had the courage to go to his suite and kill him, would they? It had to be a professional job, planned and prepared well in advance. Why were we so slow?"

Giles gave a long yawn, and rubbed his bleary eyes.

"It's easy to be smart with the benefit of hindsight, Fiona. But don't forget that until tonight we had no reason to suspect anyone other than the girls, did we?"

Fiona stopped rubbing cream into her feet to start on her ankles.

"You know, Giles, if Rashid arranged Ahmad's death, he must have known three things: that Ahmad couldn't swim; that he had a passion for Chinotto; and that the Presidential Suite has a pool. How could he have known all that?"

"I suppose Ahmad could have mentioned the first two in conversation. After all, they were colleagues and knew each other pretty well. Although the pool had only just been installed and wasn't yet on the hotel's website, a professional hitman could have studied satellite photos of the hotel."

Giving her ankles a final rub, Fiona moved to her calves.

"This cream's lovely. Bet it's expensive. It makes my skin feel really smooth. I always use the same routine—toes and feet first, ankles, then calves, then thighs, then…"

She raised her head to give him a wink.

"I hope all this stroking and massaging is keeping you awake. It was a long wait up here with only David Attenborough's nature videos for company. It's always the same stuff in those documentaries. Animals seem to do little else but eat, sleep, and have sex. Did you know, by the way, that hippos can do it underwater?"

"Yes. They can sleep underwater too—which I'd have no difficulty doing myself right now."

Giles stretched as he yawned, before rolling over to make himself more comfortable.

"Not so fast, please! As soon as I've finished my pegs, I'm going to ask you to do my bum.

"You know, there's actually something else the assassin seems to have known, which you didn't mention. The fact that the Presidential Suite didn't have any Chinotto. How could a hitman have known that?"

Fiona squeezed cream from the tube onto her thighs before continuing.

"I can't see how anyone else could have known something like that other than some of the hotel staff. Who do we have: the maid, whoever checks the frigobars, the waiters who do room service, an electrician? But surely Rashid wouldn't have risked involving people like that? It would have been far too risky. And come to think of it, how would hotel staff have known Ahmad liked Chinotto and couldn't swim?

"Okay, let's drop it for now and continue in the morning. In which case, you'll be pleased to know your big moment has arrived, Giles. Here's the cream. You can open your peepers and get going. I'm all yours."

Tossing the tube onto the bed, Fiona got up to lie on her stomach beside him.

"Did you hear me? I said it's your turn now.

"Giles, come on, I know you're not asleep. Stop teasing. It's too late.

"Giles, I'm waiting! You can return to your theories later."

She gave him a soft nudge in the ribs.

"Giles, you *are* awake, aren't you?

"Giles!

"GILES!"

Chapter Twenty-Two

Determined not to let the previous night's drama interfere with her routine, Fiona crept out before sunrise for a brisk walk in the gardens of the nearby Villa Borghese. After a gentle downhill jog back to the hotel, she made her way to the Salone di Colazione, where she found Giles well into his breakfast.

"Enjoy your jog?" he asked, his eyes fixed on his newspaper. "Assuming that's what you were doing, not flirting with one of the waiters."

"Both actually. I've lots of energy today."

"Which came first, the jog or the waiter?"

"I meant both waiters."

"Ah! Well, while you were wasting your time, I was doing something useful— thinking about Ahmad's assassin. There's nothing like an early start while the nerve cells are still fresh."

"That's what the waiters said, too. And what did those brain cells come up with?"

"As soon as I awoke, it occurred to me that if the killer knew the suite had no Chinotto, one of the hotel staff could have been involved, like whoever checks the frigobar, or a maid, or a waiter, even an electrician."

"My, that's a good idea!"

"But then I thought that Rashid wouldn't have been so careless as to approach someone like that. It would have been too risky."

"Good thinking."

"And how would hotel staff have known Ahmad liked Chinotto and couldn't swim?"

"Now you've pointed all this out, I'm beginning to see the advantages of a good night's sleep. Is there more?"

"No."

"Well, I'm sorry to have to tell you, Professor Butterfield, but it all sounds very familiar. You don't suppose you might have heard all that from me as you were falling asleep last night, do you?"

"Really? Oh…sorry!"

"No problem. You did a fantastic job with the translation. You deserved a good rest. I should apologies for the slight inebriation, by the way, but it was all I could do to cope with the tension. Anyhow, I'll go and have a shower now. Then you can show me around Trastevere as promised. See you later."

***

Arriving at the Isola Tiberina at around noon after a relaxing sunlit stroll, Giles and Fiona paused on the Ponte Cestio to enjoy the view, before sauntering through the narrow streets in search of a restaurant. When Fiona remembered she had not yet bought a postcard of the ceiling of the church of S. Ignazio, which Ros had requested for a forthcoming art class at the Ruskin, she darted into a newsagent's, leaving Giles outside to admire the local buildings. She emerged triumphantly a few minutes later waving a brown paper bag high in the air.

"Got one, and she'll love it. We must look at that ceiling again before we return. How could anyone paint like that? It's a miracle. Worth every minute of the stiff neck it gives you."

Thinking he was looking a little out of sorts, she placed a hand on his forehead to check his temperature.

"Are you okay?"

"Yes, thanks. I'm fine, just fine."

"You're looking rather pale all of a sudden."

"Have I? The damp wind off the river perhaps."

She buttoned his jacket and pulled up his collar.

"Still want to eat?"

"Of course. I'm fine. If my memory serves me correct, one called Pastarellaro is just around the corner."

Finding it packed with noisy locals, they took off their coats and hung them on the already overloaded hooks. Fiona dithered over which of the two empty tables to choose, next to a family of four that included a fractious infant, or behind a couple of businessmen in the middle of a contentious negotiation, before opting for the second.

"Hobson's choice, I'm afraid," she murmured, "but I like the atmosphere here. So authentic, and the food looks fabulous.

"Are you sure there's nothing wrong, Giles? You've gone very quiet. Something on your mind?"

"I'm fine, really. The only thing is..."

Interrupted by the waiter, Giles seemed relieved to break off in mid-sentence, offering the menu to Fiona and taking the wine list for himself.

Mindful that more exercise lay ahead, Fiona limited herself to a bowl of stracciatella soup and bread rolls. Giles was more adventurous and went for osso bucco e piselli, not heeding her warnings about his sickly appearance and recommendation to have something lighter.

By the time their food was on its way, Giles had said little more, repeatedly stifling Fiona's attempts to start conversations. It was not until he had almost finished his plate that he leant across the table.

"It's no use. I can't keep this in any longer."

"I *knew* you should have an omelette," she sighed, thrusting the brown paper bag under his chin.

"What's in my *head*, not my stomach!"

"Thank goodness for that! So, what's on your mind?"

"I think I know who Ahmad's assassin was."

"What! Who? How?"

"It came to me when I was waiting for you to buy that card, I spotted an Arab newspaper in the newsstand. It's called Al-Hayat. It's one I like to read every now and then to keep me up to scratch with the language. And in a flash, it came to me."

"What did?"

"When I was in the bar with Ahmad, Steve, and the girls in Sorrento, there was a woman nearby who had a copy of the same newspaper sticking out of her bag. I wanted to ask her where she'd bought it, but didn't get the chance. Later on, when I bumped into Steve on the terrace, I asked him if he knew her. But he didn't."

"What did she look like?"

"She reminded me of a famous Syrian singer called Asmahan, who died in a car crash during the war."

"What type?"

"Olive skin…raven hair…brown eyes."

"Pretty?"

"Yes."

"Nice figure?"

Giles gestured with both hands to leave no doubt about the answer.

"She wasn't far from our table. She could very well have overheard Ahmad going on about Chinotto."

"Was she on her own?"

Giles nodded.

"But do you think MECCAR would have sent someone so conspicuous?"

"Don't forget we were in the south of Italy. Steve thought she was Sicilian. I hadn't noticed her until then, and it was the last day of the symposium. It was the newspaper that caught my eye."

"I'll believe you! Well, if you're right, it would mean Ahmad had three women up to his room in one night. Impressive! Perhaps you should give up D 'n' S, and start drinking Chinotto instead. Was she registered for the symposium?"

"She had to be. Security was watertight. An animal-rights lot had threatened to cause problems. For that reason, the Welcome Desk was outside the hotel entrance, issuing plastic identity cards complete with a mug shot taken on the spot."

"So her name will be in the programme?"

"Only if she registered in advance. Not otherwise."

"Why don't you call the hotel, and ask if anyone with an Arab name checked in."

"Good idea. There was a woman on the front desk from England who I got on pretty well with."

"Do it now. I'm off to the loo."

When Fiona returned from the ladies' room, Giles was busy with his phone.

"Problem?"

"No, just changing the ringing tone. I've had enough of Bizet."

"Made the call?"

"Yes. She said she'll go through the records and call me back. While we're waiting, how about making our way to Caffè Greco for some dessert? I've paid the bill."

"Great idea."

They had just entered the Piazza di Spagna, when Giles's phone started playing Land of Hope and Glory. Seeing the call was from the Splendido Palace, he stopped to sit on one of the stone pillars that encircle the fountain at the foot of the Spanish Steps.

"Hello, Carol. What's the news?"

Giles placed a finger in his ear to keep out the boisterous chatter of a group of American teenagers.

"A Dr Brigitte Dubois Yusuf, you say? She was the only one. Thank you so much. It might be very important......yes, of course, I do appreciate you're not supposed to do this sort of thing. I promise not to tell a soul. Many thanks again. Good bye."

After giving a thumbs-up to Fiona, he called his office.

"Jane, it's me. I'm in Rome...yes, Rome, Italy......we *were* in Washington, yes, that's right. But after Fiona had finished her work in the lab, we had a change of plan and came here. It's to do with Fiona's lab results. I'll explain when we get back......no, I can't tell you anything right now...nothing at all, sorry......as I said, I'll explain everything when we're back......Sir Quentin? What did he want? ...... More spreadsheets? They'll have to wait. This is more important. Tell him I'll look at them in a few days. Now listen carefully. This is all *strictly* confidential. Understand? It's not possible to imagine anything more confidential than this. Nobody, *absolutely nobody*, must know about this call, or what I'm about to ask you to do—nobody in Magdalen, in Oxford, or in your village. Okay? Lives literally could depend on it......Whose? Never mind for now. But it's nothing to worry about, as long as you do exactly as I say......What? Jane, I can't hear you properly......are you still there? Jesus, why did I say that? There's nothing to panic about, Jane. As long as you do as I say, everything will be fine, and nobody will get hurt...... Yes, I'm certain......Now listen. Go into my office and find the box from that Sorrento symposium. It's in the usual place. As the next Secretary, I brought all the plastic identity cards back with me. See if you can find one for a Dr Brigitte Dubois Yusuf. 'Dubois' is a single word, and 'Yusuf' is y...u...s...u...f. When you've found it, assuming it's there, give me a call. Go and do it now, please.....and remember to keep calm. Do as I say, don't tell anyone, and everything will be fine. Bye for now."

He pulled Fiona towards him to whisper in her ear.

"According to Carol, a Brigitte Dubois Yusuf checked in just before midday on the second day of the symposium. She had a French passport, and gave her address as Marseille."

Fiona immediately snatched the phone from his hand.

"Fiona, what on earth?"

"Shush! I'm calling her again......she's not answering...... oh, yes, thank God! Jane, it's me, Fiona. If you find that identity card, whatever you do, don't wipe it with your sleeve or anything. I know what you are for cleaning things. It might need to be dusted for fingerprints......not the DNA kind, the usual ones. Pick it up at the edges with your fingertips. Put it on a clean sheet of paper on Prof's desk, and then call us. Cheers."

Giles gave her hug.

"Time for dessert!"

Fiona was making her way through a bowl of pistachio ice cream, and Giles drumming his fingers on the table, when his phone interrupted them again. Fiona downed her spoon and watched, as he pressed it to his ear.

"Well done, Jane! Now listen. In one of my desk drawers you'll find the small camera I used last year to take those shots of the College grounds. Take a close-up of the card. I need to see her face clearly. Use the zoom lens and plenty of light, and avoid any reflections. Play around with the settings, with and without the flash, with and without the desk lamp on, and so on, until you get it right. Take as many as you want. Then transfer the best one to your computer. Can you remember how to do that?......
Good. After that, do a literature search on the PubMed website to see what the lady's published. Search separately under Dubois and Yusuf. It shouldn't take long. Then email both the photo and the search results to me. And oh, yes, send me a text message at the same time to be sure I know. Thanks. Bye for now."

He looked across the table with a satisfied smile.

"I think we're making progress, Fiona. There wasn't an identity card for a Brigitte Dubois Yusuf, but there was one for a Brigitte Dubois. Black hair and dark eyes, Jane said. Probably in her forties."

"Why the name change, I wonde"Didn't want to advertise the Yusuf bit possibly. Unlike the hotel reception desk, the symposium's desk didn't require passports. University cards or just a letter from the university were enough."

It was not until around six o'clock, as they were walking back to the hotel along Via degli Artisti, that Jane's text message arrived, prompting Fiona to dart into a small Internet café. Grabbing the only terminal available, she logged into Giles's inbox while he went to buy the obligatory coffee. As he was returning, the sight of Jane's photograph of Brigitte Dubois Yusuf on the screen left Giles in no doubt she had been the woman in the bar.

"That's her, Fiona, definitely."

"Now I can see the real reason she caught your eye! A femme fatale if ever I saw one. Jane says the card gives her affiliation as Paul Cézanne University, Aix-en- Provence."

Giles raised his eyebrows.

"I had a friend there once. A very old university and very prestigious, but better known for producing poets and politicians than scientists. I'd be more than surprised if there's any cancer genetics going on there."

"She also says she didn't find any publications by anyone called B. Dubois Yusuf. PubMed listed twenty or so by B. Yusuf, but not a single one was on cancer genes. The nearest were a couple of clinical papers on breast and prostate cancer in Nigeria. Under B. Dubois, more than five hundred papers were listed, but this dropped to about twenty when she added 'cancer' or 'carcinoma' as a keyword. And as far as she could tell, none was on anything to do with genetics. She's attached the lists if we want to go through them. How about I go to the Paul Cézanne University website now?"

Giles nodded while she searched for the link on Google, and then for the university's faculty list.

"Okay, so here's the search engine for the staff. Here we go…Dubois… and then click on 'search'……nobody by that name at all. Now let's try…Yusuf…click…again nothing.

"How interesting! Why should an Arab lady, who has never done anything on cancer genetics, attend the Sorrento symposium falsely claiming she's from a French university? It has to be her, doesn't it, Giles? Presumably, the university card she used to register for the symposium was a fake."

Fiona swivelled her stool, her face flushed with excitement.

"So, let me get my head round this. Tell me if I'm wrong, but what must have happened is something like this. The girls went to Sorrento with the sole intention of filching information about MECCAR's research for Steve. They got themselves an invitation to Ahmad's suite over dinner. When they were there, one kept him in busy in the bedroom while the other one searched the study, and faxed anything that looked interesting to Chevy Chase. After they had left, Ahmad had a second visit, this time from…."

"The beautiful but sinful Brigitte," Giles took over. "She was there at the behest of Rashid, who had somehow learned of Ahmad's plan to defect and also knew he wasn't a swimmer. Being a professional, she had done her homework and learnt from satellite photos of the hotel that the suite has a new pool. Armed with a fake university card and some rohypnol pills, she had arrived with the intention of mingling with the crowd, introducing herself to Ahmad, visiting his suite late at night, dropping the pills into his drink while together, and pushing him into the pool when he was unsteady. But when she overheard him in the bar refusing a glass of prosecco and going on about his love of Chinotto and the fact there was none in the suite…"

"She changed her plan," Fiona resumed, "and did exactly what we thought the girls had done. She ran off to a supermarket, prepared two bottles of Chinotto, and the rest we know about.

"My, I wonder how she felt when she realised the key to the frigobar was in Ahmad's pocket."

Giles looked around the room to take in the scene: the walls, the pictures, the floor, the ceiling, every detail.

"You know, Fiona, it's hard to believe, but unless we've overlooked something quite colossal, the end of this saga may just be in sight. If so, this little café will stay with us for the rest of our lives."

To the amusement of a couple of students at other terminals, he asked the attendant to take a photograph of him and Fiona standing by the screen with the home page of the Paul Cézanne University on display. Then, after clearing the browsing history, they made their way out, ignoring the arrival of a thunderstorm.

"There's just one thing left to do, isn't there?" Fiona remarked, wiping the rain off her face as they turned into Via Liguria. "For Jane to get that identity card here as soon as possible, and for us take it to Virginia Brandolin to be dusted for prints. If they match any of those on the Chinotto bottle, that's it. Job done!"

Giles nodded as he reached for his phone.

"Jane, it's me again. Well done. You did an excellent job. But I'm afraid we haven't quite finished. I want you to get that identity card to me as soon as possible……Why? Because, as

Fiona said, it'll have to be dusted for prints here in Rome. I can't say more than that, sorry. You'll know everything eventually. But right now, it's urgent. Extremely urgent. I need to get it to the police, and there's no time to waste.

"Here's what you have to do. Pop it into a clean paper envelope, put that inside a plastic bag, and then give it to a courier, DHL or one of the others. It should be addressed to me at the Westin Excelsior, Via Vittorio Veneto, Rome. You'll find the postcode and telephone number on their website......yes, that's what I said, the Westin Excelsior......yes, you're right, it probably is one of the most expensive in Rome...... who's paying for it? My book, but what's it got to...... pardon?......Fiona?......yes, we are actually, because there was no point spending money on two rooms, when one would...... what?......are there two...? Jane, that's none of your bloody business! Just get that card to me, and remember, don't tell anyone...about *anything*!"

Chapter Twenty-Three

It was four days later when Fiona skipped into the lounge of the Westin Excelsior after yet another shopping spree. Finding Giles engrossed in the Corriere della Sera, she tossed her overcoat onto their favourite sofa and snuggled up to him.

"Hello, Sherlock, I'm back."

"Success?"

Nodding enthusiastically, she withdrew a pink and lime green umbrella from a long La Rinascente carrier bag.

"I bought this to brighten up those grey Oxford days. All brollies should be like this. Those funereal black things should be made illegal."

"Drink?"

"Yes, please, same as you. I'm parched. Haven't had time to stop. Shopping here is so addictive."

Giles called the waiter over and asked for another gin and tonic.

"Gone off your usual tipple?"

"No. They still don't have any ginger beer, and I didn't have the energy to go upstairs."

"Poor you. Is the newspaper interesting?"

"Quite."

"Only quite? I assumed it must be *very*, considering you picked it up just before I went out."

"There's a lot of news. And I fell asleep."

She took a bag of chocolates from her handbag.

"Like one?"

"Not with G and T, thanks."

"Ugh! Why did you have to mention those letters! They remind me of work. Four little letters: G, T, C, and A. Our lives revolve around them, don't they? Which prompts a question."

"What's that?"

"Why did Mother Nature settle on a four-letter alphabet for her genetic code, do you think, and not say six or seven letters? So many more 'words' for different genes would have been possible. Perhaps on another planet, spinning around another sun in another constellation somewhere, there are life forms like that. And they might be far superior to us, because of the greater potential for genetic variation during evolution."

"Interesting thought. You should do some of your statistics on that theme."

As she took her drink from the waiter, she stared at Giles inquisitively.

"Giles, to change the subject, there's something troubling me."

"What's that?"

"Why have you been so slow with something the past few days? You seem to have completely lost interest. As if it doesn't matter anymore. Do you have a problem I don't know about?"

He gazed into his glass, juggling what little was left of the ice cubes.

"Sorry about that, dear. But there's no problem, I promise. I've just been very tired the last few nights."

"Not that! I meant this."

She leaned over to take Brigitte Dubois Yusuf's card, carefully protected by his silk handkerchief, from his top pocket.

"Jane got it here quick as a flash, just as instructed. Why have you been so slow to take it to Virginia? Why is it still in your pocket, and not in hers?"

"Oh, that's what's bugging you? Is it so urgent?"

Giles took it from her hand and put it back, readjusting the handkerchief.

"That's what you said to Jane. 'It's urgent, *extremely* urgent,' you said."

He shrugged his shoulders apathetically.

"You know what she's like. If you don't say that, she takes forever."

"Rubbish! And grossly unfair. Be honest. For some reason, you're procrastinating. Come on, out with it. Why?"

"I'm not procrastinating. I'm just taking my time. It's not often I can do so in a beautiful place like this. Now this business is drawing to a close, I want to relax for a while, savour the moment. Nothing's going to happen if I call Virginia today, tomorrow, or the next day…or even next week, for that matter. Let's enjoy ourselves for once."

Fiona looked at him sceptically.

"Giles, that's not your style. Normally, when you've something important to do, you get on with it, whatever the circumstances. And anyway, what you've just said doesn't make sense. The sooner we've got it out of the way, and out of our minds, the more we *can* relax and enjoy ourselves."

She looked at him out of the corner of her eye.

"I hope you're not feeling sorry for her, in one of those 'there but for the grace of God go I' and 'there's good in everyone' moods that get you every now and then?"

"Sorry for *her!* Sorry for an assassin. Fiona, that's offensive."

"Sorry, but it's just that I don't understand what's going on."

"Did anything happen between you and her in Sorrento?"

"You mean hanky-panky?"

Fiona nodded.

"Fiona, *please!*"

"What is it then? You've suddenly got cold feet? You're afraid of looking like a fool in front of Virginia, in case we've got it wrong again?"

Giles shook his head.

"I stopped worrying about looking like a fool the first time I saw Henrik's photo of me shivering in a bus stop on the front page of Svenska Dagbladet."

"Then, you're being self-indulgent? You're relishing the prospect of making a kill, and you want to drag it out?"

She brandished her umbrella over his head.

"Like a victorious gladiator in the Colosseo, hovering over his defeated opponent, as he lies in the sweated dust, waiting for the steel."

"Very dramatic, poetic almost, but completely wrong. You should know me better than that."

"Yes, I do, sorry. Then, there's only one thing left. You've become addicted to the excitement, the thrill of the chase. You don't want it to end. You're dragging it out."

"Not bloody likely! You've forgotten to mention a few other things—like insomnia, heartburn, loss of weight, headaches."

He threw himself back into the deep cushions.

"I long for peace, Fiona, to get back to normal."

"Normal...or just dull?"

He put his arm around her shoulders.

"Apart from our research, it is a little dull at times, I have to admit. But Oxford will do until the great day arrives. We've got interesting work, and enough money, thanks to my philanthropic friends. And we have a nice little lab in a beautiful spot...the flowers in the spring, the trees, the deer."

He paused to add ice to his glass, as he pictured the College's grounds in his mind's eye.

"We're so fortunate in Magdalen. How many researchers can look through their windows of a summer's day to admire so many lovely, graceful creatures sunning themselves on the grass, dancing among the trees, their big brown eyes captivating you."

"Are you talking about the deer or this year's intake of female students?"

As they laughed, Fiona spilled her drink onto his shirt.

"Ouch, that was cold!"

"Sorry!"

"But seriously, when it's all over, I might just shed a few tears, you know, as I rev up the Austin Healey and zoom off to Italy."

She glanced at him, feigning indignation.

"As *you* zoom off to Italy? Won't I be going too?"

"Of course, but it doesn't take the two of us to get that old banger moving, does it?"

"Only at night, when the handbrake's on, and the windows are covered!"

"Ha! I said moving, not rocking."

Wanting to change the mood, Fiona got up to walk around and sit on the back of the sofa.

"Where are you off to?"

"Only here. Giles, seriously, going back to where we were… what *is* it? There *must* be something holding you back. Since DHL delivered that card, we've been on a coach trip to Tivoli, spent a day in Vatican City, looked at umpteen churches, and generally worn our shoes out, during which time you've hardly said a word. One of those marble dogs in the Vatican Museum would have been better company. There's something going on inside that head of yours, Giles Montagu Butterfield, and I want to know…"

"Don't mention that damn name, please! Are you deliberately trying to provoke me? You know how much I hate it. Just my luck for…"

"A Montagu's Harrier to have been circling overhead, when your parents were making little Giles in a wheat field near Chichester. I know all about it. You've told me more than once. Just be grateful it didn't make a nosedive, or should I say a beak dive, at the sight of moving flesh in the undergrowth. Otherwise you might not be here now."

"Pah!"

"And thank your lucky stars it wasn't a Leach's Petrel. Imagine that—Dr Giles Leach Butterfield. You wouldn't have had many private patients with a name like that! Or what about a Barnacle Goose? Dr Giles Barnacle Butterfield. Once he gets his hands on you, there's no getting rid of him. Ha…ha!"

"Not funny. Even a Peregrine Falcon would have spared me the lifelong pain of countless misspellings by illiterate clerks and typists. I had to return a new passport once, missing out on a much-needed vacation, because some smart aleck had assumed I'd really meant to write Montague with an 'e' at the end on the application form."

"Don't feel too sorry for yourself. I'm no better off with Oighrig for a middle name. Whenever anyone south of Skye tries to say it, it sounds like they're vomiting. But to get back to where we were…come on, out with it. What's going on?"

Giles sighed wearily.

"Okay, you win."

As Fiona returned to his side, he rolled up his sleeves and made himself comfortable, fearing that a long and difficult debate lay ahead.

"Here goes. It's like this. Before handing that card over to Virginia, I need to be absolutely sure I'd be doing the right thing."

"What do you mean…*doing the right thing*? Do you know something I don't?"

"No."

"So?"

"Well, it's like this. If we take it straight to her, as originally intended, we'd have to give her the full works about MECCAR, wouldn't we?"

"Of course, yes. That's what it's all about, isn't it?"

"Yes, it is. But think about it for a minute. The police would dust it for prints. If any match those from the Chinotto bottle, it would be cast-iron evidence that Brigitte Dubois Yusuf was the assassin. She'd be arrested and charged with Ahmad's murder. Yes?"

"Yes. And if she's guilty, the bitch will get what she deserves. If she isn't, which is extremely unlikely, she'll be exonerated. But whatever happens to her, the scandalous truth about MECCAR's methods will be out. The world will learn how it discovered *Achilles*—how its past achievements and future ambitions are all based on an elaborate scheme to steal the results of other people's ideas and hard work to get to the breakthroughs first. MECCAR will be closed. Rashid will be prosecuted. And that will be that. Good riddance! End of story."

"Yes, you're right. That's exactly what will happen. And it's the 'good riddance' bit I'm not so sure about."

Fiona's jaw dropped.

"What do you mean?"

"Look at it this way. The way MECCAR has been collecting data is highly controversial. There's no disputing that."

"Controversial! What? Only the other night you were saying it was criminal, scandalous, despicable, shameful, you name it. Now it's only controversial. Soon it'll be…I don't know what. What's going on?"

"That was my first reaction too. But since then, I've had time to think about it. And I've come to realise it's not so simple. Like most things, there's more than one way of looking at it."

"One way of…"

"Listen. When MECCAR discovered *Achilles*, albeit by putting together other people's experimental data, it did more than unearth a new gene. It also showed that Hassan ibn Sulaymaan…"

"Just call him Hassan."

"Okay. It showed he'd been absolutely right, when he pointed out that at any particular moment mountains of important data are sitting in research workers' computers all over the world, and that the delays getting them published are slowing down medical progress. It's true some publishers are setting up electronic editions of their journals, but that's a drop in the ocean. Most of the delays getting work published or presented at meetings are due to other reasons. The process is too slow and is holding back progress. He was spot on. And as he said, part of it's deliberate. It's people like us who decide what goes into our papers, when we write them, and when we submit them. Let's be honest about it. There are times when we all drag our feet before announcing important new findings. We tend to treat them as our personal property, when they actually belong to science as a whole. In fact, more than that, new knowledge belongs to everyone, the whole of humankind, including the unborn, the instant it's discovered. But we let it sit in our notebooks, computers, and heads, for as long as it suits us. Sometimes there are legitimate reasons, but too often the motivation is based on personal advantage—so the competition doesn't know a key fact too soon, for example, or to deny them a new lab method that's giving us an edge, or to wait for the most prestigious congress to be held, or to add weight to a grant application, or to enable us to file a patent, or to wait until we have more data so we can submit a prizewinning blockbuster for publication. There are so many reasons, and they've been there for so long we don't even think about them—even though we know it means some other research teams will be wasting time, energy, and money, going up garden paths and blind alleys, missing opportunities, and so on. We all want to keep our noses in front. It's indisputable. You know it is. But we accept it as 'only human,' 'reasonable under the circumstances,' 'natural,' and all that sort of crap. We treat it almost like a game. But the reality is it's immoral, because it delays progress. One can argue that anything that overcomes the problem is justified.

"If the communication of new research findings among scientists were much more efficient, faster, more open, and more complete, scientific progress would also be faster. One follows from the other. The breakthroughs would come sooner, each one bringing forward the attainment of the next. The whole timescale of progress would be compressed. That's a fact. And MECCAR has shown it to be so.

"Whatever misgivings we may have about MECCAR's methods, Hassan ibn Sulay…sorry…identified a major hindrance to the speed of medical advancement, and he found a way of overcoming it. If you open the bottleneck, if you increase the rate of flow of information between scientists, we're all going to get to the answers more quickly. As things stand at present, the method he devised, although unsavoury, is actually the only way of doing it. There was no choice. He either did it that way, or not at all. Was that immoral? Or was it heroic?"

"But, Giles, what about Ahmad's…"

"Sorry, dear, let me finish. Then you can have your turn. How long do you think it would have taken the rest of us to discover *Achilles* doing things the way we always do?"

Fiona ran her fingers through her hair as she thought about it.

"I don't know. Impossible to say—at a guess, let's say five years. It would depend on…"

"Lots of things, agreed. It might have taken fewer than five, but it might also have taken many more. It took MECCAR about one year. Therefore, let's say it reduced the time by about four years. So, it's probably taken the world at least four years closer to finding a cure for cancer. Do you know how many people in the world die from cancer in four years?"

"Let me work it out…about thirty million, I think."

"Now think about this. Before that cure is achieved, it's likely to need a few more discoveries in one form or another. When you get to one breakthrough sooner, and do the same again for the next one, and then again, the overall effect is cumulative, isn't it?

"Let's do an example, and see what might have happened if we'd all been exchanging our results at the speed MECCAR has been collecting them.

"When did James Watson and Francis Crick work out the structure of DNA?"

"We all know that, 1953."

"Now give me a really important development that took another five years and wouldn't have happened if we hadn't known the structure of DNA."

"1958? Meselson and Stahl showed how a DNA molecule is duplicated—how the two strands of the molecule, the two sides of the ladder, first separate, and then each half acts as a template for the assembly of a new one. In this way, one molecule of DNA gives rise to two identical molecules."

"Right. Now, let's jump another five years to 1963. Anything important that couldn't have happened in that year, if we hadn't known what we did in 1958?"

"Must be quite a few, but during that time, the mid-sixties, there was lot of progress on cracking the genetic code, and working out how messenger RNA and transfer RNA function to convert each length of code into a specific protein."

"Any names come to mind?"

"Crick again, Khorana, Nirenberg...."

"That's enough. Now without that knowledge, there's a whole world of things that could not have been discovered. But let's think of one around 1968."

Fiona scratched her head.

"Can't think of one, sorry."

"Nor can I, but how about the discovery of restriction enzymes in bacteria that chop up DNA, without which you wouldn't be able to do your DNA fingerprints. They were discovered by Hamilton Smith and Daniel Nathans a couple of years later. That's close enough.

"So, to get from the discovery of the structure of DNA to the enzymes that enable you to do your student classes it took a little more than 15 years. But, as a rough estimate, if each of those steps had taken just two years, it would have been only six years."

"That's probably an underestimate though, Giles, because the rate at which we humans can do experiments might well become the limiting factor. Furthermore, some developments have been dependent on technological advances in lab equipment, and so on."

"True. Let's add a couple of years then, and say it would have been eight years instead of six. That's still a saving of more than seven years. The point is this. If we were to leave Brigitte Dubois Yusuf's s card in my pocket, keep everyone in the dark, and let MECCAR and her future sister centres carry on, medical research will move faster, and the lives of millions will benefit—not just those destined to develop cancer, but also those in line to get AIDS, Alzheimer's, heart disease, diabetes, malaria, strokes, you name it. Unfortunately, of course, there would also be another consequence—Ahmad's killer and her accomplices would escape justice. The big question is this: Which is the more important?"

Fiona was stunned. He was right, of course. It was undeniable that MECCAR's methods had proven their worth. The *Achilles* gene would still be an unknown entity waiting to be discovered. Now that the world knows of its existence, thousands of scientists around the world are using that knowledge to develop a cure for cancer. Who knows what other medical discoveries MECCAR might make within a few years if its methods are kept under wraps? On top of which, its success is bound to boost the development of similar centres around the world. But was that a good enough reason to protect an assassin?

Keen to avoid rushing into an ill-considered opinion, she gave herself time to mull it over, meandering to and from the Regency fireplace on the other side of the lounge, before returning to the sofa.

"I take your point, Giles," she whispered, conscious her movements had attracted the attention of a couple playing cards, "but there's more to it than that, isn't there? You're right about that data mountain and the fact it's hindering progress. Something does need to be done. But I don't know that the right thing would be to turn a blind eye to MECCAR's other methods. Apart from the issues of morality, justice, the law, and so on, by exposing MECCAR you could use its success story as an example of what can be achieved by faster communication. If the world knew what goes on behind the scenes, that priceless information is often buried until people like us decide when to go public or release it to other scientists, we would be forced to change the system. Then, we could have a win-win situation. MECCAR could become the prototype for an international system of nerve centres, set up to receive and analyse data from all over the world. Researchers everywhere would send their latest results to the centres more or less as soon as they arrive on their desks. There would be no need for congresses and journals, just websites and networks. Everything would be shared and discussed collectively over the Internet, as it happened. It would be as if the whole of mankind had joined hands in one big research effort."

Giles shook his head disconsolately.

"Wouldn't that be wonderful? What a utopia! But in my view, Fiona, there's not a cat in hell's chance. The problem is hard-wired into our brains. *Homo* not-so *sapiens* is by nature a selfish, greedy, ambitious, competitive turd. After all, that's how we evolved. It was the survival of the fittest. In a world where food and sometimes water were scarce, the greedy, brutish, selfish apes had a big advantage over the 'you-go-first Mister-nice- guy' apes. The nice ones starved to death, and their nice-guy genes died with them. That's why scientists will always compete against each other. Intellectual athletes are no different from the physical ones. It's not the pleasure of the chase that spurs them on. It's the thrill of crossing the line first. And they're never satisfied. When they've won one race, they want to win again, and again.

"Competition in science is good up to a point—the race to have the best ideas, to do the most illuminating experiments, and so on—but that's where it should end. What we need is healthy competition to get the best out of people, and selfless cooperation when it comes to sharing ideas and data. But in my opinion, that's pie in the sky."

"Okay, Giles, well here's something else to think about. If you're going to let Rashid off the hook because MECCAR's crimes might be good for medicine, what about Steve? Pretending *Deidamia* was his invention was probably good for medicine, wasn't it? But you went after him like a Rottweiler, even though you knew it could finish his career. He wasn't the world's greatest geneticist, but he was pretty good. And what's more, he was the leader of a team. Who knows what breakthroughs he and his lab would have made in the future, if you'd turned a blind eye to what you found behind his office's curtain. But you didn't, did you?"

"No, I didn't. That's true, but you can't compare Steve's potential with MECCAR's...can you?"

"Why not? You don't know what he might have achieved. You're always telling me how scientific progress depends on ideas. Well, ideas come from individual brains. Steve has a pretty good one. When you start deciding whether a crime should be punished on the basis of what the perpetrator's future value to society might or might not be, you get into an impossible situation. What Rashid and Brigitte did to Ahmad was criminal, and the perpetrators of crimes must be punished. It's a fundamental principle. There's no other way."

"I'm not so sure, Fiona. Does it apply to all crimes? What about emailing spyware to a laptop to see if a Nobel Prize had been awarded to a crook? Should we have been prosecuted for that?"

Fiona gave a deep sigh.

"But that's in a different category, isn't it? I can see it's very difficult for you. And the responsibility is awesome. I know what I would do. But I've said all I can. You must decide. It has to be *your* decision and yours alone. But try not to drag it out, please. It wouldn't be good for you."

"I'll do my best. Now I need some exercise and fresh air. Let's go for a walk."

"Good idea."

"You'll be able to put that new brolly to good use. By the look of the couple who just walked through the lobby, it must be pissing down. Which reminds me—before we venture out, I'd better offload those gin and tonics."

Chapter Twenty-Four

It was almost midnight by the time they were at the top of the Spanish Steps, sheltering from another downpour under Fiona's purchase. They had been admiring the skyline with the moonlight glistening on the rooftops for several minutes before Giles took her hand and broke the silence.

"I think I've made my decision, Fiona."

"What? About MECCAR?"

"Yes."

"Oh, thank goodness for that!" she gasped, propping her head against his shoulder.

"I was dreading you'd be brooding over it for days."

"It came to me when we were looking into the fountain down there."

"I had a sneaky feeling it might have done. On the way up, you stopped fidgeting with your keys like a string of worry beads, and started chatting again."

"There was something about the water—its movement, the sounds, the coolness on my fingertips — that uncluttered my mind, helped me to think more clearly. After so much turmoil in my head, suddenly everything fell into place."

"I'm so relieved."

"I've decided…"

"Shh…! Not just now. It can wait. I don't want to influence you. Even if I don't say anything, my body language might give something away. What you've decided isn't important. There'll always be two ways of looking at it. Different people will have different opinions. That's inevitable. The only thing that matters is that you do what *you* feel is right—that you're true to yourself."

She nodded towards the window far below, through which the sun had last shone on John Keats' pale emaciated face.

"Truth is beauty, beauty truth…isn't that what he said?"

Giles smiled reassuringly as he gave her a gentle squeeze.

"It'll do. Fair enough, I'll do as you say. Let's forget about it for now, and enjoy ourselves. Carpe diem!"

"Or at least carpe noctem! Let's move, before we get soaked."

As they neared the bottom of the Steps, Giles stopped to take his handkerchief from his trouser pocket, and held it to his nose as if about to sneeze. By the time it was clear none was coming, Fiona's eyes had been riveted by the sight of Brigitte Dubois Yusuf's identity card lying in a puddle at his feet. As he re-folded the handkerchief, seemingly unaware of what had happened, she wondered why he had transferred both it and the card to his trousers, when both been in his top pocket all day. There was no doubt it was the same handkerchief. The red and green check pattern was unmistakable.

Fearful of what it might mean, it was not until they were half way down Via dei Condotti that she had recovered her composure sufficiently to speak.

"Giles," she said hesitantly as he was admiring some leather goods in a shop window, her voice betraying her uneasiness, "a few minutes ago, when you…stopped, back there with your handkerchief…"

"Beautiful handbags, aren't they? Yes, sorry, dear, what was that?"

"I said…a few minutes ago when you stopped to sneeze, but didn't…did you notice…er…there was a light on in Keats' room?"

"No, I didn't, actually. Why?"

"It's just that…there was a shadow of somebody on the wall inside. It looked like a very thin young man, bent over as he shuffled around."

"Probably a cleaner, I suppose. If you're thinking what I think you're thinking, I stopped believing in them a long time ago."

"Did you? I believe in them. Always will. What was really strange is that a light was flickering inside, as if it was from a candle."

"Must have been something fluttering in a draught."

"It didn't look like that. Would you like to go back so we can take another look?"

"All the way in this pouring rain?"

"Yes…it would have to be to the very same spot at the foot of the steps, of course."

She took his hands in hers and squeezed them tightly.

"But it's entirely up to you, Giles. I just thought before we continue on our way, I would give you the opportunity… that's all."

As a rumble of thunder warned of worse to come, he looked into her eyes, but only fleetingly, his gaze soon dropping to the pavement.

"I'm worried about your wet dress and your feet, dear. Those new shoes are so light, and they're sopping. Don't you think we should get back to the hotel?"

She smiled and kissed him softly on the cheek.

"Perhaps you're right, Giles. Perhaps we should let it all 'fade far away…and quite forget the weariness, the fever, and the fret.'"